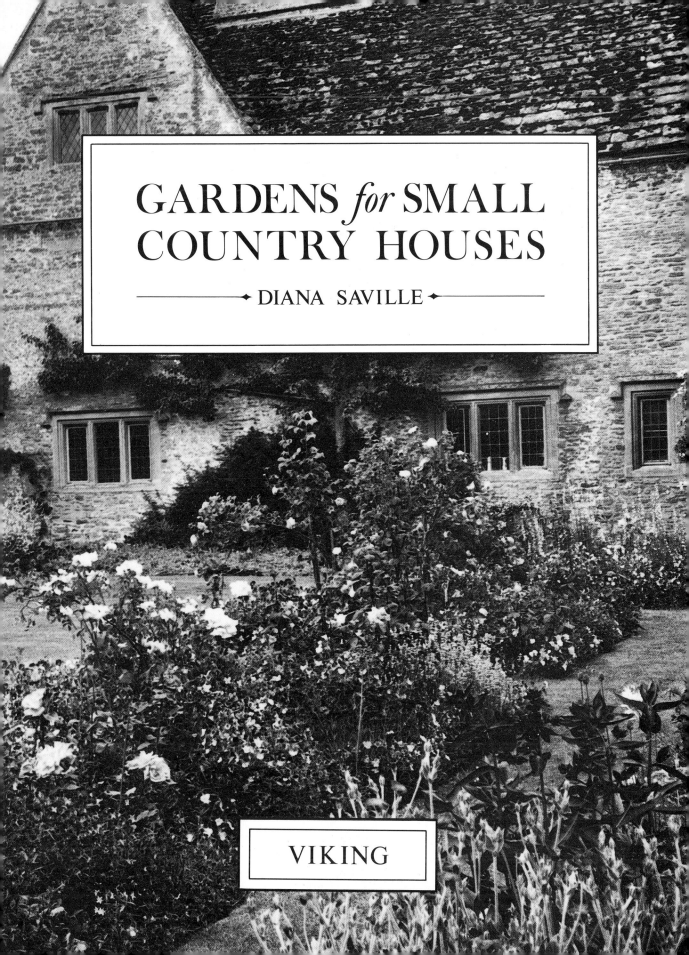

GARDENS *for* SMALL COUNTRY HOUSES

— ◄ DIANA SAVILLE ► —

VIKING

VIKING
Published by the Penguin Group
27 Wrights Lane, London W8 5TZ, England
Viking Penguin Inc., 40 West 23rd Street, New York, New York 10010, USA
Penguin Books Australia Ltd, Ringwood, Victoria, Australia
Penguin Books Canada Ltd, 2801 John Street, Markham, Ontario, Canada L3R 1B4
Penguin Books (NZ) Ltd, 182–190 Wairau Road, Auckland 10, New Zealand
Penguin Books Ltd, Registered Offices: Harmondsworth, Middlesex, England

First published 1988
Text, photographs and illustrations copyright © Diana Saville, 1988

Designed and produced by Robert Ditchfield Ltd
Filmset by Action Typesetting Ltd, Gloucester
Printed and bound by Mandarin Offset, Hong Kong

BRITISH LIBRARY CATALOGUING IN PUBLICATION DATA

Saville, Diana
    Gardens for small country houses.
    1. Country gardens. Cultivation
    I. Title
    635

    ISBN 0–670–81097–5

Contents

❧ Acknowledgements ❧

Many people have helped me and I should like to thank especially: Mr Tom Bartlett, Mr Alan Beussom, The Hon. Mrs Anthony Biddulph, Mr Peter Borlase, Head Gardener of Lanhydrock Gardens; Mrs Oliver Colthurst, Mrs Robert Chris, Mr and Mrs Christopher Dumbell, Mr and Mrs Richard Edwards, Major and Mrs T. F. Ellis, Dr Brent Elliot, Librarian of the Lindley Library at the Royal Horticultural Society; Mrs A. Galliers-Pratt, Mr Adrian Garnett, Mr and Mrs Desmond Godman, Mr Milton Grundy, Mr and Mrs John Harper, Mr and Mrs John Hill, Mrs C. N. Hornby, Mrs Daphne Hoskins, Mr and Mrs Michael Hughes, Mrs C. G. Leach, Steven McDonnell who has worked with such industry and intelligence in our own garden; Mr and Mrs Bernard Maconick, Mr and Mrs Nicholas Mander, Mr and Mrs Thomas Messel, Mrs A. Otter-Barry, Mr Martin Puddle, Head Gardener of Bodnant Garden; Mr F. W. Shepherd, Mrs J. C. Smith, Mr Paul Smith of Dean Forest Studios, Mrs Martin Turner, Mrs Joan Wilder, Captain and Mrs Eldred Wilson, Mrs Peter Wright.

All the photographs are my own except three (which are reproduced from old books) and I should like to thank the owners of the following private gardens which appear in the book. In certain cases, the owner has requested privacy, so not all the gardens can be included in this list. I should nonetheless like to record my thanks to them.

Cornwall: *Headland; Penpol House; Trewithen*
Cumbria: *Levens Hall*
Gloucestershire: *Bagendon House; Bradley Court; Great Rissington Manor; Hodges Barn; Kiftsgate Court; Misarden Park; The Old Manor, Twyning; Rodmarton Manor; Ryelands*
Gwent: *The Yew Tree*
Hampshire: *Merdon Manor*
Herefordshire: *Dinmore Manor; 2 Dalebrook, Gorsley; Kingstone Cottage; Shieldbrook House; Well Cottage*
Kent: *Hever Castle; Waystrode Manor*
Norfolk: *Besthorpe Hall*
Oxfordshire: *Beckley Park; Haseley Court; Pusey House; Rousham*
Powys: *The Walled Garden*
Shropshire: *Lower Hall; Mawley Hall; Pitchford Hall*
Somerset: *Hadspen House*
Sussex: *Borde Hill; Great Dixter*
Wiltshire: *Kellaways*
Worcestershire: *Burford House; The Priory*
Yorkshire: *Newby Hall*

Other photographs include features in the following gardens:
Angus (Tayside Region): *Edzell Castle* Gloucestershire: *Hidcote Manor, Westbury Court Garden* Hampshire: *Mottisfont Abbey* Herefordshire: *The Weir* Northumberland: *Wallington Hall* Somerset: *Barrington Court, Hestercombe* Oxfordshire: *Oxford Botanic Gardens* Sussex: *Nymans, Wakehurst Place* Wiltshire: *The Courts.*

Introduction

THE IDEA and, indeed, the title for this book arose from an inspiring prototype that was first published by Country Life in 1912. This original *Gardens for Small Country Houses* was the result of a collaboration between Gertrude Jekyll and Lawrence Weaver, the architect. Their book which ran into six issues in all appeared during an era of passionate interest in garden-making and lavish expenditure on the country house and its land. If nothing else, their era has that in common with our own, though on a much grander scale; and I have therefore long wanted to re-examine the same theme from the gardener's point of view.

What I have attempted to do is to write a late twentieth-century *Gardens for Small Country Houses*, making allowances for the vast differences that three-quarters of a century have produced since the earlier book was published. Mine is certainly not an exercise in nostalgia, nor a plea for neo-Edwardianism. Neither approach would make sense in a world so unbridgeably different from that period, and, in any case, no previous era should have a fossilizing effect. Rather my intention has been to write a book aimed entirely at today's needs, yet also one which does not ignore the traditional values that the Jekyll and Weaver book affirmed. Those values are still of concern to us and, I would argue, increasingly so in the country. The general importance of appropriateness is worth reiterating, of the integration of the house with its garden and its buildings. So too are Miss Jekyll's more specific points. She deplored silly fashions, she pleaded respect for the natural world, she stressed the need for tranquillity in a garden.

In our own current revival of interest in gardening, I feel these values need re-emphasis, for we seem as much at sea as ever, being prey to a host of exaggerated styles and greedy for an over-proliferation of tricks. We are investing more cash in our gardens than we have for decades (or, as one spectator put it, today's gardeners have green fingers from digging them in so much money). Yet the result of all this is that many of our gardens are being ruined by cosmetic additions and copycat contrivances, regardless of their suitability. The aesthetic tenets of the Edwardian age – those of simplicity and restfulness, no matter how prodigal or profusely planted their schemes – are too often eluding us.

I have therefore tried to take a fresh look at as many aspects as I can of the country house garden nowadays, covering not only the relevant topics that appeared in the original book but adding those which are of appeal to our own age. Like the prototype, I have confined my range to the ornamental garden, excluding the kitchen area; for one reason, I explored the fruit garden in an earlier book, for another reason, my own vegetable garden which resides in the sheep paddock (where else?) exists for produce not beauty. Peering, however, at the country garden through the hype of manure, urns and asparagus that go to make up our perception, my intention has been to sort out the best and most realistic proposals for today. In doing so, I have striven not to be rude (there are enough writers around with a pH of 3.5); though in all honesty stating any opinion sometimes involves criticism of things that many gardeners hold dear. If this has been the case, I apologize, but feel that the country garden must keep its rank as an ideal. It would be a cause for regret if its name could only launch a thousand catalogues.

I. Terraces and Gravel Gardens
Their Materials and Plants

IT IS AXIOMATIC (though not always true) that you start your journey round the garden from a terrace, so it is here that I must begin this book. A terrace, however, is a changeable not to say moveable feast. For at different eras, the area beside the house has been a quiet battleground for the needs of humans, plants and the building. Three hundred years ago, terraces were status symbols, tiers of plateaux affording walks and a prospect to provoke the it-all-belongs-to-me syndrome. A century later, and the terraces were gone from rich and fashionable establishments, for Mr Lancelot 'Capability' Brown had restored grass to your doorstep. Since then, the terrace has hovered between these two extremes, being at one time scarcely distinguishable from the house, and at another inseparable from the garden. To Miss Jekyll there belongs the credit for achieving that almost perfect balance of power in the conflict, masonry admittedly getting the upper hand near the house, but always gentled and made sympathetic by plants. To our own era, there is the discredit of having largely returned the terrace into the hands of the builders' merchants rather than the gardeners.

For the fact is that a post-war basilisk has visited the terraces of the land and, in recent years especially, the idea of an outdoor room has been interpreted rather too literally in its wake. The emphasis on hardware and convenience in this area has put the squeeze on our plants and we have forgotten that a terrace is best presented as the garden in its most civilized yet alluring idiom. This modern tendency is regrettable enough in a town or suburban setting where cement so often wins the war against plants near a house. But, in the countryside where the great outdoors exerts a rather more seductive pull, it flouts the whole idea of a garden. Here, a terrace can truly belong to the garden as much as to the house. And its challenge to the owner is to link it with equal success to both.

A terrace that harmonizes with its house must take its lines, its proportions and, if they're nice, its materials from the adjacent building. These are the facts in hand, ready to be heightened by you to the zenith of their own particular beauty. No stereotype will help you do this. Nor will received dogma. Le Nôtre's much quoted dictum, for example, that the width of a terrace should be equal to the height of the building from ground level to cornice, can be dismissed for a start. Two of the most delightful private terraces I have ever seen, one at Hodges Barn in Gloucestershire and the other at Waystrode Manor in Kent, make an irrelevance of such rules.

Take the first as an example which is shown in Plate 2 and Colour Plate I. Here you can

1. Waystrode Manor, Kent: yew hedges contain the profusely planted terrace.

2. The semi-circular grassed terrace at Hodges Barn, Gloucestershire (see also Colour Plate I).

see that the terrace at Hodges Barn is neither square nor rectangular, nor even paved – apart from a narrow strip beside the house. Instead it is keyed to the beautiful peculiarities of its adjacent house. A sixteenth-century columbarium in its former existence, the house wears a crown of pepper-pots with domed tops. The terrace at its foot is thus aptly semi-circular, reflecting the domed outline above it, like a huge shadow on the ground. It was a wonderful idea which most owners would have celebrated by spoiling with overall paving. Instead, this first good idea was capped by a second here: for this terrace was grassed rather than paved, its greenness a life-giving contrast to the stone uprights of the house facade, the balustrade and the old walls round the flanking garden.

The terrace at Waystrode Manor is equally individual (see Plates 1 and 3). Here you will find a profusely planted and ornamented area which flows into a long paved aisle, the whole hedged with high yews leading from the back of the old brick house – a perfect choice, for the dark green of yew is at its richest against warm brick. This aisle's length is broken into self-contained areas, and doors in the yew hedges on either side of the axis permit views to left and right into the garden. Your perspective thus runs through flowers and shrubs not only the length of the axis but to the world beyond on either side. What is special here is the sense of momentum, which contrasts with the stasis of most terraces.

These two examples are memorable because they are enchantingly individual, not in a forced way but simply because their owners used the special facts of their setting and made something beautiful out of it. This is a message that is reinforced by other examples which are described at the end of this book, which include a formal herb parterre, a green-foliaged gravel garden and a sunken terrace. Not one of these has arisen out of a stereotype.

Warmth, yet provision for shade, seclusion, wind shelter, convenient access to the house, room for sitting, all these are admittedly constants; but if you put these aside, there is in fact no reason for the standardization that threatens this area of the garden more than elsewhere. You can wall your terrace into a courtyard, partially enclose it with hedges, give it changes of level within its own area, sink it or raise it and treat it to steps, endow it with a formal water garden or carpet it with plants, all possibilities that are explored in their own chapters in this book. And, as a basis for all this, you have also a large number of paving possibilities at your fingertips, as shown at the end of the chapter.

It is, of course, this paving underfoot which makes the terrace belong to the house, just as it is the plants which should unite it with the garden, two intermingled layers making simultaneous links in opposite directions, so that, whether you approach your terrace from the house or from the garden, it should feel a well-adjusted transition. This is the reason that paving should be suited to the house and, if patterned, perhaps take its scale and lines from the building, door, windows etc. My own feeling, however, is that all patterns (whatever the complexity of the house) should be kept to the simplest. Whilst it is tempting to devise a knitwear of stones, it is the plants which give life, diversity, constant change to the terrace and it is with these that you embroider. And, as in all embroideries, they are at their most distinctive set in padded relief against a quiet background.

Planting the Terrace

There are two solid arguments for planting a terrace for maximum interest. Firstly, you are spending lots of time here, not just visiting or passing through. Secondly, it is a place of rest and your idling eyes should be amused by what they see whilst your body stays put. Neither reason means that your plantings need be exaggerated. A cottage cottage, for

3. Even in October, the terrace of Waystrode Manor is full of interest.

example, may well be at its happiest with a foundation of unpretentious plants before it like lavenders, rosemaries, ballotas, the hardier tree heaths like *Erica arborea alpina* or *Erica australis* for evergreen cover, and an underlayer of ajugas, pinks, thymes, thrifts, and dwarf campanulas. A mix of the more ornamental food plants is always convenient and suitable here, like giant chives, lovage and fennel or, in shade, decorative mints and alpine strawberries. The latter are perfectly sited in paving which will keep the berries clean; and, if you mix them with the cream-and-green-leafed form, *Fragaria vesca* 'Variegata', and perhaps the double-flowered form, *F.v.* 'Flore Pleno', they will be very decorative too. In the paving cracks, assuming there is light soil, you might encourage plenty of humble self-sowers which will spread without your having to bother with planting in holes. If you start with contrived harmonies, not random subjects, good looks should be maintained by the plants' own opportunism. The best are those self-sowers that will harmonize in colour, contrast in shape and match in speed of reproduction – such as the prostrate *Sedum acre* 'Aureum' with golden new shoots and golden flowers, and the vertical grass-leafed, blue *Sisyrinchium angustifolium*.

With plant infestations of this kind, there are always two risks. The first is that you get neurotic visitors or traumatized plants, depending on whether your guests try to avoid trampling your flowers. The second risk is on a higher plane altogether: that the picture may simply fail to coalesce. However, both these risks are avoidable if you keep empty of plants certain paved spaces throughout the terrace. I am not just talking about the gap for table, chairs, and human access which is often a somewhat ill-defined vacancy. What I mean are those spaces, defined by the managed absence of plants, which will balance other similar spaces nearby. If the large majority of plants are evergreen — as they should always be near the house — then such spaces will keep their status throughout the year.

There is also another means of keeping your picture in sharp definition despite the proliferation of plants. This method involves controlling the pattern of the flower colour and is therefore entirely seasonal. Sophisticated handling of the values of foliage colour, size and scale can have the same effect; this operates over a far longer term, but is less eventful. In practice, you will probably rely on both methods, but in either case, your choice of flower and foliage colour can only be made in relation to the house or the rest of the garden, or both, depending on the context. However, it is worth remembering that on the usual west or south-west facing terrace, fantastic effects can be struck from certain colours with a lowering sun behind them. Maroon flowers and dark-leafed plants in particular have a luminosity here to be attained in no other position. The purple-leafed clover becomes burnished and looks wonderful with one of the double-flowered helianthemums like 'Cerise Queen' which retains its flowers to sunset (which is when you intend to exploit these effects) instead of shedding them early like the single-flowered cultivars. The same is true of trees like the purple Myrobalan plums which can look lovely in such areas when formally clipped; in paving at Penshurst Place in Kent, they were trained as mop-heads on stilts with pale blue violas as a foil.

Planting the Terrace of a Formal House

Such a building demands a formal terrace. The balance of the plants, too, needs to be tilted in favour of those with sculptured leaves and/or flowers. Zantedeschias with their carved white blooms, waxen magnolias, crown imperials, pillars of eremurus, large and small

4. Topiary is perfect for a formal terrace and an ideal background to pale furniture.

euphorbias of architectural appearance and, if there is plenty of room, a tree like *Cunninghamia lanceolata* (suited to the shelter of this position), its precisely structured leaves like a monkey's puzzle. The long-leafed *Podocarpus salignus* would be another beauty here, so would *Pinus patula*, a tree of strong presence and texture and, like the other two suggestions, a conifer (see also page 71).

Topiary makes, in my view, the perfect idiosyncratic prop in this setting (see Plate 4), but if the thought of clipping is irksome and waiting for the results impossible, then try certain shrubs or small trees of naturally distinctive form. You might include the weeping domed elm, *Ulmus glabra* 'Camperdownii' (if you will risk elm – I have admired some very healthy specimens of this tree); or *Viburnum plicatum* 'Mariesii' for its horizontal spread; or the even wider vase-shaped yew with drooping branchlets, *Taxus baccata* 'Dovastanii'. Such subjects are star performers with curiosity value. As such they lend themselves to specimen display and may be far more at home on a terrace with its resemblance to a stage, than in the open parts of a garden.

The same is true of certain flowers whose beauty is of the kind of intensity that demands close and all-round inspection. The kind of subjects I mean are tree peonies, fairly brief in flower but worth the spotlight at the time. It is important to choose cultivars with strong stems such as the white semi-double 'Tama Sudare', the dusky coral 'Mme. Louis Henri', the huge carmine semi-double 'Sitifukujin' or the beautiful lilac-lavender 'Montrose'. Or, later in the season, the most glamorous of the cistus are well worth a position here. *Cistus* x *aguilari* 'Maculatus' is a lovely thing, bushy with a large white bloom splashed with ruby, its only drawback a shortish flowering season compared with its peers. Try if you can, rather, to get hold of *C.* 'Paladin' which is of the greatest beauty – white with an inner stain of velvety maroon, a gleaming golden boss of stamens in its centre, and semi-double petals. Or, from a different genus, try the tenderish *Lavatera maritima* (syn. *bicolor*) in a sheltered position. All summer and autumn it produces large silky lilac flowers with a claret eye.

On any terrace, fragrance is a luxurious extra, though so many of the sweetest-smelling plants have a dowdy appearance that they are best kept at bay, such as chimonanthus, *Lippia citriodora*, mignonette, night-scented stock. Depend rather on the shapelier evergreen *Sarcococca hookerana digyna* for late-winter scent, on the evergreen daphnes over a long spring period, from *Daphne odora* 'Aureo-marginata' through the prostrate *D. cneorum* 'Eximia', the round bushes of *D.* x *burkwoodii* (deciduous) and *D. tangutica* and the vase-shaped *D. pontica*, though its elegant creamy-green flowers are less showy than the rich pink blossoms of all the foregoing. For summer, try the small philadelphus such as the lovely 'Sybille' with white, purple-stained squarish flowers; or the scented-leafed geraniums for bedding out (see page 146), pots of lilies and even, for the very ambitious, pots of daturas (see page 108). Other 'pot' suggestions are in the chapter on 'Garden Ornament'. All these will effect that true seduction by plants that is the first duty of a terrace.

Gravel Gardens

But of all hardware areas, it is the gravel garden that can offer the most lavish of plant effects. This is because it can absorb the greatest number of plants whilst remaining accessible to human beings. I would offer one caution, however: that the gravel should be married with paving if the area has a direct entry to a house, otherwise you and the gravel will enter together. Sited elsewhere, gravel may well look best when used by itself.

These gravel gardens can be virtually vast borders, and it is a dream-like experience to enter them (indeed sit within them, eat within them if you have left a nook unplanted for a table and chairs) and be assailed by colour and leaves, scents and butterflies. What's more, if you have prepared your ground, these areas, though fully planted, can be virtually weed-free and require very little maintenance. Thus you can sit without the threat of impending toil clouding your outlook.

The weed-proofing method which I tried out first in a previous garden and now use in three areas of my present home is to lay the gravel over polythene. The best preparation is to dig the entire area first, eliminating perennial weeds with glyphosate. Rake it level, ideally rid it of all surface stones (an impossible job in genuinely stony soil, but be prepared for those you leave to puncture the polythene in time), give it a 1in /2.5cm topping of coarse sand (counsel of perfection) and cover it with a stout grade of polythene sheeting, overlapping by 1ft/30cm all joins. Use black polythene if you can, for clear sheeting tends to encourage germinating weeds, suckers etc. to seek the light if gravel gets displaced and force a hole. Finally, finish off with a layer of gravel. This should be about 2in/5cm thick where the planting area is, thinning to 1in/2.5cm thick where you walk (assuming you are not using a paved path).

You then plant in holes which you cut in the polythene, varying your diameters according to the size of plants. For larger shrubs and trees, I would allow up to 3ft/90cm across, but for very small plants, 1ft/30cm should do. (If the holes are not large enough, the plants will not thrive, so be prepared to cut out extra room if they need it.) Add peat or a well-rotted compost and bonemeal to the earth. Keep the gravel away from these planting holes if you are doing the job in a cold spring and on heavy soil. Like a mulch (which it is, in effect) it would keep the soil cold for the next few months. Let the soil warm up immediately below the plant, though not dry out, and then smooth the gravel

5. Planting clothes a swimming-pool terrace: *Buddleja alternifolia* and *Cytisus battandieri* partner each other on the wall, *Taxus baccata* 'Semperaurea' is the vertical conifer.

6. A gravelled and paved terrace: note the mix of upright growers (grasses and conifers) with low shrubs of neat, mounded habit.

7. Our own gravel garden, laid on polythene, includes irises, libertias and *Artemisia canascens*.

across. You will have to keep these planting holes weeded until the plants can smother the usurpers themselves, but the gravelled surface makes it easier and this is nothing compared with the usually onerous task of weeding or mulching whole tracts of bed. If you want to feed and mulch around the base of plants, you can of course still do so – and you should protect the plants against slugs.

In my experience, plants do extremely well under these conditions, having hot heads and moist feet. I feared initially that a permanent polythene cover across much of the bed could lead to sour, sweaty earth, but I have given it a seven-year trial and have seen no ill-effects from this as yet. The one precaution I would advise from experience is to ensure absolutely free drainage, however, for without it, puddling could occur in the holes. I cannot speak with the same confidence about surface-rooting trees, and in this respect, I have planted a magnolia which will act as a canary down the mines. Time will tell whether it will stop singing or not.

Certain plants have become *de rigueur* in gravel, for their natural habitat is characterized by hot, dry, stony conditions. Anything with a meridional flavour is right. Prostrate junipers, cistus, genistas, cytisus, helianthemums, rosemaries, lavenders, santolinas, helichrysums, rues, tree heaths, osteospermums and species pinks are all admirable. For height, have eucalyptus trees in large areas, *Hippophae rhamnoides* on small sites. The spikier varieties of euphorbia look appropriate, for the strong, stony surface needs aggressively distinct plants to master it: *Euphorbia myrsinites* is ideal together with its upright relative

16

E. rigida (syn. *E. biglandulosa*), and, on a larger scale, add necessary bulk with *E. wulfenii* or *E. sibthorpii* (very similar except the leaves of the latter have a bluer cast and the lime-green bracts lack the black eye). *E. mellifera* is a good addition in a sheltered corner, though even if it gets cut to the ground in winter, I have never known it to fail to re-shoot to 4ft/1.2m in summer. Add *Yucca gloriosa* for height and *Y. filamentosa* for repetition on a smaller scale. *Helleborus corsicus* will give you an early start to the year, its serrated leaves appropriate companions for eryngiums like *E. serra, E. agavifolium*, the tall *E. pandanifolium* and prolific self-sowers like *E. giganteum*. *Libertia grandiflora* with its white flower spikes in early summer and stiff fans of evergreen leaves is good for clumping, reinforced perhaps by *Sisyrinchium striatum* (self-sowing in abundance), by the beautiful Pacific Coast irises, and, for late blossoms, by schizostylis which is at its very best in the tall, vigorous, coral-pink form called 'Sunrise'. *Kniphofia northiae* makes a grandly exotic, if untidy, specimen and is fairly hardy; so does *Fascicularia pitcairnifolia*, a bromeliad with blue flowers in autumn at the heart of reddened leaves, but it is semi-hardy and only worth trying with winter protection. However, you can rely on succulent-leafed, frost-hardy plants to make good carpeters whether sempervivums or *Sedum rhodiola* (the rose-root) or *Sedum* 'Ruby Glow' or 'Green Mantle' or the creeping *Crassula sedifolia* or the bizarre *Saxifraga spathularis* (a parent of London Pride) with its spiky spoon-shaped leaves. And in the flattest areas, you might give intermittent height with the gnarled little *Crassula sarcocaulis*, a miniature succulent tree-like plant with starry pink flowers; though unlike its relative mentioned above, it is tender in cold places without winter protection.

Not everything should be aggressive enough to poke your eyes out. Round-headed alliums and soft plumy fennels (the giant *Ferula communis* as well as the culinary green or purple *Foeniculum vulgare*), biennial angelicas and lots of grasses are soothing additions. An area like this can take large grasses like the 8ft/2.4m *Miscanthus floridulus* (syn. *M. sacchariflorus*) making a high screen every summer; or the graceful and somewhat shorter *M.* 'Silver Feather' which flowers so well each year. *Stipa gigantea* with its evergreen leaf sprays and 5ft/1.5m oaten sprays, and the blue grass *Helictotrichon sempervirens* are lovely pouffes on the ground. Pampas grass might be replaced in milder areas by *Chionocloa conspicua*, a New Zealand grass which is valuable for its earlier-flowering plumes.

Some of the best soft-looking carpets for these areas are to be found amongst the acaenas. My favourites are *A.* 'Blue Haze' with tiny blue-grey leaves, *A. buchananii* with pea-green leaves and yellowish-brown burrs, and the largest and bluest of them all, *A. adscendens* (syn. *A. affinis*). All are comfortingly rampant over the stony surface and are the kind of plants which help to ensure that the coverage is as wide as possible on the ground. Gravel, after all, especially if unshaped, is no more attractive to look at than bare earth.

A gravel garden which is filled with such plants as all the above has a supercharged presence and is perfect in an enclosed area. But this is rarely the setting and such gardens are often open on one or more sides to the garden as a whole. In this case, the planting should not be as consistent. To avoid it resembling a theme park, you can introduce plants which are not inappropriate to the adjacent area, even though they are not usual 'gravel' subjects. One has to exercise a degree of tact about introducing one guest to another in these circumstances, but it is fairly obvious on the ground; floribunda (or cluster-flowered) roses would be shown the door, rugosas pressed to stay. An enclosed garden, of course, poses no such constraints, which is one of its most exploitable assets – but on that topic, there is much more to be said in the next chapter.

Paving Materials

Cost, convenience, ease of maintenance and suitability in colour, texture and period feel to the house or paths are all factors to influence your choice.

PAVING Paving slabs can be artificial or natural, the latter much more expensive. There are lots of sizes and colours, but avoid the ice-cream coloured extremes of the artificial slabs and opt for a quiet fawn or grey which may weather comfortably. A roughened texture to the surface, simulating the flaking of natural stone, is also preferable and more slip-proof. If the paving borders a step and its edges are exposed, choose pavers which copy the worn edges of natural stone. Don't mix natural and artificial slabs; the proximity will expose the unnatralness of the latter in all its horror. Even the application of tea-leaves, dung and yoghurt will fail to age its appearance satisfactorily.

SLATE Usually greyish-green but also dusky blue. Best when it can be incorporated in discrete bands or edging strips, where it makes a subtle rather than startling contrast with the main paving. Strong, durable and obtainable in random sizes, usually squares or rectangles.

GRANITE SETTS A smaller unit than the above varying from 6in/15cm square to 16in x 8in/40cm x 20cm. Natural or artificial, and usually grey or a blend of rust colours, they make attractive panels, borders or insertions (see Plate 18) and can be used as relief areas in the same way as cobblestones (see below). Used on their own in a large terrace, they are less distracting if their pattern is broken up at intervals by plants.

BRICKS Generally, old bricks have a softer warmth than new, though there are exceptions to this. If old, they must be in good condition, frost-proof, free or free-able of mortar, suitable for external use. Grey, donkey brown, rust to fawn are all possible, but the glaring yellows are dreadful. A good subject by a brick house, or where paths from the terrace are also brick, so long as both the colour and feel harmonize. As small units, they can be laid to form curves or irregular lines.

QUARRY TILES These look so domestic that they are best confined to a small area by the house, perhaps within a verandah or under a balcony. Square or hexagonal, they range from terracotta to blue or grey-green. Check they are frost-proof.

COBBLESTONES Highly decorative when alternating with slabs, either as blocks of pattern or as a circular surround to a tree or, perhaps, as a perimeter border. But they make a difficult surface for wheelbarrows, prams, trolleys etc and are therefore best kept away from the main traffic lines of the area.

GRAVEL Stone chippings in sizes from 1in/2.5cm to ¼in/6mm, a pea-sized gravel so small it may stick to shoe soles and be walked into the house. Shades include pinks, rusts, grey-green, buff and grey. Choose to blend with surrounding materials. Cheap, easy to lay and a first choice where the surface cannot be accurately levelled. It does not need maintenance as such, but unless it is laid over polythene, it will become infested with weeds. It will also need intermittent raking to keep it evenly distributed.

STONE ROOF-TILES Treat as paving slabs, though their comparative fragility means that the whole tile needs to be bedded in mortar.

Costing the operations

Calculate paving slabs, slates, setts and quarry tiles from a scale drawing of the area. Bricks are usually supplied in multiples of 100; very roughly, 35 laid flat cover a square yard. They look better used on their side, but this can double the cost. Err on the generous side in your estimate. Builders' merchants will give guidance on cobblestones and gravel for a given area and can also help in calculating sand and ballast.

Laying the materials

PAVING SLABS   If the ground is soft, roll in 4in/10cm of hardcore topped with a fine material like ashes or sand. Check level. Bed slabs in a mix of 1 part cement and 6 parts sand to a depth of 1in/2.5cm in traffic areas. To the sides of the terrace or where it will be planted, use this mix in dabs under each corner and in the middle of the slabs. Keep lines straight with pegs and string. Tap slabs into position using a hammer with a block of wood over the slabs to prevent damage. Fill joints with sandy earth for planting, or on traffic lines brush 1 part cement to 3 parts sand into the joints and water with a fine-rosed watering can. Otherwise, joints can be filled with gravel or river sand if you are using this in adjacent areas, but it will overflow.

SLATES   Excavate 3½in/8.5cm (or half as much again, depending on depth of slates, steadiness of soil and heaviness of traffic) and lay 2in/5cm deep (or 4in/10cm deep) concrete base (a mix of 1 part cement, 3 parts fine sand, 6 parts ½in/12mm aggregate). Top with 1in/2.5cm mortar bed (see mix under paving slabs) and bed slates.

GRANITE SETTS   Prepare base as for paving slabs but make the mortar bed 2in/5cm deep. Put setts into bed before it hardens. Finish by brushing cement and sand into joints and watering as in paving slabs.

BRICKS   Treat as for paving slabs, using rubble or hardcore topped with ashes or sand. Either bed the bricks in 1in/2.5cm deep mortar (see mix under paving slabs) or dry-lay the bricks on a consolidated coarse sand bed. Fill the ½in/12mm joints with sand or point on traffic lines with a mortar of 1 part lime and 4 parts soft sand. Wash off any mortar that stains the surface at once.

QUARRY TILES   See instructions for slates, but point as for bricks.

COBBLESTONES   Bed the stones in a mortar base over hardcore as given under 'Paving slabs', but the mortar base should be 3in/7.5cm deep. Cobbles should be sunk into the bed before it hardens to at least half of their own depth. Work with the cobbles sitting in a bucket of water to stop them drying out.

GRAVEL   Put down a layer of sand over 4in/10cm depth of hardcore and then pour in one layer of gravel to the thickness of 1in/2.5cm where you walk and two separate layers elsewhere. Water each layer, ram and rake even. If you want to avoid weeds, cover the sand with a sheet of black polythene before adding the gravel. You can plant at any time by cutting holes in the polythene and scooping out the hardcore etc. below and making earth pockets here, but confine your plants to those which will tolerate such conditions. For a full-scale gravel garden, the preparation should be different; details are given on page 14.

II. Walls and Entrances
*Decoration, Wall Climbers and Shrubs, Retaining Walls
and their Plants*

PICTURESQUE OLD GARDEN WALLS deserve the same respect as a cherished antique. They too have been built by good artists and craftsmen and they too have acquired a long history of their own. Sun-warmed, lichened, colonized by lizards, insects and plants, they have a private life that you can only guess at. My own fondness for them, which took root during a period spent building two garden walls, is not merely fanciful. Walls, after all, are part of our artistic culture.

Until the last two centuries, for most of the civilized world and for much of its history, gardens have been, almost by definition, walled. They were green and private fastnesses against bad weather, animals and human beings. And, even though the eighteenth-century English landscape movement overthrew this tradition by offering a magnificent alternative, the craving for the formal garden surrounded by walls could not be held at bay for very long. Walls were revived for numerous reasons. They were practical rabbit- and deer-excluders. They were useful in designing a garden. They were legally advantageous as boundaries, defining a property's extent. And in due course, as gardens became smaller, they were a social necessity to avoid dealing with cheek-by-jowl human beings. But these reasons were trivial compared with the force of a subjective impulse: an ineradicable yearning to rejoin that old world of simple geometric outlines which spelt snugness, security and shelter.

By the end of the nineteenth century Miss Jekyll and other gardening writers were advocating a return to the old system of separate enclosures in a garden. It was in this persevering climate of opinion that the great enclosed compartmental garden of the early twentieth century was built, Hidcote Manor Gardens. Sissinghurst Castle Gardens, similarly enclosed, followed some several decades later. Both are National Trust properties and are of inestimable public influence.

As the National Trust has expanded, these two examples (occupying arguably the foremost positions among its gardens) have especially conditioned present-day gardening taste, with the result that the fashion for gardens made on cellular (or linear) enclosure systems, is even now all the rage. The smallness of the individual gardens is obviously a main reason, making them easy for us to digest and reproduce. But I should guess they have a subconscious appeal as well. Firstly, we respond to their snob value. Secondly, we

8. 'All see-through gates say come hither.'

too have the old psychological need of their shelter, privacy and continuity with the past – probably far more now than before. Most of us therefore have good reason to love a walled garden, but put it out of mind if we don't have or move into an existing one. Is it not virtually out of court except at huge cost?

Not in my own experience. One is rarely barmy enough to take one's more expensive advice, but whilst writing a book called *Walled Gardens; Their Planting and Design* (1982), I became sufficiently spellbound by my subject to have one built. Quailing at the potential price, I set about trying to limit the costs. Without going into too much detail, this involved using two low walls in one area and raising them to 7ft/2.1m, linking existing barns to each other and to the house, buying local materials (red sandstone to conform with the house and barns) and keeping the design simple.

The results were dramatic. One example suffices. Look at the before and after Plates 9 and 10 of the entrance to the walled area. You can feel how the eye is bored by the view it gets for free in the first picture; and how, contrastingly, the intense concentration of the view in the second photograph lures you into wanting to know what is behind the concealing walls. It is indeed the same old boring view, but now it takes on the spurious glow of a discovery.

I could have bought this dramatic effect more cheaply. Either by having the wall built with a single thickness, though this is only possible with bricks and to a limited height and with buttresses (see also page 24). Or I could have planted hedges (see pages 128-133) partly or wholly round the area. But this would have forced me to wait for the effect and involved me in labour for ever. Walls, whilst expensive to erect in the first place, are your main allies in cutting costs thereafter.

For those considering the plunge, there are two warnings however. Firstly, in the countryside especially, a wall has to look comfortable rather than just arbitrary. If it will always have the air of a planned imposition (even when weathered), it will lack the liveliness of something which could have grown up over the years as an expression of true need. Secondly, there is now a real danger of getting so crazed with enthusiasm for the enclosure system, that one disregards contemporary obstacles. Our gardens are usually much too small to take more than a very few compartments at most. Don't forget that Hidcote is ten acres and Sissinghurst is twelve acres and both put a strong emphasis on vistas and axes. In our own copycat impulse, we ignore this need for space. As a result, too many of our aspiring reproductions look not, alas, like their prototypes but more like ye olde boutiques. Wary of this danger in my own case, I have tried to keep certain areas of the garden open and uncluttered, as breathing spaces.

Yet having fired off these statutory warnings, I can only encourage by writing of my own delight. With a walled enclosure you gain an addition which will extend your use of the garden. It allows the experimental gardener a tremendous run of vertical space on which to grow climbing plants and shrubs – and on both sides, if the wall is internal, in sun as well as shade. It provides a variety of warm and sheltered nooks for plants, and gives you the bonus of snug burrows where you can sit and bask and soak up that delicious feeling of heat and shelter (even though walls, and especially doorways, will cause severe wind turbulence in parts). It can also offer you a manipulated view out, for you can arrange your doorways, gates, windows, clairvoyées or simply gaps to frame part of the outside world to its most artistic advantage. Most crucial of all, a walled garden bestows on you the freedom to dictate your own terms of reference – precisely because it excludes all of

9 & 10. A before-and-after demonstration of walling our own garden.

the outside landscape except those parts you manipulate into view. You have your own secretive microcosm, to shape as you want.

One can take the word 'shape' quite literally here, for walls (or hedges) around an area define not only its extent but its form. If you are starting from scratch you can make a garden which is square, rectangular, round or oval. The latter is very rare though a marvellous example exists at Netherbyes in Berwickshire where the internal flower-beds echo the curve of the wall. You could even opt for an alcoved garden, a most dramatic version to be found at Wroxhall Abbey (now a school) near Warwick. Designed by Sir Christopher Wren originally, its semi-circular bays now house roses and fruit trees. This use of brick is more lavish than any but a few could envisage on private money, but a more economical variant is the serpentine wall which was favoured as a purse-saver. This needed only a single flank in protected areas, though piers are necessary if it rises above 3ft/90cm. It has a quaint appeal, offers warmth and shelter to tender plants in its hollows, but its swoops can be visually disturbing and difficult to accommodate successfully in a garden (though Plate 46 shows an ingenious way to do so).

Adornment

Most gardeners who opt for walls are going to drape them with plants, not only the cheapest form of ornament but the only cure for the stage-set quality of a newly erected structure. But if you do want architectural adornment (and can afford the cost which, in terms of space occupied, is all out of proportion to the body) then discipline it to a single type of motif. This adornment usually embellishes the top of the wall, often resting on the coping itself.

So long as you avoid horrible battlements (the male castellation complex) the potential is enormous and can range from exuberant obelisk finials (such as the spires on the round walls of the Coronal at Athelhampton in Dorset) to decorative balustrades – both of which are very expensive indeed. Alternatively, decoration can often be built into the flank of the wall itself. It can take the structural form of a niche for a figure or a seat. Or it can be a more superficial addition. This is at its most delightful when it is made personally relevant or even usable, as in the case of the walls of the 1604 pleasance at Edzell Castle in Angus (see Plate 11). These not only carry the family motto (*Dum Spiro Spero*) but canopied oval panels of sculptured symbolic figures which alternate with square cavities in a chequerboard pattern representing the family arms. Some of these recesses were nesting-places for doves, others acted as flower-boxes. All of which is impossibly elaborate for today, though it could be the source for some simplified ideas. Otherwise, you could go for another option which is to build ornament for its own sake into the wall itself – say, a pattern of flint and bricks which is often found in certain counties where flints are a natural product of the land.

You have to be sensitive, however, if you plant up a wall of architectural beauty; indeed, sometimes so wary of intruding that you leave well alone. Such restrictions may hamper your scope too severely. For this reason it can be more convenient, not to say cheaper, to keep your ornament to the tops of gateways or doors. You will probably need two or more of these, for they exist not only to allow you to enter and leave at different points, but to give views (sometimes linked if you can line them up). This last purpose is an important one, enabling you to avoid the deadening introspection of a closed walled garden.

11. Edzell Castle in Angus has the most elaborate of all wall treatments.

However, it is worth giving some thought first to the kind of doorway required, which in itself may provide all the decoration you need. You have a basic choice between solid and see-through doors. A solid door emits the warning to keep out, whilst giving security to those within. In cold periods, however, it has to be left widely ajar to let air escape on freezing nights, for without this free egress, the area is liable to become a lethal frost-pocket. A see-through door solves this problem. But it also says come hither and permits views, so it is only suitable in the right place. It can be made of iron or wood, and architectural salvage traders are a good source of supply for the former, especially if you need a decorative door in keeping with a period house. (Modern doors tend to be made of steel not iron and, unless designed by artists, their patterns are often bereft of vitality.) Otherwise, you might get away with a home-made one using old materials. The little gate in Plate 12 with the charming lacy pattern could have been made to a full-length shape if necessary, and is simply the result of welding old horseshoes together. Wooden doors can be equally patterned and see-through, perhaps latticed or Chinese Chippendale; but to allow frost to escape, this openwork must run the full length of the door otherwise the solid wood could act as a trap at the bottom (see Plate 13).

I, in fact, have left my doorways unblocked (doors being too much of a nuisance with through-traffic) but have nonetheless had immense fun with the actual surrounds. I have three. One is a simple arch through which one sees the green, glinting water of a large pond and its small cargo of sailing ducks. The second is merely a gateway between piers through which a road runs to connect with the third, a much larger pedimented arch on the other side of the walled garden. Both this entrance and exit are decorated with paired balls. For a time the exit wore one ball only, when it looked both foolish and melancholy like a lop-eared dog. And also embarrassed (or do I mean me, for there is nothing like a one-ball gate to expose the absurdity of your pretensions).

12 & 13. Contrasts of simplicity and sophistication in openwork gates.

14. Pineapple finials (in reality the fruits of the stone pine) are well partnered with the mop-heads of blue and white agapanthus.

Balls aren't the only possibility for finials and the reconstituted stone merchants sell a range of items including baskets of fruit, falcons, lions and eagles. They also offer the ubiquitous pineapple finials. If you look at these closely, you will see that these pineapples are rarely the fruit we eat (*Ananas comosus*), but are modelled on the cone of the stone pine (*Pinus pinea*), the seeds of which symbolized fertility in the Roman cult of Mithras. This doesn't exactly spoil the ornamental charm of these finials, but it does bring me to my main point that so many of these fancy finials are barren of significance nowadays and therefore unlikely to be suitable. If nothing else, they flout one key rule for ornament that I mention at the end of Chapter IX – that it should arise out of the main item itself.

For all these reasons you might choose to dispense with finials and concentrate on decorating the doorway itself with an imaginative and patterned combination of materials. Sir Edwin Lutyens, for example, sometimes used tiles edge-on in fans to give a sunburst effect. Or you could make the shape of the door a decoration in itself. The Chinese were wonderfully inventive in this respect, though the only simple and lasting shape they bequeathed us was the moon-gate. This kind of doorway is fairly uncommon, one of the most readily accessible examples being at the National Trust property of West Green House in Hampshire, though a very lovely modern version is in the Moon Garden at Drenagh in Northern Ireland where the circle frames paired summerhouses in the garden beyond. Hill Pastures at Broxted in Essex contains another which was carefully positioned to 'hold' the moon within its curve as it rises from a group of trees, planted to give this effect. Any moon-gate must be given an equally romantic and tranquil setting. Originating possibly as a beautiful focus for meditation which could be practised whilst the moon passed within the frame, it cannot be introduced where bathos is a risk.

If you are working in stone, you have another decorative approach in prospect. That is to sculpt a relief design on selected individual stones which can be set around the gateway. If these can be made personal or relevant to the area, rather than mere catalogue copies, so much the better. My own temptation is to take cue from the red sandstone carvings around several old churches near my home. These embodied incubi and medieval bestiary beings which were used to keep the evil spirits outside the church, barring their entry to the pure sanctuary. Quite useful in a garden at a time of personal crisis, not least if one feels a smattering of Pantheism which affects most of us who have lived long enough in the country to acquire it.

Another method is to incise your decoration, deeply so that ravaging weather will not blur it away. This will only be easy on soft stone, which correspondingly is the most likely to wear. As a precaution against this, our own stonemason incised his name on a stone in the wall and prudently soaked it in a chemical which has ensured his immortality even if the wall falls down.

All the foregoing may seem lavish attention to a simple wall, but remember that, short of faulty construction in the first place and Act of God thereafter, it will be lasting far, far into the unforeseeable future.

Organizing the Formal Garden

I admit, though, that after the addition of these intricate extras, the fancy approach has to stop here. For the main obligation a walled garden confers on you is to be simple in its treatment. Unless it is very big, keep to one theme. If you pack it with a sea of plants, tune them into unity (like the wonderful rose garden at Mottisfont). If you make a topiary garden, then orchestrate the impact. And if you keep it open, make its internal lines simple and geometric. Formality in this case begets formality. Straight paths and beds will reinforce a square or rectangular perimeter. Or if curves are used as in a round or oval central pool, they have to be symmetrical. Warring informality will destroy that secluded calm which is the *raison d'être* of a walled garden.

If you have more than one enclosure, you are in the enviable position of being able to use each for a different purpose, season, theme or time of day. But the principle remains the same in each: that a simple, unified treatment is important. You are building a harmonious world.

Planting Within Walls

One or more trees of the canopy type are essential in any but the very regimented garden, in my view. Not only will they give height and shade but, if placed near the edges so that they spread outside the area of seclusion, they will counteract that feeling of claustrophobia induced by so introverted a world. Unless the enclosure is exceptionally large, small trees are best for you don't want the top-heavy dominance of taller trees. I myself have *Magnolia salicifolia*, three hornbeams undergoing the process of formal clipping and an opening into woodland in one corner. The first is invaluable for its starry scented flowers (and elegance throughout the year); the second, the short run of clipped hornbeams, gives useful structural shape; and the third, the woodland opening, a surprising encroachment.

A fair number of the wall plants should have equally forceful and differing personalities, for they have lots of aggressive hardware to cover. With these shrubs and climbers, one has to keep the balance in favour of heavy, stabilizing evergreens like clipped yews, *Magnolia grandiflora* (in one of its early-flowering clones), *Fatsia japonica*, *Hedera colchica* 'Dentata'; and all these can be reinforced in summer by heavy-foliaged deciduous plants like figs or *Aristolochia durior* (syn.*A. sipho*). You can add to this the kind of deciduous froth supplied by the ferny, pinnate-leafed *Albizzia julibrissin* with pink mimosa powder-puffs, or by *Robinia hispida* (also pinnate-leafed but with luscious pink racemes) or by the elegant grassy *Caragana arborescens* 'Lorbergii'. Wistaria, as befits this greatest of wall plants, eludes these simple categories, for its leaves are refined in form yet have a strong presence in the mass. Those cultivars with very long racemes (*Wistaria floribunda* 'Macrobotrys') are especially lovely trained over doorways so that you can drift back and forth through a curtain of trailing tresses.

With such plants as these in the majority, there is room for personal favourites or indulgences, even though these may not contribute much to the main effect. The gourmet might plant for a harvest of apricots. The plantsman would rather earmark his southern nooks for tender plants, since these walls drink in the sun's warmth during the day and radiate it out at night, thus helping to ripen the wood of the plants against them.

But whatever the choice of wall plants, the best effects are conjured when plants in both wall and border beneath it are colour- or leaf-related. Thus wall plants become actually part of the border beneath them. You could try, for example, the white lace-cap *Viburnum plicatum* 'Mariesii' (it looks marvellous trained against a shady wall) with *Myrrhis odorata* for ferny foliage and white geraniums like *G. sylvaticum album* for milky blossom at its feet. Or, beside a sunny wall, the climbing form of *Rosa* 'Souvenir de la Malmaison' with

15. Tall, old trees soaring beyond a smallish walled garden break its introversion.

huge blush quartered blooms, and banks of maroon double peonies as a skirt ('Knighthood' for early display, with 'Dr. Barnsby' to take over later). Or, to give an example of a leaf-related wall and border, I have the ferny-foliaged, velvet-stemmed *Lomatia ferruginea* on a north-west facing wall with ostrich ferns (*Matteuccia struthiopteris*) and hostas in variety around its base.

But one can have too much attention-getting and I aim for soothing effects by having a dominant reliable theme in parts anyway. A 50ft/15m wall run is entirely covered in my garden with grapevines, boring perhaps to many but valuable to me as they fulfil the same calm function as grass, giving a green uniform expanse. The bonus of sun-warmed grapes in October is a joy, though a family of small arboreal mice always beat us to the last bunches.

You can achieve the same restful effect with cool colour, with for example the blue of massed ceanothus. The incredibly beautiful garden of Kerdalo in Brittany has these blue cascades in repeated waves in spring. In any cold climate, these shrubs really must have wall protection and even then certain cultivars aren't reliably safe, especially the most glamorous which is *C. arboreus* 'Trewithen Blue'. There is now, however, a new form called 'Ray Hartman' which is supposed to be equally prodigal and large in its flower-clusters though reputedly hardier. *Clematis montana*, though enveloping in its potential size, is also worthy of a similarly repeated grouping if your canvas is of a scale to house them. The loveliest of all the cultivars, better than 'Tetrarose' or 'Pink Perfection' in my opinion, is the deep pink *C.m.* 'Percy Picton', originating in the famous nursery whose late founder-owner could still remember his early days with William Robinson at Gravetye Manor.

We expect a lot of all these wall shrubs and climbers, for the ground is often dust-dry at the foot of a wall; and even if we feed it during the planting ceremony, it rarely gets the same top-dressing that one accords a large border. Yet we plant our performers, jump back and ask them to amuse us. Many will oblige but even such stalwarts as the tougher roses may fail without an annual mulch and feeding. This is equally true of the large hybrid clematis which also share with camellias a need for a moist soil. The latter are often grown by a north-facing wall to shelter early blossoms and sometimes, in the case of certain cultivars, by a hot wall to initiate bud production, but whatever the aspect, they will be subject to bud-drop if their soil dries out.

Plants that will naturally grow within the wall itself will give you no such work, yet often good coverage. The crumbling mortar and crevices of an old wall can provide perches for sempervivums (I have seen them completely embossing a wall), the invasive pennywort (*Umbilicus rupestris*), hart's tongue fern in shade, *Asplenium trichomanes* and *A. ruta-muraria*, Cheddar Pinks (*Dianthus gratianopolitanus*), the ubiquitous but always graceful *Corydalis lutea*, the invasive *Sedum acre*, prettier and pendulous *Sedum album* and the equally encroaching *Cymbalaria muralis*. The latter is an interesting case of a plant so adapted to its environment that it holds its ripening fruit away from the light, thus increasing its chances of finding a crevice to invade. Quite a few of these plants can be found in the wild, and are therefore a charming way of tying an old garden wall to the countryside behind it.

Retaining Walls

Of all walls, the retaining drystone wall is the plantsman's paradise. One flank thick (if two, it is normally mortared, given weepholes but no plants in its sides), it can be planted above, between and below to make an exuberant crinoline of flower and leaf. It can lend itself to alpine plant treatment (see Chapter VII), but a larger wall is better clothed with billowing shrubs. The latter was Miss Jekyll's forte and her *Gardens for Small Country Houses* shows repeated examples of her brilliant schemes. Her walls are vertical borders, burgeoning with life, supporting great colonies of colour-related plants.

This is an ideal which is difficult to pursue, for in my experience it is virtually impossible to establish plants in the body of a wall (save self-seeders which do the job for you) unless you can plant in the course of building the structure. With an existing wall, you therefore rely on cascades from above which intermingle voluptuously at certain points with ascending growth from below. The top growth might consist of *Ceanothus* 'Cascade' (or *C. thyrsiflorus repens*), or tamarisks, tree lupins, fabianas (needing humus, lime-free soil and moisture), *Cytisus* x *kewensis* with its cream skirt in spring, *Genista lydia*, *Acer palmatum* 'Dissectum Viridis' (or one of its garnet cultivars), artemisias, rosemaries, sprawling roses

16. Walls at different angles and of varying heights are drawn together by a box hedge.

like 'Raubritter' with its pink globular shells or the pink 'Scintillation', *Senecio* 'Sunshine', phlomis, santolinas, gypsophilas, nepetas, *Alchemilla mollis* and *Campanula porscharskyana* (the last two making a very easy and lovely combination of lime-yellow and blue), white foxgloves and, for later in the season, fuchsias, perovskias, phygelius, caryopteris, and *Lespedeza thunbergii*, its arching branches pendulous with the weight of its long rosy-purple panicles.

These can be related to plants at the foot of the wall (if any) whether by colour, by fruit or by leaf or species, as, for example, in the case of trailing x *Fatshedera lizei* at the top of the wall falling towards *Fatsia japonica* at the foot. Or, for variety, those at the foot might be chosen for their contrasting shape: abrasive spires from below, be they *Eremurus robustus*, foxgloves, the tallest eryngiums (*E. pandanifolium*) or even the grassy sheaves of *Arundo donax*, will prevent it all from becoming too soft and monotonous a pillow.

Indigestibility is far worse than monotony, however, and there is sometimes a case for scoring a line through plant lists and recalling those strange yews on the terraces of Powis Castle — dark and overwhelmingly greater than the sum of all the flowers you might imagine. There are certain plants which, when given a prime position, express the character of a garden in an unforgettable way and these are just such an example.

But my own partnership is a conservatory above a retaining wall related to an oil tank beneath it. Though helped along by plants, they remain a constant warning to me that gardening is not a fine art, as is so often claimed. It is an applied one and therefore only the art of the possible.

31

III. Paths
Their Materials and Plants

TO BE BOTH USEFUL and beautiful at the same time is a difficult task, for like serving God and Mammon, it is bound to cause conflict at some stage. Yet the best sort of paths are just that, appealing to your sense as well as your sensibility. They are logical yet elegant extensions of the house into the garden, and from one point of departure to its destination.

A path's logic, however, must take precedence initially over its looks, because it is there for a purpose. It is an object of use, whether a straight run to provide urgent access, or a meandering way to give you lungfuls of air after a day indoors. Its elegance is, as it were, a superimposition, derived from its own internal pattern, from the rightness of its line or position in relation to buildings or the garden, and, not least, from the way it both organizes a garden and sets it in motion.

If judged by usefulness, many paths would fail. The reason is that feet can't read books or drawing-boards, and those paths which appeal on paper may be rejected by humans on the ground. There is a lesson to be learnt on this subject in hundreds of public parks. Here, 'Do not walk on the grass' notices supplement paths which were planned by clerks trying to make you walk two sides of a triangle instead of the hypotenuse. Such inconveniences can never work long-term. The moral is not to be apoplectic about the offenders, but to make sure that one's ideal path chimes with the user's self-interest.

The following, then, is my first rule when making a path. I either accept that convenience in path-using is essential. Or, alternatively, if I want to make a path which gives slow and circuitous access (the usual reason for this is to compel a particular angle of view on the walker), then I can only enforce it by blocking the walker's escape route. I can do this by walls, or deterrent plants (hedges), or with untraversable materials such as painfully lumpy cobbles or incommodiously long grass, as in an orchard.

Hidcote is an excellent illustration of this method. You don't think of it as a garden of paths and alleys because it is the hedges that are the evident feature. But it is full of restricting walks from which you have little escape, thanks mainly to the hedges. These compel on you in certain areas an enfiladed view of the flower borders, by far the most attractive way of viewing them. Without these hedges, you would be breaking from your paths and predetermined viewpoints, and the garden would seem a great deal less beautiful.

There is another path-making ideal to aspire to, but it is usually only a possibility in a larger garden. It entails having a path which leads you by one route from the main point

17. A beautiful and complex brick path using basketweave patterns to border a central elongating strip laid in stretcher bond.

of departure (the house) and enables you to return by a different route. In a large garden of varied parts, such a path will almost certainly take different forms in its circuit, for this arterial flow should harmonize sensitively with the spirit of each section it penetrates. For a start, its shape will change. If I can make a rather clichéd analogy with a river flowing into a sea, this path may in some areas (most probably near the house) change its linear character into a spread of paving or an equivalent material. And even where strictly linear, the width of the path will change in different areas of the garden. At some points, it could hold three of you abreast; at others, in woodland perhaps, where silence rather than sociability is appropriate, it can shrink to a single file. You might even care at some stage to dabble in *trompe l'oeil*, narrowing the furthest end of a straight run to reinforce the illusion of distance.

The path will also change from formal to informal in different self-contained areas; from straightness, which Ruskin claimed suggested restraint, to very gently sinuous where no urgent access is needed. Even its materials will alter, for it may be gravelled here, paved there, grassed in a third place, barked perhaps in a copse, non-existent in some parts, but with sub-plots to left and right elsewhere. It may therefore change its clothing, but at all times the thread should be sufficiently persistent and coherent to enable you to make your journey. And seeing it as a link helps you to preserve the unity of your garden.

Formal Paths

The handsomest clothing of all is to be found in the formal garden, where the path can be the main object of beauty. It may have to be, as it can be the most prominent ingredient, will be seen from start to finish and, in its role of delineating the shape of the garden, will determine the appearance of the surroundings. Here, this skeleton can be made an integral part of the design on a horizontal canvas. In some of the lovely turn-of-the-century gardens, for example, the paths are like an ornate picture frame around formal flower beds. Such paths are made from masonry which is treated as an art form, and they are ornamental not merely in themselves, but part of a larger overall pattern, reinforced perhaps by low formal hedges or borders.

Even in the formal garden, there is a degree of flexibility and paths do not have to be straight. Where they debouch from a house, for example, a gentle fan can be a lovely outward-flowing shape, but the curves must be geometric or symmetrical. A visit to Sulgrave Manor in Northamptonshire, home of George Washington's ancestors, throws light on this fact. Its garden was the work of Sir Reginald Blomfield, the architect who championed the return of formality at the end of the nineteenth century in an illuminating book called *The Formal Garden in England*. The design of this simple garden demonstrates the use of curves, circles and straight lines, particularly in paths, and would furnish anyone with ideas for possibilities.

Materials

The materials at your disposal include most of the range and its combinations outlined in Chapter I on terraces and courtyards; and the methods of laying are the same with equal stress put on the importance of good drainage. At the risk, however of stating the obvious, omit or keep to the side any materials which are awkward to walk over like protruding

18. *(above left)* 'Where paths debouch from a house, a gentle fan can be a lovely outward-flowing shape.'

19. *(above right)* ' The paths are like an ornate picture-frame around formal flower-beds' (Hidcote Manor Garden).

Fig. 1. (A) shows a pattern which elongates a short path. (B) is less elongating but more ornamental. (C) shows the basketweave in its simplest form. (D) is a herringbone path.

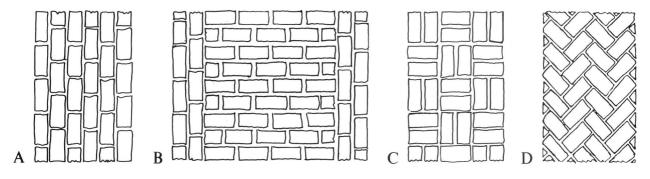

cobbles, or potentially dangerous where children might run, like slippery stone. Another obvious point is that the level of laying the path may be different from, say, paving. Where it is next to grass, a path needs to be slightly lower to avoid it scraping the mower's blade.

Similar materials, then, but you can ring the changes by using them in a different way. Bricks, for example, or any small rectangular units such as setts, can be laid to give the optical illusion of greater width or length than exists. Laid in the kind of bond shown in Fig. 1A, they will elongate a short path. Set crosswise, they will shorten and widen it. You can combine the two directions as in Fig. B to give a more ornamental as well as elongating effect (this device is used in a long path between borders at The Salutation, Kent, a garden originally designed by Lutyens). You can opt for one of the variations on basketweave patterns as in Fig. C which is the simplest form, a contrast with the path shown in Plate 17, a beautiful complicated variation using bricks in basketweave patterns bordering a central elongating run. Or you could choose a herringbone path, Fig. D, though its triangular ends need careful cutting and fitting, and you may prefer to omit them. In all these cases, the bricks can be laid in coarse sand (of a 3in/7.5cm depth, firmed and consolidated), but if you add a special selvedge, it is wiser to hold this in place by setting it in mortar which can be tinted to match the bricks with a suitably coloured sand. And if you want to keep the cost down, use the bricks flat rather than on edge as the latter method can more than double the number required.

Square units, such as paving slabs, can be given a fresh and original appearance if they are assembled in a diamond sequence. These lozenge shapes are wonderful in a path because they give a rhythmic movement, drawing you along. Another possibility is to incorporate the kind of eccentric additions which only come in small quantities and use these as stepping stones. In his garden at Stonypath in Scotland, the poet Ian Hamilton Finlay laid a path of diamond-set concrete slabs in grass, each unit incised with the name of an old sailing vessel. On a homelier note, Plate 56 shows staddle stones in a thread through a white border. Plate 20 shows circular slabs through a topiary garden. And, still on a rounded theme, at Portmeirion in North Wales, the grand architectural folly built by the architect Sir Clough Williams-Ellis, you will find concrete circles laid in a widely-spaced linear sequence within a cobbled path bordered by kerbstones. In all these cases, the stones are used as individuals and it is this that makes them so arresting.

Paths of Softer Appearance

Grass paths are another possibility, used as often in the formal as informal garden, for they do more for its tranquil atmosphere than any amount of hardware. They are the most labour-intensive of paths, however, and need regular fillips if subject to heavy wear for which they are scarcely suitable. Modern sportsfield treatment for whacked grass involves feeding it generously, cutting it less closely and less often, and using light rotary mowers. But this may be a recipe you would rather avoid in your own garden. Besides, if the grass path is bordered by beds, you already have the regular labour of edging it and keeping the gully clear. To ease your lot, mower-slabs lining one or both sides, are a great asset.

Woodland and Wild Garden Paths

Informal winding paths through long grass can simply be made by the mower. Such paths, however, being defined solely by the height of the adjacent grass in summer, do not exist at any other season. This temporary characteristic appeals to me, for seasonal change is one of the great pleasures in the temperate parts of our world.

In woodland, a grass path is also possible though it is inclined to wear out to a mix of mud and moss. And it shows the less acceptable face of seasonal change when it degenerates into an unnegotiable quagmire in winter which will follow you into the house around the ankles of your boots. You can try sowing it with a shade-bearing mix of grass, but this still requires mowing and may not work for you. In this case, pulverized bark (expensive but agreeably dark) or sawdust (cheap but rather obtrusive in cool, green woodland) can be used instead. (Threave Gardening School in south-west Scotland have used the latter over ashes as a labour-saving measure.) But both materials are certainly comfortable to walk on and can either be left untreated as a medium for woodland plants to colonize in parts, or treated with herbicide.

Some people use slices of tree-trunks as stepping-stones in this setting, but these become

20. Round stepping-stones make an apt path when bordered by rounded topiary shapes.

slippery under tree-drip. In my view, they also give the inappropriate air of corpses among the living, for an unfortunate event has clearly occurred. It afflicts me with the kind of unease I feel when the butcher delivers a leg of lamb in front of my paddock of pet sheep.

Gravel: the Happy Medium

Gravel comes somewhere between these soft surfaces and hard-edged paving etc. For the method of laying, please see page 19, but on a path keep this gravel to a thickness of about 1in/2.5cm otherwise you will roll and wallow in its give, especially uphill. If the slope is very steep (and especially on drives) the only lasting method is to bond the gravel with a bituminous surface and then top this with an extra sprinkling of gravel. The colour range of the material includes dusky tones of red, green, yellow, violet and grey; the best is the one which blends quietly with your house (if in stone or brick), and the cheapest is the one which is local.

Though it is relatively maintenance-free and can be kept clear with herbicides, it has several main drawbacks. Firstly it is inclined to infiltrate adjacent material, especially grass, and for this reason it is best to give it a firm raised edging to control it. Secondly, it slips into open sandals when you walk on it (sometimes, mysteriously, even into gumboots and hoovers). And most obvious of all, its surface smoothness is easily displaced. The only answer to this is a relaxed attitude, or you will be provoked into frantic raking whenever

21. The spikes of yuccas are a skyline contrast to a gravel path.

you or your friends arrive or depart. Walter, the husband of the gardener Margery Fish, would hold an inquest and a raking whenever they had a party which left tyremarks on his gravelled drive.

The big plus with gravel paths is that they can become gravel gardens (see page 14). In this case, the path comes into existence through omission; that is, it is defined solely by being the one portion to be left unplanted. I hesitate to call such a path a line, for its flow is usually inconsistent and interrupted. Rugs of plants break up its edges completely, sometimes the vanguard of dense planting behind. And, among these plants, the paths (or to be precise, the unplanted areas) can run as rivulets, enabling you to make incursions into different parts.

Plants to Border Any Path

Assuming you want the path to dominate plants, opt for a precisely defined edging to follow its line along either side. If, however, the plants are to rule the path, you can choose them to mutiny against its restraint. Thus, either you use plants to enforce its hard angularity and to give it direction: or your plants can blur its edges and purposefulness. An extreme example of the first category is a flank of low, formally clipped hedging such as box beside a straight path. But any tidy plants used regularly, even if placed at intervals, will do a similar job, whether clipped, as with a series of box puddings (the best known example is at Tintinhull in Somerset) or whether used as a free-growing edging. Lines of giant chives (*Allium schoenoprasum sibiricum*), thrifts (the bigger forms like *Armeria* 'Ornament' or *A. hybrida formosa*) or pinks or London Pride or short hebes like the glaucous *Hebe albicans* or rich green dwarf *H.* 'Edinensis' are candidates. Fairly neat, domed or angular in growth, they will not interrupt a decoratively laid formal path which is designed to be seen in full from side to side and from start to finish.

These are biddable plants, chosen for their subservience to the path. But you can extract

22. The extreme softening effect of the pendulous, delicately textured *Equisetum telmataia*.

dramatic effects of a different kind by using less tractable plants which oppose their situation. Plate 21 shows a path at Penpol House in Cornwall. The gentle curve of the gravel path here is framed by the hard, uneven spikes of yuccas, following its direction high above the ground. It is the contrast here that makes it interesting – the horizontal curve on the ground marked out by spiky uprights in the sky.

With a straight path, you would achieve your contrast by using instead collapsing, irregularly billowing plants for a deliberate softening job. Extreme softening effects are possible if you plant very delicately textured, pendulous plants such as *Equisetum telmataia* (Plate 22) – not delicate in its growth, I must add, being highly invasive, though it would not offend me were it to take over much of my garden. It is the contrast between path and plant that startles: the adornment of hardware with lace.

There are yet other means of achieving the same soft effect. Bulky shrubs can be allowed to encroach right across the path and I have seen *Daphne pontica*, *Acer palmatum* and *Choisya ternata* in such positions. In truth, shrubs such as these are rarely intended to encroach, but are planted too close to the path in infancy and virtually seal off access in maturity. Yet, unless the path is a piece of rigid decoration, free growth of this kind has an appeal to be exploited. It results in that special charm of building work rightly welded through time to the plants that live by it. It is apparent symbiosis of this kind that makes a place lovable and lived-in.

The real softeners are indeed those plants that live off the path or in its crevices, such as thyme mats, longer-lasting pinks (in well-drained positions) like *Dianthus gratianopolitanus* and *D. neglectus*, the smallest thrifts, pads of aubrieta, purple-leafed clovers and a creeping campanula like the thimble-flowered *C. cochlearifolia*. More of these are suggested in Chapter VII on alpines and rock plants. Whether you can bear to tread them is another point. They look marvellous rampaging over a large area in full flower, but keep them near the edges in a path subject to constant use throughout the year. To come back to where I began, most paths have to be utilitarian.

IV. Steps, Staircases and Banks
Designs, Softening Plants, Ornament, and the Ha-ha

THE BUSINESS of impressing one's identity on a garden can take perverse forms. It often expresses itself by turning the site into something it isn't. Thus a flat town garden is massaged into tiers of different heights. And a sloping country garden is all too often bulldozed without reason to a uniform level and consequent blandness. Such an action shows a complete misunderstanding of what a country garden is about. One of the (intractable) delights it gives you is that it shows its relationship to the rocky substrata of its land; it conforms to its contours, to those oolitic or sandstone layers which are the patient accumulation of millions of years.

Now, this may be a hyper-rosy description of a site which is simply a horror to mow, but there is an interest and variety in such a garden which is worth retaining. The difficulties that accompany these charms can at least be tamed into convenience. The means you use to do so – whether steps, staircases, banks etc. – depend on the immediate surroundings. They also depend on the price you are prepared to pay, though, as always, it does not follow that the best effects can be bought. Rather, they are contrived out of an artful design, apt materials and an understanding that steps etc. are there to be used safely. They are not just executive toys, one function of many garden structures these days.

Steps

Their siting matters. Where circumstances don't dictate a particular position (as in the continuation of a path), it is sensible to build the steps where they will be assertive. There is a sound argument for this. Safeness is essential, and a bold and spacious design lessens the risk of mistaking levels and tripping. This is true even in woodland where the appropriate steps ought to be tastefully self-effacing. Cryptically camouflaged and slimy with tree-drip, such treads can be lethal on a wet day.

Most steps, however, are in the formal part of the garden near the house. Here, they are most frequently needed as a lead from the terrace into the open garden. In theory, this is always a downward movement, everyone assuming that all houses are built on the classical ideal of raised ground. In practice, in a garden at the bottom of the hill, the steps may rise. Unfortunately, this usually restricts your scope for design, quite apart from challenging your drainage system in heavy rain, when a positive cascade may threaten.

23. 'The use of the semi-circle has an almost liquid effect on stone, as though it were spilling forward very slowly into the garden.'

From the terrace, the change of level rarely involves a drop of more than a few feet. Yet this small space can be turned into a work of art.

The fortunate owners of old formal houses might have a look at some turn-of-the-century examples for ideas. Few have exceeded the reverence which Sir Edwin Lutyens accorded his steps. His characteristic look was dramatic but simple, and arose out of the balance he achieved between straight and semi-circular or circular treads within the short drop. This use of the circle or its segment is treating masonry as though it were a sort of drapery, and it is only possible with steps. You cannot do it with paths, nor with walls, nor even doorways, since these are horizontal or vertical; but steps can flow, and the use of the semi-circle in particular has an almost liquid effect on stone as though it were spilling forward very slowly into the garden, impelling the feet that tread it onwards – and also outwards. For the important point about semi-circular steps is that their focus of attention is not just straight ahead, but also fans out to the left and right. This gives you an expansive angle of vision over the full extent of the territory before you. In addition, this symmetrical bulge gives the steps a profile when approached obliquely from a distant point. They can act as a visible drawing-force from far off, being a focus of order, purpose and beauty which the area beside the house is supposed to represent.

This use of curving steps was taken to its full extent in the gardens of Bodnant and Renishaw Hall, the Sitwell home in Derbyshire. Both have landings on steps in the form of complete circles, a wonderfully opulent device. And at Great Dixter in Sussex (see Colour Plate IV), the circular landings are made of grass within stone, an ultimate and, alas, labour-intensive refinement.

In a very cramped or simple setting, the rich effect of these curves would be quite inappropriate. But even with straight-edged steps, a feeling of comfort can be conveyed by a spacious tread and a shallow riser. Lutyens' steps, for example, have 18in/45cm treads and 6in/15cm high risers. They were designed for walkers who have the time to linger over changing their ground levels. Indeed, at times, the invitation to linger became a message to rest a while. For where piers or low walls gently grasped the straight steps, the effect was almost that of winged armchair comfort. Or the ease of a deep sofa might be a better analogy, since the width of these steps was normally ample enough to allow several people to rise or fall in companionship. Indeed, in *Gardens for Small Country Houses* Miss Jekyll expressly warned against 'the common mistake of making them too narrow'.

Given the space and an appropriate setting, it is not difficult to achieve similarly expansive and even curved designs, though the latter will inevitably use more stone or bricks, and more ground space. By selecting your materials carefully, you may modify the difficulties and the costs, though the need to key the steps to the materials of the adjacent terrace, paths and house will leave you little room for manoeuvre.

Large, real stone slabs are the most awkward to use for curved steps, though perversely perhaps the loveliest. Each slab will almost surely have to be cut to fit beside its neighbour and form a symmetrical 'rib' within the semi-circle. Actual stones, whether semi-dressed or undressed, are also possible, though they should be of roughly equivalent size, not *too* large, and with two flat faces. Even supposing they are obtainable, their rusticity will be an advantage in one garden, and a drawback in another. Frost-proof bricks, laid on edge, are simpler by far to handle and, with patience, could be assembled by an amateur, so long as he never puts the spirit-level down. Or another possibility is to modify the full-blooded semi-circular outline and use instead a segment (a shallow curve which is simply part of a circle); such an outline can easily be laid with small symmetrical setts (such as those shown in Plate 18) which are positioned to form a fan.

For all the above, it is essential that any stone, bricks etc. are weathered. If stone, for example, is taken straight from a quarry, it can crack, which is especially dangerous on steps.

Miss Jekyll judged that 'the decorative value of steps consists primarily in the alternation of horizontal bands of light and shade – shining treads and dark risers'. And it is true that the risers are very much part of the whole design. This is usually more evident in a staircase where the upper steps may well be at eye-level or higher; here, it is the risers that you see first. You have the option of treating these risers discreetly, using a stable and conforming material, or of devising deliberate ornament for them. I cautiously opted for the latter in the case of a long step in my own garden, for which I planned to use large natural stones. They needed extra height, however, so for their base we decided on a cement riser which would be studded with closely set pebbles. It sounds rather too cosmetic, but it was especially appropriate beside a gravel garden where the materials are the same in colour and shape and only differ in scale. Besides, you will find a similar treatment was given to the great Lutyens staircase at Home Place, Norfolk, a photograph of which was published in the 1912 edition of *Gardens for Small Country Houses*.

If you try this treatment yourself, keep the pebbles in a bucket of cold water as you work. Press them closely together into the moist but firm cement. They must be inserted to at least half their length or they will fall out. It is quite a heavy job as the firm cement exerts resistance to them.

Yet the most enchanting contrast I have seen between treads and risers is at Misarden Park in one of the highest parts of the Cotswolds. Two of the many flights of steps in this hillside garden are made with wide, shallow, mown grass treads. At each of the right-angles where tread and riser meet is a necklace strung from side to side of non-trailing, deep blue lobelia (see Plate 24). The gardener here suggested to me that a permanent planting

24. Grass treads with stone and lobelia-planted risers.

of crocuses in the lines of these crevices would be equally appealing. The effect is the prettiest staircase imaginable, reminding one of those medieval turf seats studded with miniature flowers and courtly human beings. It is as labour-saving in its design as possible, for you can see how the grass steps are keyed into the gently sloping flanks of the bank either side, to permit easy and continuous mowing. What is more, its cheapness to erect and the charming simplicity of its appearance could make it a choice for many country homes.

Staircases

However, the demands of maintenance remain a top concern for most of us and, faced with the need for a large staircase, we would probably opt for hard materials that don't need aftercare. Stone or brick are indeed very hard if you fall on them and a flight of steps will need to be winged with some kind of wall or edging which will warn the eye and steady you if you trip. This eats up a lot of materials and all must be securely assembled, which means that it must be a professional job. The staircase is, however, quicker to erect (and therefore cheaper) than you might imagine. My own, for example, walled either side, eleven treads high running to a maximum height of 7ft/2.1m and width of 10ft/3m, took two men three and a half days to build.

The kind of balance between treads and risers that the Jekyll/Lutyens partnership practised and that many garden designers now recommend (treads three times the height of risers) is a luxury for a staircase with many steps, because it will consume so much ground. It will also have a somewhat ballroomy impact and one cannot for ever be sweeping into one's garden for the grand entrance. My own rather more modest staircase has 16in/40cm treads (made of setts) and 6in/15cm risers, and I find that the slope is gentle enough for comfort. In practice, the 16in/40cm treads are reduced, of course, because the back part is buried (the front overhanging by about 2in/5cm).

When these steps were first built, the uniformity of the setts I used gave them a dismaying resemblance to teeth, but they began to settle into their surroundings quite soon. Two measures help this softening process. Both concern the materials. My setts have a rounded edge and riven surface; the latter is not only safer in bad weather, but gives a softer, aged appearance. Secondly, the grouting is simply a mix of sand and cement (no water), brushed into the cracks between the setts after they are laid upon wet cement. Rain or simply damp in the atmosphere will harden the mix. Again, the effect is soft. Weeds will of course seed into it in due course and so will acceptable plants, but simazine will keep undesirables out.

There are a few more softening devices you can resort to. Most steps march forward; I designed mine instead to fan out. Again, as with curved steps, they are leading you not only onwards but outwards. The masonry is in effect telling you to look about you. The other measure you can take is to trail climbers down the sides. Wistaria and *Clematis montana* are sometimes used, guided down on wires. Ornamental vines are also possible. This kind of abandoned festooning looks very lovely in flower or leaf, but a monkey's breakfast in winter. An ivy with elegant leaves, such as the feathery *Hedera helix* 'Green Ripple' or the architectural *H.h.* 'Hamilton' would be good all-year-round candidates. *H.h.* 'Manda's Crested', a vigorous clone with curly leaves is another possibility.

You can also introduce flowers – perhaps filmy and frail-looking self-sowers such as

25. *(above)* Tiled risers with plain stone treads flanked by clipped yews.

26 & 27. *(above left)* Steps which are banked and *(below left)* edged with wistaria.
28. *(right)* The repeated use of the simplest of ornaments suits this stone staircase in a tree-hung setting.

Erigeron karvinskianus (syn. *E. mucronatus*) in sun, or in shade *Corydalis lutea* (*C. ochroleuca* with white, yellow-tipped flowers is less common and even more charming), both of which will surely take over. Or you could plant in the angle between tread and riser; encourage ivy trails, creeping campanulas, creeping mints, and add ferns, tight-leafed sedums like *S. dasyphyllum*, sempervivums, pads of aubrieta, hummocky thymes such as *Thymus caespititius* (syn *T. micans*), and other foliage cushions towards the extremities, perhaps on the treads themselves. But the creepers need regular attention to stop them straying outside the area. And cushions near the edges force you to walk down the centre of the steps, perhaps riskily far from the rail or guards. Neither prospect is ideal in certain circumstances.

An impression of bosomy leafiness may be more prudently achieved by planting bushy shrubs to flank the steps, particularly at the landing point. *Choisya ternata, Ozothamnus rosmarinifolius, Daphne* x *burkwoodii, Pinus mugo* are the kind of subjects I have in mind.

Or, if you have built the steps into the bank (as opposed to making them a projection from it), then you could plant up the sides of a gentle slope with dome-forming helichrysums, the spreading *Euphorbia cyparissias*, the cascading *Artemisia* 'Powis Castle', genistas like *G. lydia*, rounded hebes such as *H. rakaensis*, the grey *H. albicans* or the similar *H.* 'Pewter Dome'. A steeper slope would need clinging cover such as *Cotoneaster congesta* or drapings from plants like the prostrate rosemary (*Rosmarinus lavandulaceus*). Given a high enough perch, sun, well-drained and light soil and fairly mild winters, this will live to make a long, tapering curtain of grey-green. The hardier, bushier but low-growing *R.* 'Severn Sea', a form with rich blue flowers, is also excellent in colder places: mine catches the scourge of an icy north wind as it whips round a wall, yet has never shown signs of bad needle-loss or burn — only lorry roll-over. Helianthemums and the lower-growing cistus such as *C.* x *corbariensis, C.* 'Silver Pink', *C.* x *loretii* (white with a maroon blotch) and *Halimiocistus sahucii* (*Cistus rosmarinifolius*) will add summer colour. They are also especially suited to droughty situations of this kind, if in sun. All the above, too, are evergreen, so the steps will keep their soft furnishings in winter.

The other type of staircase ornament is the dead adornment of stone, terracotta or similar hard materials. It is likely to take the form of pots (see Chapter IX) – almost always acceptable if they are unpretentious, but perhaps difficult to water if planted — balustrading which can be horizontal or ramped, and obelisks or balls etc. These will be appropriate or absurd according to their surroundings, though, on a staircase, my own feeling is that the grander elements only slide into place in the Italianate garden where all decoration is formal, even the plants. And, even there, until the ornament is weathered and lichened, if you have any finesse you will still cringe at the raw *nouveau-riche* quality of it all. The weathering process can be sped on its way with an application of milk, watered-down dung or strong tea. A liquid chemical to give instant antiquity can also be used. Haddonstone, the reconstituted stone manufacturers, gave me this after I took delivery of two excruciatingly new-looking balls, resembling a pair of tomatoes. It works, though nothing equals the comfortable patina of age and well-aimed bird droppings.

Whatever adornment you choose, do confine your purchases to one type of ornament. There is nothing like an overdressed staircase for monumentalizing conspicuous expenditure. Lucky those who need only a relatively short staircase (see Plate 28) and settle either for an undecorated low stone ramp or the simplest of adornments as sufficient. It will be assimilated far more easily into its surroundings.

Where great length is required, a terraced staircase will be necessary, complete with landings. My own, which is eleven treads high, is quite enough to manage without pause. If you can afford to make the landing spacious enough, then a bench or seat is a welcome human touch, inviting you to sit and look from a height, reminding you that steps can provide you with unfamiliar vistas. The landing is also a necessary device in a staircase that has to change direction, crooking at right-angles.

Trees overhanging or flanking steps are lovely; for they dwarf any large hard structure which always threatens to step out of scale with the natural world. For this reason we have retained a big ash whose branches sweep forward beside steps; but in a wet November, the dead leaves are admittedly a hazard as they pile on the steps, and this would be yet truer with a larger-leafed tree whose dead foliage was too heavy to be blown away in the wind.

This is the great drawback of steps in woodland. Leaf-drip and fall are especially dangerous on stone steps. Timber steps are often used here as an alternative – made perhaps from railway sleepers, though any timber must be fully treated with preservative if it is to endure in the ground. But even these will get slippery. Gravel steps edged with timber are a safer option in this part of the garden, unless they offend the spirit of the setting. Keep these very shallow, and in icy or wet weather, you can step confidently into the gravel area, passing over the slippery edge. Colonies of ferns can be built up at the edges if the steps are long enough, and the centre can be kept free with a contact and residual herbicide. Steps dug out of earth alone will never work. However firm and dry in summer, they will soon melt into a series of muddy bumps in rain.

Ramps

In comparison with steps, ramps are bereft of aesthetic possibilities. They belong to the first technological society, that which discovered the wheel. They are destined for prams, wheelchairs, bicycles, cars and wheelbarrows; feet take a poor second-place to machines

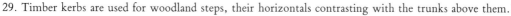

29. Timber kerbs are used for woodland steps, their horizontals contrasting with the trunks above them.

30. The roof of a summerhouse at Pitchford Hall, Shropshire, appears above the bank like a mushroom.

here. It follows that they should only be built with a very shallow rise, otherwise you will be straining your load uphill and out of control downhill. And, as befits any service area, it is best to keep them out of sight if possible, perhaps by giving them flanks of shrubs.

Banks

Green banks, when used in a deliberate design, can be quite beautiful and in Britain especially, where most years we have the climate for a lush sward, we underestimate the potential of grass works. Gardens of changing lawn levels, banked into squares and rectangles like small tiltyards, can be attractive in themselves without further adornment. The play of sunlight and shade across these green undulations does not occur to you until you see it. In this respect, we ought to regain the picturesque sensibility of the eighteenth century which was aware of and exploited changing light on the landscape. It is one of the great charms of such green-banked gardens that, even on frenzied days and despite the scudding of light and shade, they have the power to impart a sense of calm. Their one drawback is that they do force you to depend on a hover mower, and even though these work on a cushion of air, some people find them heavy to manipulate on anything but a small scale. In less organized parts of the garden, it would be best to let the grass on a large bank grow long and only cut it twice a year. With this method, if you plant small bulbs and wild flowers on the upper reaches of the bank, they will in time naturalize down the slope if in congenial soil.

Sometimes a mower is out of the question, yet the situation demands action. In this case, you can plant the bank up. On a high, very steep slope, plants are your best insurance against soil erosion and subsidence. This remains true, even though, paradoxically, the act of planting precipitates erosion at first because you have to break into well-compacted soil and apply water to settle the plants in.

The simplest approach to planting is to apply a contact and pre-emergence weed-killer (I will do anything to avoid chemicals on my beds, but this is one area which does defy one's conscience) and then dig holes for the plants at close intervals to encourage early union. They must be watered in not only very thoroughly, but very slowly too. A trickle or continuous spray will be absorbed (it must penetrate to at least 12in/30cm for ground-cover plants, considerably more for trees): but a heavy hosing will not, for the water will simply run down the slope. You may need to puddle the plants in in dry seasons or dry areas, and then apply water afterwards too. If you are not using a pre-emergence weed-killer, then mulch with sheets of black polythene, with holes cut out for the plants. Remove this when they start to get going.

You can use scrambling plants and spreading shrubs, but include a high proportion of those whose roots will colonize and knit the soil together. Pampas grass has proved a first-rate subject in this test; Algerian ivy is also good, though not suited to the coldest regions.

In formal parts of the garden, a once-and-forever solution is to wall the bank's surface with slabs, leaving planting holes for the subjects. But this is so often a favourite option for municipal amenity officers, that, as a private gardener, one has to select one's plants, one's slabs, one's mortar with great care to avoid a Shopping Centre impression. Keep to evergreens but avoid any of those indestructible subjects with a vandal-proof tag. This means no berberis, shrubby potentillas, hypericums, commonplace cotoneasters or large-leafed vincas for a start. A careful assemblage of tumbling and slab-obliterating conifers could work, using such types as *Picea abies* 'Reflexa', prostrate blue spruce, *Juniperus sabina tamariscifolia, Pinus mugo*. But these look unacceptably foreign in a country garden unless they are in a self-contained area and are related thematically to other parts of this garden. A mix of maquis-type plants – brooms, artemisias, senecios, lavenders, rosemaries, rock roses, evergreen achilleas, stachys – may blend in better. So might the use of trailers, such as ivies, x *Fatshedera lizei, Aristolochia durior* (syn. *A. sipho, A. macrophylla*), *Hydrangea petiolaris*, clematis species, *Rubus cockburnianus* and *R. tricolor* though all these will soon intertwine in an inextricable embrace unless you curb some exuberance.

The Ha-ha

Those few with an unspoilt view over undulating pasture may settle for the ha-ha, which is a bank you cannot see. To be more precise, it is a sunken ditch with a vertical walled side (usually about 4ft/1.2m deep) and a gentle slope for its other side. Its virtue is that it allows not only unimpeded views from the garden out to the land beyond, but also permits the impression that these are an extension of the garden. But beware. Nowadays, most open land in the country is subject to industrialized farming; this is much more obtrusive than the managed drift of browsing cows and sheep over green turf. The result is that, unless you own the land you overlook, you may be periodically shocked by your views. For two months of the year, you are likely to survey ploughed earth. For the rest of the year, who knows what? Some possibilities can look very lovely such as wheat; and it is salutory to remember that Humphry Repton exploited this by retaining cornfields between the house and the wooded hills at Sheringham Hall in Norfolk. But other possibilities are much less engaging. Your pride in false ownership of the land you survey is likely to tumble when the fields beyond are put on a rotating cycle of cabbage, swedes, potatoes etc. or whatever the Ministry of Agriculture encourages next.

V. Water in the Garden
Natural Water, Waterfowl, Wet Ditches, Bridges, Formal Water, Swimming-pools

SEVEN YEARS AGO we made a pond. By usual standards it is large; nearly a fifth of an acre, originally 6ft/1.8m deep in the middle, fed by a wet ditch and rainpipes, and drained by a 12in/30cm bore outlet. Though the slough of despond in winter, it is transformed into a glittering mirror in summer when we call it a lake. Its status therefore fluctuates, but at all times it gives me more real pleasure than anywhere else in the garden. It has the negative charm that it doesn't have to be mown. And, looked at more positively, it has the unique capacity amongst all the other ingredients of the garden to take one back to childhood. Prone on its banks, a Pimms in one hand and *The Observer's Book of Pond Life* in the other, you revert very easily to that infant state of just watching and wondering.

Our pool is 'natural', by which I mean that the ingredients already existed in a raw state which could be turned to advantage. We had impermeable Herefordshire clay, a wet ditch down sloping land, a puddle at the lowest point and a site nearby which could be exploited to give fine reflections if flooded with water. For its shape, we decided on a great irregular bowl, narrowing like a teardrop at the main source. It would be rounded but not too much, following the dictates that a 'natural' pool should be contoured to the land rather than to man's geometry. If shape was important, size was yet more crucial. The pool must cover the largest possible area, for the surrounding scenery would have dwarfed a smaller pool to dinkiness, a fate all owners of large or merely open country gardens should beware.

Decisions such as these can be worked out in advance using hosepipes as outlines on the ground, but in practice, given the astonishing flexibility of a Caterpillar earth-moving machine in capable hands, finishing scoops can easily be made on site. If you want an island, however, or a peninsula (or even an archipelago), you must plan well beforehand, so that the earth can either be left in its place or piled there in the process. Of the two, a peninsula has the obvious advantage that you can trot across the isthmus to tend the plants or whatever. An island in contrast needs a large pool to justify its existence and can only be reached by rowing-boat, delightful adventure though that is in one's own garden.

Whatever the shape of your pool, its sides are formed from the banks of excavated earth, massaged to your purposes. A shallow and shelved rise, on some sides at least, is best for pool life, whether this takes the form of marginal plants or of ducks whose offspring must be able to climb out of the water or they will die from exhaustion. If you don't plan well

31. *Déjeuner liquide sur l'eau* — not quite Manet, nor even Monet (see page 53), but a supreme pleasure in your own garden.

in advance, the top of this bank will be sub-soil and a poor growing-medium for plants. You avoid this (I didn't and am paying for it now) by arranging for your digger to transfer the top-soil to a separate area, so that you can 'ice' the sub-soil with a layer of 9in/22.5cm, at the very least, of top-soil after the other earth-moving operations are over. This will enable you to establish plants more easily round the entire perimeter of the bank, a necessity in most cases, but certainly if you are lining the pool (see below) with butyl-rubber or PVC. Both of these need to be concealed by weeping, smothering foliage at their top edge. Only really pendulous plants will do this job adequately for the water-level drops considerably in summer, even in a deep pool, and lining (or concrete, mud, shingle etc.) can be extensively exposed.

There is another factor you may have to anticipate at the digging-stage and that is erosion of the banks by moles, water voles or rats, pecking ducks or simply by the water itself — though this is not a problem with a concrete pool. You may be able to live with this if the pool has lots of surrounding space, and plants will in any case help to bind the banks of the earth — unless they are eaten too. But if not, a stone or block wall may be necessary, if not all the way round at least on the side taking the greatest pressure. In Beth Chatto's garden in Essex, concrete blocks were used which were stabilized by angle irons driven through the blocks and into the mud. Alternatively, the banks can be lined with a closely packed wall of preservative-treated timber stakes or planks which are pushed vertically into the mud.

The digging of our own pool took merely two days, so the labour costs weren't too high. As it was a large job, the operation was carried out with a JCB and a Caterpillar in a dry August to avoid the risk of the machines sticking and sliding in wet clay. I then had a month to agonize over the huge unvisualized bomb-crater we had bought. It seemed the driest August in years. Why didn't it rain and if it did, would it ever fill? Within two months the answer was yes to both and, had I but known this at the time, my experience of lake-making was as painless as it is possible to be.

The reason for this lay in the soil. Our own earth, Herefordshire clay, is so impermeable that it holds water without further ado. Freer-draining soils have to be lined either with the expensive but durable, matt-black butyl-rubber or the inferior, shorter-lived PVC alternative. (Lay off the gaudy colours.) Polythene liners are also sold, but forget them; they have a life-span of only a few years and are easily pierced.

Otherwise, pools can be constructed of concrete, a tricky operation requiring punctilious care if it is to be successful. I have seen several empty concrete basins of poignant appearance in people's gardens which never quite made it to the usable stage.

A fourth option is to line free-draining soil with imported, puddled clay. In the past, this was applied whilst damp over a coating of soot, devised to deter worms who habitually punctured the clay layer. Water would then be poured into the pool and the level of puddled clay checked for a match with the surface of the water. In sun, any clay exposed above the water surface to the air, would contract and fall off. In practice, this meant that even with an established pool, a hosepipe had to be ready to replace water which had evaporated on hot days. It is not surprising that this operation was (and still is, when practised) notorious for its failure rate. ('Capability' Brown would sometimes receive letters from clients to the effect that his lake had lost its water; very sorry he would reply, and have another go.)

In the United States, however, a soil sealant is available which has eased this method of constructing a natural, unlined pool (to the best of my knowledge, not yet available in the UK). An emulsified polymer which acts by binding the particles of soil together, it is used on all but very sandy or stony soils and cuts seepage by up to 95%. After the excavation has finished and the soil has been compacted to the fullest extent, the pool is half-filled with water whereupon the sealant is added and mixed with the water. The process of stirring to ensure complete distribution is continued as more water is poured in and the level of water is kept topped up for between twelve and twenty days. If the surface drops, the exposed area will be insufficiently sealed. For a month or perhaps more, the water is milky and toxic to fish, but this is not the only problem. If the pool dries out, the sealant can be affected; and algaecides and chemical treatments are not recommended. In addition to all this, it is an open question whether plant roots can also cause damage, but the method has been tried for a number of years in the construction of man-made lakes and lagoons in America.

These, then, are the practical steps involved in making a pool. What is its potential and why is it worth making? There are several answers to this, one to do with beauty, the other about fun.

Monet's garden at Giverney is the most persuasive of the artistic arguments. It contained the ultimate in waterlilied pool beauty and was to prove to him an inexhaustible source of inspiration for over thirty years. Yet its origins were the most prosaic imaginable. The original pool, a tiny embryo near the River Ru, lay in a field on the other side of the railway line beyond his house. He bought and planted it, but soon grew dissatisfied with its size and symmetry, and planned to divert the river and shape the pool to his own requirements. French peasant arguments ensued about Monet's plants which might poison the cattle's drinking-water or pollute the river for women who washed their linen there. Then finally, daunted by the artist's persistence, the Parish Council permitted his plans to divert this branch of the Epte.

Out of these wranglings, so familiar to those who live in a village, grew Monet's paradisaical pool. He enlarged it repeatedly, he shaped its edges to the curves that he needed, he ensured that tree clumps and twisting paths gave a sense of space. The arched bridge with its superstructure, inspired by a Japanese print, was smothered in pendent mauve and white wistaria weeping into their reflection. Poplars, willows and alders stood further afield. Rhododendrons, and azaleas, weeping willows, great ferns, massed roses (bushes and ramblers – he grew 'Belle Vichyssoise' like a tropical climber over his trees, so Miss Jekyll was not the first to popularize this method of growing roses) and bamboo jungles clustered in groves round the edges. Meadowsweet, irises and the fragrant but rampant early-flowering petasites covered the banks. And in the surface of the pond floated the waterlilies that he painted again and again. Almost until his death, he recreated this water-garden obsessively in his paintings, the art of gardening and of painting interconnected in mutual nourishment.

This is the kind of perfection that we nearly all fail by, not simply from lack of imagination, but through insufficient time, labour and dedication. But something can still be extracted by those who seek to make a beautiful natural water-garden – if they remember the profusion of his planting, his mingling of native and exotic plants, and the way he used the connection between a subject and its reflection in the water.

This last is the most important, and its success can in some cases depend neither on time nor on effort (which plants require) but simply on the imaginative placing of a pool in the first instance. In our garden, for example, the pool was positioned to reflect the pink stone walls of house and barns. I saw this as a daylight asset, but it was at night that it surprised me with its beauty. Here, after dark, I often walk on the far side of our pool and watch the golden lights of the house and barns moving dreamily in the blue-black water, now sharp and starry in outline, now dissolving out of focus as a breeze shifts the surface of the water. It is one of the loveliest sights that we have and the more valued by me for being an effortless way of achieving a spectacular effect.

Waterfowl

But there is another way of dramatizing informal (and unlined) water and that is to populate it with waterfowl. It is not trouble-free – they will require feeding once a day in summer and double that rate in the six winter months. And the birds, which are often bought with one wing pinioned to prevent them flying away, are a responsibility in a way that plants are not, for their lives depend on your care and protection, perhaps for years. Yet their presence is rewarding beyond belief and will introduce you to a world outside the narrow constraints of 'gardens mean plants' and in this case 'pools mean waterlilies'.

Which species of birds you choose will affect the look of the pool enormously (see the table), and I am not referring simply to the appearance of the waterfowl. Diving-ducks (*Aythya*), for example, stir up mud or deposits continuously at the base of the pool in their search for food, with the result that the water is mostly cloudy and brown. In contrast dabbling ducks (*Anas*) up-end themselves in the shallows and cause much less churning all round. Swans, despite their size, disturb less pool mud than the divers, even in spring when the joy of their own and every other kind of rising sap will make them charge round the pool, rolling over and over like porpoises in the fountains of water they create. In other respects, however, they can be one of the most problematic of wildfowl to keep in a domestic setting; for, like geese, they can bark trees and crop more than just grass.

Over the years, I have kept a fair selection of waterfowl (though not geese) and am now down to a hard core which are hardy, usually healthy, unaggressive and without the inclination to roam dangerously which makes them such easy prey for foxes. (It is this last habit which prevents me from keeping entrancing, painted ducks like Mandarins or the Carolina Wood Duck, for they wander and our pond is not surrounded by fox-proof netting, essential for all small ponds in fox-ridden areas.) My own include free-winged white, apricot and silver call-ducks, European Pochards (diving-ducks), the engaging black and white Tufted Ducks with a trilling call (also divers) and the South American Rosybills (of the *Netta* group, halfway between divers and dabblers). The male of this species is a glossy black with a large carmine bill.

Until a couple of years ago, I had also a pair of black swans, dazzling Australians with ruffled wing-feathers and lipstick-red beaks. Of all swans (except possibly the little white Coscoroba) they are thought to be the best suited to a relatively small pool as they need less space to breed. They are not without drawbacks, however, for the cob develops in early adulthood an aggression to match the drama of his looks. My own was no exception. After a warning period of months when he had savaged all males in sight but left me unmolested, my own crisis came when I was sleeping beside the pool one afternoon and woke to find his wing-span lowering above me, his beak mutilating my big toe. Until then, it had been a case of him Tarzan, me Jane; but now, no Leda I. Both cob and pen (who mate for life) had to leave for a home where the pool was not part of the garden itself.

A Beginner's Selection of Ducks for the Pond

You can best assess ducks of different species at a specialist breeder's or wildfowl park between October and May when the Northern breeds are in full plumage, which is in most cases lost during their summer eclipse. (The South American ducks in the list below have no eclipse.) Most ornamental waterfowl are sold with one wing pinioned to prevent them flying away. This leaves them defenceless against predators, so ponds must be protected with high, out-turned netting against foxes. If this is impossible, consider the following: keep only free-winged domestic birds such as call-ducks or, on a large deep pond, diving-ducks which will spend virtually their entire life on the water and keep part of it unfrozen in winter; or geese, or ornamental domestic fowl (see also page 105) which must be shut up at night.

In the list of suggestions below, only the plumage of the drakes is described: the females are usually self-effacing in comparison though they have their own quiet beauty.

Diving ducks

These need at least 2ft/60cm depth of water for feeding and preferably much more as they will dive to 6ft/1.8m plus.

TUFTED DUCK (*Aythya fuligula*)   Black and white with eyes like yellow liquorice allsorts, and a pigtail.

COMMON POCHARD (*Aythya ferina*)   Chestnut head, grey body.

Midway between diving and dabbling ducks

RED-CRESTED POCHARD (*Netta rufina*)   Larger than the above and with a domed golden-red head. There is also a blonde-bodied form. Both can wander so should only ever be kept under netted conditions in fox-ridden areas.

THE ROSYBILL (*Netta peposaca*)   Blackish South-American duck with a carmine bill. No eclipse plumage.

Dabbling ducks

CALL DUCKS   Brown, white, silver, blue and apricot forms. Females have a loud quack. Domestic birds which should be kept free-winged if possible.

PINTAIL (*Anas acuta*)   Chocolate, white, grey and black bird of great elegance.

BAHAMA PINTAIL (*Anas bahamensis*)   South American with no eclipse in plumage. Half the size of the above. Dark and mottled tawny brown with white cheeks and neck and blue and red bill.

CHILOE WIDGEON (*Anas sibilatrix*)   South American with no eclipse dress. Dark green head, tan and white flanks, upper parts black with white.

Perching ducks

MANDARIN *(Aix galericulata)*   Most ornamental of all waterfowl with elaborate markings of chestnut, white, green, blue and black, with crested head and chestnut 'sails'. Has great personality and fascinating courtship rituals.

CAROLINA *(Aix sponsa)*   Another beauty with 'painted' head and drooping crest; purple, green, blue and olive.

Months later, pining with memories – the feel of their deep, meltingly soft breast-feathers; the slap of their feet on the stairs of the house; their Exocet charge at a visiting heron in the twilight – I rang the headquarters of the British Wildfowl Centre at Slimbridge in Gloucestershire for advice. I was told my problem with the black swans was common and one which they faced themselves: nonetheless, they still recommended this species of swan as the most suitable for a garden pool.

Since then, I have not dared re-introduce any swans, though my endearing ducks do not quite make up for their loss. But I content myself with the thought that these are still worth the forfeit of aquatic flowers that I cannot plant lest they are gobbled in an expensive banquet. The play of their personalities, their courtship rituals, their individual voices and their animated beauty are infinitely more interesting than the static perfection of a flowery picture. The latter is my aim, certainly, in other parts of the garden. But here (by the pool), it is a place for childlike fun. A small rowing boat, dragonflies and tadpoles, and a perimeter fringe of shrubs and gunneras beneath whose green umbrellas the ducks and I commune, all these are quite blissful enough.

Wet Ditches and Brooks (or the Over-mallarded and Under-sniped Problem)

No man is an island, or in this case a pool. In converting our wet ditch into a lake, I was one of thousands. All over the country in the last few years, a pro-pool and anti-ditch movement has been taking place and it has brought in its wake an unforeseen development. In the words of the Countryside Commission, we are now over-mallarded and under-sniped. Though not quite in the realm of an affliction, the term has a gruesome ring to it, with its suggestion of alarming excess on the one hand and deprivation on the other. Foreknowledge of this state of affairs would not actually have quenched my desire for a pool. But all this has brought home to me the truth that fashions in the garden (as on a farm) have a quantifiable effect on all the other populations it supports.

Snipe-lovers should therefore protect their territory and keep their wet ditches in unadulterated form. This does not preclude planting the sides with moisture-loving subjects and developing a bog garden. But it needs to be said that this is an extremely demanding form of gardening. Weeds grow rapaciously in this kind of situation and the area has to be under continuous cultivation if it is to look pretty. Nor are such places the simplest to work. The banks are muddy, slippery and their lower reaches can be inaccessible to any but the most agile – such as moorhen (snipe, too, I daresay) which may nip off some herbaceous resting-buds as they start to develop.

Really rank plants are therefore your main asset here, but even these can fail to thrive if you plant them in the middle of unoxygenated gunge in the central channel. Keep this clear and put the plants instead into a peaty soil-mix above the winter prolonged-saturation level. Useful plants include coarse-leafed ivies like the Irish or Persian varieties (*Hedera helix* 'Hibernica' and *H. colchica* 'Dentata'), gunneras, ferns such as *Dryopteris filix-mas*, *Blechnum chilense* and *Matteucia struthiopteris* (which is slow to get going but colonizing when it does so). Add *Darmera peltata* (syn. *Peltiphyllum peltatum*), *Iris pseudacorus* and its dazzling variegated form, the yellow inulas (especially the rank *I. helenium*), ligularias, *Lysimachia punctata*, lysichitums which when truly established will need a JCB to lift them, the invasive *Heracleum mantegazzianum*, *Butomus umbellatus* (needing sun to flower well), and the more aggressive grasses such as *Carex pendula*, *Glyceria aquatica* 'Variegata' and *Phalaris*

I. Hodges Barn, Gloucestershire: the semi-circular shape of the terrace is keyed to the beautiful peculiarities of the house, which was a former columbarium.

II. Spired plants like foxgloves and the erect shoots of *Lychnis coronaria* are a welcome contradiction to the horizontal lines of walls and box hedges in this garden.

III. Part of the formal rock-plant arena at Kingstone Cottage, Herefordshire, which holds the National Collection of pinks. Plants include *Salvia haematodes* and the true antirrhinum species in the background, also *Tanacetum densum amanum* (syn. *Chrysanthemum haradjanii*), *Sedum* 'Dragon's Blood', *Campanula cochlearifolia* and *Iris pallida* 'Variegata', as well as dianthus in great variety.

IV. *(opposite above)* The circular landing-steps at Great Dixter, Sussex, lapped by the orchard. They are grassed, an ultimate and labour-intensive refinement.

V. *(opposite below)* Massed *Primula vialii* beside water — a luxury planting as it is usually a short-lived perennial.

VI. Primulas, irises and hostas fringe the banks of a water garden which reflects the sky at its centre.

VII. The beautiful swimming-pool at Mawley Hall, Shropshire: since it is black rather than the customary too-blue-to-be-true, it is like a quiet, old looking-glass.

arundinacea 'Picta'. *Rheum palmatum*, especially in one of its improved crimson forms, is handsome in the first half of the summer, but loses its leaves early, thus failing to earn its keep properly. The wild brooklime (*Veronica beccabunga*) will tolerate almost any treatment; also the invasive pink or carmine *Impatiens glandulifera* (syn. *I. roylei*) which spreads everywhere by exploding seeds. In the silt itself, the bog bean (*Menyanthes trifoliata*) is equally invasive. In fact, the aggression of this last trio will certainly need watching.

As a contrast to all this coarseness, add some of the tiny-leafed but heartier growing cotoneasters such as *C. microphyllus* or even *C. horizontalis*, though the latter may need its surrounds temporarily polythened against weeds until it has extended enough. Amongst these, tall white foxgloves and the more vigorous candelabra primulas will look lovely, especially the richest carmine forms which glow intensely against green companions; named forms such as 'Valley Red' or the taller 'Fiery Red' or 'Miller's Crimson' look marvellous in May-June. The lavender and white shorter-growing *Primula iossa* is one of the more reliable perennials among the prettier bog primulas, a compliment one cannot pay to the most gorgeous of all, the scarlet-tipped mauve-pokered *P. vialii*, flowering in June-July. The latter is temperamental to a fault and unlikely to last, though if you plant it, why not do it in style and wallow in a dramatic mass for at least one season (see Colour Plate V for a splendid example).

If the area is part-shaded and the soil laced with masses of peat, try too some meconopsis here. *M. betonicifolia* has a tendency to die out even if you religiously prevent it from flowering the first year, largely because it needs so much food and moisture to produce enough offsets to compensate for its dying parts. But *M x sheldonii* particularly in the 'Slieve Donard' form is a perennial of the richest blue, and also a glorious, numbered and expensive form called *M.* GS600 ('Branklyn' is a selection from this). In my garden the latter has developed heartily though it is in a position where it has to survive alternating drought and moisture. It is these extreme conditions – saturation for one half of the year when a plant is dormant followed by drought during its growing period – that make this kind of bank-planting difficult to manage. My own inclination would be to keep the treasured plants to limited and accessible patches which can get 'spot' attention whilst the coarser plants thrash it out below.

Finally, don't neglect the value of trees lining the banks of a runnel. Their trunks will emphasize the ribbon of water, reinforcing it if its course is serpentine, or softening a straight run so long as they are planted in wayward clusters rather than lined up like railings. Keep them well to the side so that their foliage and roots cannot choke the rivulet. Avoid willows which sponge up quantities of water, but the rather less greedy birches (like *Betula costata*) and alders, especially one of the cut-leafed forms (e.g. *Alnus incana* 'Laciniata'), both amongst the trees used at Longstock Water Gardens in Hampshire, are beautiful subjects and fast-growing. Admittedly trees block sunlight, but you are not growing surface-water flowers here which need still water and sun to thrive, but merely plants on the bank and most of those mentioned above will enjoy part-shade.

Bridges

This ditch, stream or small pool will probably need a path to carry you across it. In many cases, all that is necessary will be a weathered, wide and stable plank of wood or stone, sprouting ferns where it enters the earth at each end. On a longer stretch, however, where

32. A curved small stone bridge has a balustraded inset for the straight run at the apex.

a crossing is vital and looks so, you have the perfect excuse to devise a bridge.

Bridge-building stirs the Brunel in one's silt. In truth it is a many-sided business and draws not only on your reserves of taste but your engineering skills. Taste, first. The trouble here is that most well-known models for bridges are foreign in origin. Too many resemble souvenirs in a holiday-snap and the more extreme *touche de Venise* or even *du Japon* will not be what one needs unless it is part of a coherent whole. Guard therefore against excess whether this takes the form of the over-sophisticated or aggressively foreign. Or whether, at the opposite extreme, it is the rustic knockabout – usually larch timbers which are nailed to form diagonal crosses. Avoid, too, flimsy structures which sway the minute a toe is laid upon them.

What you are aiming for is a sturdy building, wide enough to give you room to pause without falling into the grip of vertigo, simple and lovely in outline and in its inverted reflection. This last is important and is one reason why the curved Palladian stone bridge of the eighteenth century and the arched wooden Japanese bridges were such perfect partners for water. Their shape meant that the curve in the air dipped to meet its inverted arc in the pool and united to form an oval or flattened circle.

You can in fact buy made-to-measure bridges although they are expensive. In Britain, for example, Tiger Developments designs individual, mild steel bridges costing about £100 per foot at the time of writing. The footboards are of pickled pine and the whole structure is designed to rest on concrete piers in the ground. David Baker, the designer and owner of the company, builds for looks and safety; and, both visually and structurally, he believes

33. Merdon Manor, Hampshire, where a roofless barn was turned into an Anglo-Italian water garden.

the ideal shape to be a shallow curve the radius of which is twice the length of the bridge. Elegant and airy in appearance, the bridges have to be strong enough to withstand a 3 ton weight which he places in the middle 'just in case someone decides to have a party on it'.

If you bear in mind this need for elegance and safety, there is no reason why you should not make your own bridge, probably in wood, and working the design out with a capable carpenter. (You can actually buy a book of plans, published in America though obtainable in Britain, but many of the designs are horrifically ornate.) One warning, though. Should your bridge be on a bridleway, it will have to conform to the safety regulations, but it is wise to check these anyway for your own protection.

Formal Water

At Merdon Manor in Hampshire, there is the most surprising formal pool garden I have yet to see. Enclosed in a topless barn, its very discovery is startling, for it is revealed only by opening a heavy door in the barn wall. The area that then lies before you is divided into two, with an ante-room preceding a main chamber and separated by an ornamented iron screen. This larger of the two sections is the pool garden with two rectangular waterlilied stretches of water, surrounded by raised beds (originally feeding troughs for the cattle but now filled with lime-free soil which permits the growth of calcifuge plants like camellias and rhododendrons). Tender plants (crinodendrons, caesalpinias) have grown lushly against the walls in this sheltered micro-climate. Trailers like the long-flowering hot-pink

Verbena 'Sissinghurst' cascade down the sides, climbers festoon the walls about you. Pots and urns act as formal correctives to the exuberance of the plants. And in the background – in effect topping the end wall of the barn – is the scenery of the high trees in the green park beyond, a long perspective to the gallery around you.

This pool garden originated some thirty years ago and was planned as an Anglo-Italian garden. The concept was ingenious, an example of what can result when an imaginative gardener exploits a disaster (losing a barn roof) and turns it into an opportunity.

The key to this garden's success is that it was devised as a whole. This ought to be a rule when designing all formal pools. They are not simply geometric patches of water which are added to other ingredients in a garden, but are at their most successful only when they are the *raison d'être* of the surrounding area. One such example was built at Milton Lodge in Somerset, of the simplest design, easy to maintain and immensely effective. The rectangular stone-edged lily-pool was centrally placed in a small gravelled terrace. Clumps of self-sowing, creamy-flowered *Sisyrinchium striatum* were grown in the gravel, their colouring echoed by the huge *Phlomis fruticosa* in the corner. Tubs of agapanthus were placed to flank a seat. The whole scene was wonderfully framed by distant blue views, but even without this uncommon asset, the pool at the heart of the picture could pull in the outside world, reflecting sky, clouds, sun and moon.

These continuously changing reflections bring any clear water to life and can make plants superfluous. The shadowed dog-leg pool at The Priory in Worcestershire, for example, depends on unplanted simplicity for its serenity. Where an ornately shaped pool is concerned, this is even more obvious: it is almost always best left bare. In the patio gardens of Southern Spain (and 'nowhere' wrote Miss Jekyll rather ungrammatically 'can better lessons be learnt of the use of water in small gardens') pools of elaborate outline have been refined to an unplanted perfection. Sparse amounts of crystal-clear water trickle down staircase channels or lie cupped in lace-edged stone pools. Even more decorated devices to contain water can still be seen in the gardens of Mogul India; foliated octagonal pools, tiny stone ponds embellished with carved stone lotus buds, serpent rills coiled in upon themselves.

I don't suggest that all these ornate containers, often of mystical significance, would be suitable in a damper, cooler climate. They answer a hot country's need not only for water in a garden but for frugality in its use – whereas we can be relatively profligate. But I do stress that formal water, skilfully presented, can be a highly decorative and enchanting addition to a garden even when bare of surface and surrounding plants. (Fish – which need a minimum depth of 18in/45cm to survive winter – and underwater oxygenating plants are all you need to keep it clear.) Such schemes give the greatest pleasure if the water is held above the ground in a raised container, curbed with a stone edge on which you can sit, trailing fingers in the glinting depths. Feeling as well as seeing water casts a spell. So does hearing it for many people; it conveys coolness, hence the popularity of fountains and sprays. To me the sound of a parsimonious trickle rather than the roar of Victoria Falls is only an irritant. The surface mirror is shattered, calm dispersed and you start totting up the cost of the electricity.

Where you do choose to plant the surrounds of a formal pool, go for architectural subjects where possible. Irises in variety are ideal and include the aquatic *I. laevigata* and the moist-border or marginal varieties like *I. kaempferi*, *I. kermesina* 'Versicolor', *I. sibirica* ('Gatineau', rich pale blue netted with gold and 'Helen Astor', a pinkish-plum, are very

34. Examples of two formal pools of different geometric shape, echoed by their enclosures: a square set simply into grass and...

35. ...a kerbed circle with a gravelled perimeter.

36. Consistent design at Hodges Barn: curved ends to the swimming-pool and the pepperpot tops on the pool house repeat those of the former columbarium which is shown in Colour Plate I.

lovely) and *I. setosa*, an underplanted, vigorous, rushy-leafed and purple-flowered variety. Add zantedeschias, hemerocallis and hostas with blue leaves especially and, as a fine contrast to the latter, *Asphodeline lutea* with glaucous, grassy foliage and yellow spires. For dry surrounds, you might opt for the bearded early summer irises (*I. pallida dalmatica* has bluish leaves which are much more resistant to leaf-spot than many hybrids); or choose globe-headed alliums (*A. aflatunense, A. giganteum, A. rosenbachianum* and the huge *A. christophii* [syn. *A. albopilosum*]), yuccas and, for richer soil, agapanthus.

Shadier courtyard pools would have their surrounds better dressed with rugs of mossy saxifrage or small-leafed ivies fingering their way toward the pool. Ferns of contrasting shapes are an elegant addition including the hart's tongue fern (*Asplenium scolopendrium*), the fluffy *Athyrium filix-femina plumosa* and the feathery forms of *Polystichum setiferum*. These usually have '*plumosum*' as a suffix, but since they can vary, ask for the nurseryman's most plumose form in stock. *P. s. plumoso-divisilobum* is a distinct variety and the most glamorous of all. *Dryopteris pseudo-mas* in its crested forms makes a handsome vertical break against the more horizontal growth of the plumose *Polystichum* or *Athyrium*. Forms with *'grandiceps'* in the name have the largest and most showy terminal crests. In the case of all the above, limit yourself to a few good companions and use them rhythmically for maximum impact.

The surface of a pool which has mid-day sunlight can be permanently water-lilied with hardy cultivars, chosen to suit the size and depth of the water. But for summer enchantment in areas with long hot summers (or for a conservatory pool) you could try instead tropical waterlilies which are stored during winter in damp sand in a large tin. The advantage of these is that the flowers are held poised above the water and some bloom in a colour outside the usual range – *Nymphaea* 'Blue Beauty', for example, which is a deep blue with a golden disc, to be planted in water some 2½-3ft/75-90cm deep. An intensely romantic addition would be the night-blooming tropical waterlilies (the milky *N.* 'Missouri', the purplish-rose *N.* 'Emily Grant Hutchings' or the huge purple *N.* 'B.C. Berry'). Opening in the evening, lasting all night and folding again the following morning, they flower for insomniacs. Those who love the spiky, starry outlines of the tropical waterlilies yet cannot provide the warmth in which they thrive might care to try a new, very beautiful and very expensive American cultivar called 'American Star' – pink, perfumed, hardy, of medium vigour and for a planting depth of 6-18in/15-45cm.

Swimming-pools

Swimming-pools rarely adorn a garden and most owners sensibly tuck them away in a separate enclosure, especially if they are sized for a dunk and a wallow rather than a swim. But there are two examples I have admired as exceptional ornaments. Both illustrate how a thoughtful and sensitive owner can convert these garden accessories into objects of some loveliness. The first is at Hodges Barn in Gloucestershire, shown in Plate 36. Here the curved pool-ends tie in with the twin pepper-pot tops on the charming pool-house. These, in turn, repeat the columbarium's roof-top outline on the house, shown in Colour Plate I. This inspired consistency of design has achieved a remarkably unified house and garden.

The second example shows brilliant treatment of the pool itself, resolving a frequent difficulty. In a cool, grey climate, the choice of pool colour can be a problem. The ubiquitous too-blue-to-be-true can be very disruptive to its surroundings in a cold country. It needs at the least a wide blue arc of Mediterranean sky above it; and, at best, the turquoise and gold domes of the East crowning its shallows, as I realized when I visited the gardens of Isfahan in the 1970s. But if not blue, what can one choose? At Mawley Hall in Shropshire (Colour Plate VII), there is a wonderful example of a black swimming-pool. Not only does it make a sympathetic partner for its old stone and brick backcloth here, but the colour must help it to retain warmth. Better still, its mysterious depths are highly reflective. In it you see the white obelisks that corner it, the luminous beds of flowering shrubs at either end, and the octagonal summerhouse in the far background. It is like a quiet, very beautiful old looking-glass as well as a swimming-pool.

VI. Trees and their Selection
Multi-stemmed Specimens, Functionaries, Open-ground Planting, Avenues

I N 1833, the Director General of Gardens in the Kingdom of Bavaria deplored a change in the English landscape garden:

The immense multitude of plants which since the commencement of the present century have been brought from all parts of the world to Europe, and more especially England, supplies the landscape gardener with an inexhaustible fund for decorating his grounds. There are thus to be found numerous varieties of trees and shrubs, which, either by their elegant growth, the picturesque disposition of their branches and foliage, or by their beautiful flowers, belong to the first class of ornaments for landscape gardening ...

It might have been supposed that this richness of vegetation would be highly advantageous to landscape-gardening in England, where formerly the most classical modes of the natural garden style were to be found; and that it would have given immensely increased facilities to the artist for the execution of his work; but according to my experience, I found quite the contrary. Amidst the disproportionate abundance of his materials, he knows not which to take first: one is scarcely chosen, when he is attracted to another; then to a third, a fourth and so on. Each tree and each shrub, has some particular charm to recommend it, and finally, that none may be lost, he grasps them all.

Thus I found the English gardens a real chaos of unconnected beauties.

The Chevalier Charles Sckell was writing a hundred and fifty years ago. His censure strikes with even greater force today, when our supply of trees is overwhelming.

With trees our errors are especially apparent, since these are big, obvious and fixed plants. We blunder twice over. First, we select in the random way the Chevalier described. Next, we dot the ground with lots of different varieties – usually one of each. The foreigner would shake his Bavarian head. So too would 'Capability' Brown, working in the previous century with predominantly oak, larch and Scots pine on a huge canvas, though a canvas (as the landscape architect, Hal Moggridge, pointed out in relation to Blenheim) planned with such precision that a single tree added or detached from his groups would have had an adverse effect on the view. We would have earned a further ticking-off from a number of garden-writers and designers around the turn of our own century, Miss Jekyll included.

We are apparently irredeemable, lapsing every time we are re-educated whether by our

37. Certain trees set their stamp upon a garden. Here *Pinus radiata*, a large fast-growing conifer, has given an almost Mediterranean feel to the high cliff-face at Kiftsgate Court Garden.

own ranks or by clear-sighted foreigners. But, then, why not? We avidly enjoy our vast variety of plants. Business buzzes for nurserymen in this leisure industry boom. So why not? Only because it makes for such poor gardens.

Appealing for self-restraint is clearly not the answer. Perhaps compromise has a better chance of success. For my own part, I try to achieve this by imposing on my garden twofold controls. The first concerns the selection of individual trees. The second has to do with the thematic background use of trees which will give a coherent look to the garden. This is crucial if you want to grow many different varieties (and for more on this subject, please see page 75).

Selecting trees

There are two good ways, I would suggest, of choosing trees. Employ both together and you will inhibit that random, personal choice that results in a garden peppered with different items.

First, you choose the position in which you require a tree, seeing this position as a hole which needs a certain shape in it. If you have more than one position (which is likely) relate it to the others, visualizing them filled with tree shapes, both at eye-level and against the skyline (for the latter must always be taken into account with trees). Now it follows that all the saplings you intend to plant in the spaces can be considered as building blocks whose span, mass and outline are more important at this stage of planning than their flower, leaf and trunk. These blocks will be shaping your garden and forming its spaces. You can plan their looks quite precisely by sketching them into their setting or by inking their shape onto a photograph of the garden. You can also get a three-dimensional idea of their effect by walking out their future span on the ground. Gauge their effect from a distance by marching far away in one direction and then in another. Only now, after you have visualized as entirely as possible the shape and scale you are choosing, should you find the trees to fit.

This takes us onto the second stage – choosing the actual tree. Rather than picking something to fit that you have always fancied (or that some writer like me fancies), it helps now to sort trees roughly into categories. I define these categories as honours lists in trees. At the top come those on whom one would confer the more serious sort of knighthood. As distinguished individuals by habit or human association, these can stand alone. The next category is the highly commended chorus line; elegant creatures which are best in groups or as backgrounds to others. Lastly, you have the hard-working functionaries with a job to do, be it fruiting, screening or wind-deflecting; attractive they may be but reliability of job performance is their main asset.

In the Appendix, you will find a table of trees divided into these three main categories. But here I aim to concentrate on certain examples and use them as a peg to make some more general points. Let me start by selecting certain aristocrats from the first group in the table to explain what I mean. The Cedar of Lebanon is the most obvious example. With its great, dark, layered plates of branches and its history of dignifying the stateliest of houses, it is a first candidate to ennoble surroundings that are grand enough to give it a foster-home. But conifers as a group include a number of fairly close rivals of very differing aspect, having powerful yet less class-conscious personalities. Among these, I believe it is certain pines which deserve to be planted most widely.

38. *Picea brewerana* has long pendulous branchlets.   39. 'Banana' cones on *Pinus wallichiana*.

There are many candidates. *Pinus wallichiana* (syn. *P. griffithii, P. excelsa*) is one of my favourites for a large garden, whether used as a specimen or in a group (for it has the rare advantage of adapting to either category). Its appeal lies in its highly ornamental pendulous cones, 8-12in/20-30cm banana shapes (see Plate 39), and its long glaucous needles bound in groups of five, which give it a feathery feel and appearance. It is a fairly fast-growing tree and tolerant of most soils except shallow chalk. If grown as a single specimen, it will keep its far-flung lower branches. Group it and it will lose these unless very widely spaced. Nonetheless, such a group will make one of the most beautiful screens a large garden can include, airy and graceful on its own, or a wonderful foil to a group of a different species. At Kew, for example, it was partnered by a collection of the short, wide-spreading *Prunus* x *yedoensis*, its horizontal branches clustered with large white flowers in March. The upright paired with the horizontal may be a cliché (it is one of the main choreographic principles in ballet duets), but its childlike simplicity is always effective in the garden.

For much smaller gardens, I would recommend a three-needle pine with shorter leaves, but they have the kind of furry texture which invites caress. *Pinus patula* can grow to about 30ft/9m in Britain, has rich, bright green, pendulous needles, a reddish bark and a broadly conic shape. It is slightly tender, does best in mild areas and indeed can only be relied on in a sheltered position. A pair which I admired in a chilly garden some 900ft/275m high and subject to freezing winds were scourged to death a couple of winters ago but they had at least thrived for about thirty years. Nonetheless, it is a lovely tree for the side of a terrace in a sheltered spot, where it will soften stonework.

Singling out a third example (a large garden subject), *Cryptomeria japonica* is usually planted in its slow-growing dwarf form called 'Elegans' with permanently juvenile, soft, fluffy foliage, bronzing in winter. It is not a patch on its big relative if you have room for its height. Its rich, reddish-brown bark, conical outline with heavy, tip-tilted lower branches skirting round its base and its branchlets like Rastafarian dreadlocks earn it a site which it can dominate with its own character.

Those who have less space and are prepared to wait for their effects, might prefer *Picea brewerana*, one of the most beautiful of all conifers with its weeping branchlets which can extend to 7ft/2.1m (Plate 38). These are a deep intense green, blackish in some lights and positions, and look exceptionally lovely in rain. The one drawback of this spruce is that it is very slow-growing and can look puny when young, especially when grown as a drooping-topped graft rather than a seedling (superior but it doesn't take on its distinctive form for some years). A specimen or dominant small group of these most graceful trees in a large enclosed area would be a wonderful heritage for the future.

As this selection of species shows, conifers are an enormously varied and exciting group, but two points must be stressed about them. Firstly, the majority of those sold in garden centres are no good to you as a country gardener; namely, those factory clones used as accent plants. These are suburban tools for mass-duplicated gardens. Secondly, those striking and individual species that do deserve your attention need thoughtful positioning.

You need to start from the point that nearly all conifer species are exotics in this country. Unlike many deciduous trees, they are no good whatsoever at melting the typical country garden into its background. Don't therefore use them as boundary trees unless you deliberately want to emphasize the difference between your garden and the land beyond. In this case, use conifers with broad crowns or a broad base. These, as opposed to totem pole conifers, will ride the land in a comfortable attachment. Secondly, use them within distinct areas of the garden as a means of summarizing their mood, a task at which they excel, for the personalities of many conifers are so strong. Harness them, too, to reinforce the period of a house and its garden (see the comments beside some trees in the table): don't let them fight it. Thirdly, take deliberate advantage of their clear and very varied profiles near a house (the outline of deciduous trees is confused by comparison). Think how one profile will relate to the next when snow lies on the ground for several months on end in winter. And on a fourth count, get the maximum impact from their marvellously varied textures, whether furry, feathery, scaly or spiny. This is a feature that makes them especially valuable for the kind of modern garden which over-depends on labour-saving masonry whether it is gravel, paving or brickwork. Such dead hardware in our gardens needs a constant electric charge to bring it to life, and strongly textured evergreens are one means of doing so.

With this last point in mind, it is no surprise that the Japanese make such emphatic use of textured conifers (such as *Pinus thunbergii, P. densiflora, P. parviflora, Cryptomeria japonica, Chamaecyparis obtusa, Tsuga canadensis* and *T. caroliniana*); for they have created an art form out of solid stone and gravel and selected its plant complement to perfection. Their treatment of these trees is quite as precise as their selection, and they shape them to a particular configuration. This is extreme artificiality and to be rejected in all English-style country gardens except those with entirely enclosed courtyards which have no other disparate terms of reference. Admittedly, it is no different in principle from our native topiary (see Chapter X) but it has an exoticism that could never become naturalized and a tree thus treated would jar unless it is kept on a tactful rein.

Purists might say that these trees are too tortured for *anywhere* in our country gardens.

40. A multi-stemmed tree can give a highly dramatic viewpoint to a formal garden.

They forget that the so-called normal shape of our trees is artifically encouraged anyway. You don't get those upright, ramrod-straight stems of standard trees without the nurseryman's intervention.

Multi-stemmed Trees

Whilst we are on the subject of tree-trunks, it is worth pointing out that a multi-stemmed tree can make a most decorative specimen planting, even if the species lacks individuality in its usual single-stemmed form.

A multi-stemmed tree occurs in one of three ways. It is normal for some trees simply to grow this way. *Tsuga canadensis*, the Eastern Hemlock is one conifer which usually forks low from its base. *Podocarpus salignus*, a slightly tender but lovelier conifer with deep green willow-like leaves is another. *Eucalyptus niphophila*, the Snow Gum with a python-skin bark, is an evergreen with the same habit. And *Pterocarya fraxinifolia* (and *P* x *rehderana*) is a deciduous example, a graceful pinnate-leafed tree with long catkins of fruit in summer and the habit of producing a cluster of boles from the ground.

Other trees, however, become multi-stemmed when the leader is removed in infancy and it is under a couple of feet (60cm) in height. This can happen by accident or by deliberate act on the part of the nurseryman or gardener. A third method is for the tendency to be induced by pruning a year-old tree to the ground and encouraging it to develop a cluster of stem-growths, a practice (called stooling) that is often tried on *Paulownia tomentosa* and *Ailanthus altissima* (syn. *A. glandulosa*) to give rise to huge, tropical-looking leaves. As you may know from experience, it induces such bushy growth, that, if your aim is a good-looking tree, you may have to weed out all but three or four stems which you wish to become the principle tree-trunks.

Certainly, one has to be selective with one's subjects for multi-stemming. The nobility of particular tall landscape and forest trees is such that they should be tamper-free. But the

73

range of possibles is still wide. Suggestions put forward by John Bond, Keeper of the Savill Gardens in Berkshire, include a wide variety, but if they are to be destined for star treatment, I would single out those with ornamental barks. Their impact will be stunning when those barks are multiplied on two, three or four trunks. The following would therefore be ideal; our native white-barked birch (*Betula pendula* (syn. *B. verrucosa*); *B. nigra* with a shaggy pinkish bark which deepens with age; *Acer davidii*, one of the snake-barked maples with a dark green stem striped in white; the red-barked evergreen strawberry tree, *Arbutus unedo*, and its rather larger relative, *A. x andrachnoides*.

It is not easy to track down examples from nurserymen, particularly when a particular species is the object of your search. In this case, John Bond suggests the do-it-yourself method. You could either grow your own from seed or buy an infant single-stemmed variety from a garden-centre and remove its leader. If the tree is expensive and grafted, this exercise of cutting it down to 12in/30cm high is an agonizing one. Less expensive, however, than a third way of securing a multi-stemmed specimen which is to plant three or four standard-stemmed saplings (of the same species, need I say?) in one hole. The overall profile they develop will seem exactly the same as an individual tree which has produced a handful of trunks from the base.

Trees of this kind are extremely adaptable from the point of view of design. They can be given spotlit isolation in rather artificial surroundings, or, if deciduous, can emerge in glades which are backed by an inchoate mass of woodland. As aberrations of nature (sometimes), these multi-stemmed deciduous trees can do a very good job melting that abrupt transition between garden and wilderness beyond.

Seasonal Embellishments

Other trees demand a star position because of their extreme glamour when in flower. This is especially true of some of the magnolias in the table on page 198. Cultivars are now generally available which have such huge (yet unvulgar) flowers that they seem hot-house material, though a number are as cold-hardy as their more self-effacing relatives. *M. x soulangiana* 'Sundew' is one with scented, up to 8in/20cm wide flowers which are white with an apricot shading throughout or simply at the base. 'Burgundy' is another wondrously beautiful form, thought to have originated in New Zealand, with large, deep rose flowers. *M. sargentiana* 'Robusta', an older variety, is a larger shrubby tree with a huge spread; it is breathtaking when covered in April with its 8in/20cm wide, pink and white waterlily blossoms (see Plate 41). It has in turn given rise to an even lovelier hybrid, *M. mollicomata* 'Caerhays Belle' with rich salmon pink flowers, though its slightly earlier season of bloom puts its display at risk outside mild areas. One could continue without pause enumerating this marvellous group of trees most of which are cold-tolerant, clay-tolerant and so prodigal in their riches. Any of those in the table which includes summer as well as spring-flowering examples is a superlative treasure.

Some of the shrubbier types are sufficiently adaptable to lend themselves not only to specimen planting but to groups. And at Lanhydrock in Cornwall, there is even a magnolia tunnel (*M. x soulangiana* 'Lennei') where the low-spreading branches have been trained to canopy a path (see page 98 for details). It is a device that I yearn to copy, but have had to abandon for lack of a suitable position.

Many pines make marvellous evergreen backgrounds to these early-flowering trees with

41. The huge open pink blooms of *Magnolia sargentiana* 'Robusta' are presented on bare branches.

pale blossoms on bare branches. Though you have to ensure that, if the flowering trees are low-growing, they are paired with conifers that retain their lower level or descending branches as they grow older.

Grouping Trees

More frequently, however, glamorous display is not the object in grouping trees. Instead you seek an effect that you wish to reinforce by numbers. Or you wish to bulk extreme thinness of individual outlines into more comfortable contours. Or, more importantly, you are hoping to give a coherent look to the garden.

As I said at the beginning of this chapter, this last point is crucial if you want to grow a number of different trees. These trees will make your garden spotty and fragmented unless you plant them in large related stands or place them against a thematic background, the theme to be provided by a particular recurring tree which is present in large enough numbers to knit the different kinds together. What you are doing is grooming the garden, or parts of it anyway, into a kind of uniform.

Some trees are naturals for grouping (see page 200 of the table in the Appendix for suggestions). The birches are one example, especially those that are slender in growth, having airy foliage and barks whose lovely markings bear repetition. The various white-barked species are more widely available, but it is worth seeking out *Betula ermanii* with an apricot pink trunk and *B. nigra* with its pink shaggy bark which is an excellent subject for wet land. The terracotta-barked *B. albosinensis* (and its variant *septentrionalis*) is perhaps even more splendid. Some proud owners prize the sheen on its bark so highly that they give it the scrubbing-brush. Whether or not it involves you in housework, this birch is ideal for grouping, fairly quick-growing and shows its trunk colour early, so you can choose good

75

specimens. It will distinguish itself from surroundings, however, and in country gardens on sandy soil in a lightly wooded area, our native birch (*Betula pendula*) may be more useful in reinforcing a background theme. As one of the first trees to colonize such grounds, it is also an effective means of ensuring an easy transition between garden and woodland beyond. In fact, in the open woodland garden itself, these birches with spectacular barks come into their own. This is because you only see trunks, not tops in such circumstances.

Another more common purpose in grouping trees is to reinforce autumn colour. *Acer* and *Sorbus* (of the *Aucuparia* section) are the most frequently planted in this respect. Unfortunately grouping is not enough to achieve the best effect. Too often they are plonked down in a squadron, whereas their brilliant reds and yellows would be far more dramatic if they were planted in drifts among darker-leafed trees for contrast. Make sure, too, that these groups of trees shape spaces in their midst, so that you can see these autumn effects from a distance as well as close-to.

Trees for Open-ground Planting

We now move on to the functionaries. Given a piece of open ground in the countryside that you wish to plant, what steps can you take? You have four main options. Most people choose the first, which is to plant according to private choice, unaided by grants but correspondingly unrestricted by strings. In this case you may well need windbreak trees to make part-perimeter clumps; these act as shelter belts for the choicer interior material and, if planted in curved blocks themselves, perhaps with tapering ends, will form handsome backgrounds as well. (See page 201 of the table for a selection of subjects for inland and maritime areas.)

In Britain however, you have at the time of writing three other main options. (Other countries will obviously differ and readers should investigate their own national schemes.) Here, you can plant under the auspices of the Ministry of Agriculture, the Forestry Commission, or your local county council which operates a Countryside Commission scheme. Each of these runs a grant system and you approach the body most suited to your planting purposes.

If, for example, you have farming or smallholding land, and want trees for shelter belts, for stock protection, or for landscape use to hide eyesore buildings, you might apply to the Ministry of Agriculture which gives either a 30% grant for (at the time of writing) a total cost of £750 of work (or 60% in less favoured areas). Alternatively, on even a small scale, if you have part of a garden (over six-tenths of an acre) or more land that you want to plant for timber use, try the Forestry Commission which gives (currently) the huge grant of £1250 per hectare for broad-leafed trees (much less for a mixed planting that includes conifers). You can choose any trees you like so long as they are suitable for timber; not, for example, willow or poplar, but certainly wild cherry and sweet chestnut. Don't imagine the planting can be ornamental, for maximum spacing is set at 10ft/3m, though the trees are thinned as they grow, resulting in a final spacing of forty to eighty trees per acre, depending on the species and its length of life. To some extent, you can redress this stiffness by making the outline of the plantation shapely and flowing, never geometrical – but you will still have to cut the trees before they have reached attractive maturity.

Otherwise you can try the Countryside Commission scheme operated by the local county council. Grants vary according to different areas, but you will get a subsidy for planting native trees in the countryside (and maintaining them properly). Alternatively, some schemes operate Tree Kit sales for very small scale planting, whereby a selection of ten infant trees suited to different soils, complete with stake and rabbit guard, is sold for a minimal price.

Don't dismiss these schemes as pedestrian, simply because you cannot plant wellingtonias at the tax-payer's expense. All are worth investigating as an extension to land or the garden, and play their part in the crucial re-introduction of native broad-leafed trees to our under-treed landscape. Here is your raw material for the woodlands and landscapes of the future. And with the exception of the Forestry Commission option which determines your spacing (if not your outline), you can organize your clumps and belts like an eighteenth-century aesthete to follow the contours of the land.

Fruit Trees

Fruit trees are also functionaries which look lovelier when grouped into shapes. Any orchard has great charm, but if there is space, it is a pity for example to plant an orchard so that it looks like a tree factory, when, by gathering the trees into clusters of three or sometimes five (spaced within to allow air and light for growth and ripening, and room for picking) you can form one of the prettiest parts of the garden.

All fruit trees are decorative in flower and in fruit and your choice will be governed by taste, climate and a suitable site (be it for fig or apricot, cherry or quince), but for year-round productivity the humble apple cannot be excelled. At Lighthorne in Warwickshire, for example, the Dews have planted their cottage garden to contain thirteen varieties to provide an apple a day throughout the year. Beauty of Bath in July is followed by Discovery in August, Worcester Pearmain and James Grieve in September, Ribston Pippin, Allington Pippin, Sunset, Blenheim Orange, Egremont Russet till the New Year, then Tydeman's Late Orange and the mellow Ashmead's Kernel from January to March and Sturmer Pippin in April, May and June, with the circle complete in early July by Orléans Reinette. The surplus is converted into sparkling dry cider.

You can grow these fruit trees in a variety of ways – as cordons, espaliers, dwarf pyramids, standards etc. – but they also make charming borders either side of a straight path. Grown here in the garden proper rather than segregated into a commune (the orchard), they will impart a sense of productive abundance. Even if they are not actually apple trees, they summarize that mix of Pomona and Flora which is the quintessential English country cottage style. I prefer the unaffected simplicity of the bush form here, but they are often trimmed into espaliers so that the path is flanked by see-through walls. In this case, they are forming an avenue, though, like all straight and orderly roads, they should lead the eye to a little crescendo at the end that gives the illusion that the journey there will be worthwhile.

Avenues

The above scarcely conforms to our notion of a conventional avenue: namely a tree-flanked road in a seventeenth- or early eighteenth-century garden, a symbol of omnipotence thrusting out to the horizon, dominating all sign of visible Nature. Avenues, however, have since taken more variable forms and scaled-down versions of short trees are credible

42. *(above)* Old hornbeams clipped into mushrooms make a one-sided avenue.

43. *(below left)* Trees for impact at different heights: *Pinus sylvestris* against the skyline and . . .

44. *(below right)* . . .*Prunus subhirtella* 'Pendula' with its extraordinary spreading hummock.

even in a small garden (see page 204). There is even the one-sided variant shown in Plate 42). Here, a short line of clipped hornbeams in a raised bed ornaments one side of a gravel walk. This unilateral version is something I have included in my own garden to redress a slope within a formal walled area. A two-sided 'avenue' at the lowest point of this garden would have emphasized the slide of the land; the one-sided version acts instead like a buttress.

A conventional avenue, however, does not fool about with a handful of trees, but is long, wide, usually straight (though, if curving, bends gently yet boldly like a motorway) and leads somewhere necessary, like a house. Its looks will depend on the trees you choose, their spacing and the number of rows. At one extreme, you can have an avenue made of two or even three rows, with the line/s of smaller trees inside the large. Ample space is essential here, to avoid an over-furnished and cluttered appearance. At the other extreme, you can plant a single row to achieve the effect of a high tunnel. I rather like this etiolated Gothic impression of very closely planted trees which grow tall, thin and small-headed under the restraint, and have aimed for this with our own planting of Scots pine, partly from choice, but equally from force for the space available was desperately narrow. In fact it is restrictions such as this which often limit the gardener's choice of tree in such a situation; not just lack of space, but possibly changing soil over a long run or exposure to violent wind. But where a free hand (and purse) is possible, you can in theory choose almost any tree there is, with one proviso. Namely, make your choice as risk-free as possible.

For myself, I would avoid a rich diet (such as that mix of embothriums, ilex and *Eucryphia glutinosa* which was planted at Castle Kennedy in Scotland). I would also eschew oddities like the monkey puzzle avenue of Murthly Park, Perthshire, or the wellingtonias which now puncture the skyline in a straight line beside so many Victorian houses, or even the avenue of Leyland cypress at Bedgebury Pinetum in Kent. Like a ribbon-development of modernist buildings, bulk conifer plantings of this kind, unsoftened by kindlier neighbours, rarely settle comfortably into the landscape.

So, despite even the most successful plantings of the last century – such as the avenue of *Cedrus atlantica glauca* in 1866 or the quarter-of-a-mile-long one in 1868 of *Abies procera* (syn. *nobilis*) *glauca* at Madresfield Court in Worcestershire – I would still settle for those trusty deciduous avenues with an even longer past. Elm, the staple avenue tree of the seventeenth and eighteenth centuries, is sadly no longer with us, but lime which can also be traced back to the early seventeenth century for avenue use, remains a firm favourite. (*Tilia platyphyllos* or *T. cordata* tend to be used now, not the original *T. vulgaris* which develops bushy clumps at the base nor *Tilia* x *euchlora* which is canker-prone.)

Other possible varieties are suggested in the table, some of the loveliest of which can be the large, domed forest trees that have been felled in such numbers since the last war. It is another way of giving back to the countryside the noblest trees it has lost. Only plant them if you have the space to position them so that they can spread their great, deciduous canopies either side of the road, cradling between them, not squeezing, the view of the house at the far end.

I nearly bought a house once on the sole strength that it had an avenue of sweet chestnuts. Romantic indeed but certainly wrong. Or was it? You need plants that will force your gaze up and remind you of your humble position on this planet as a smallish, short-lived organism.

45. One of the great rock gardens shown in the Jekyll and Weaver *Gardens for Small Country Houses*.

VII. Alpine and Rock Gardens
Plants, Carpets and Arenas

ALPINE GARDENING is on the increase. Reason here for surprised delight, as it requires plantsmanship and skilled husbandry to be practised with success. Herein, however, lies the snag, every silver lining having its cloud. Such is the craft that it tends *per se* to be seen as self-justifying, the result being that the art of this form of garden-making is thereby diminished. Alpine gardeners are so often knowledgeable growers rather than the creators of what is potentially a most beautiful form of garden.

Different styles of rock gardens have always caused contention, and various writers (notably William Robinson, Reginald Blomfield and Reginald Farrer) have sniped in print over the last century and a half at inferior examples. Nevertheless, if you look at the photographs in the Jekyll and Weaver *Gardens for Small Country Houses*, it is hard not to conclude that the standard of rock gardens was much higher then than now. (The chapter was written, incidentally, by a specialist contributor, Raymond E. Negus). Here you will find some magnificent examples as the reproduction of one in Plate 45 testifies. In several, huge rocks were used to form small cliff faces, their foreheads festooned with blossoms, their fissures jewelled with flower necklaces. This was rock gardening for large gardens where gargantuan stone formations, assembled and stratified in wilder reaches of the estate, could have a more plausible existence. By their treatment of such stones (often imported at huge expense), the creators of such rock gardens paid tribute to the wildness and sublimity of the origins of these plants.

For many reasons, we cannot contrive such august settings for these plants nowadays. As a general rule our gardens are not large enough; our countryside is tamed and, except in certain areas, an absurd environment for a burst of Nature at her very Rudest; more practically, rocks are usually even more expensive to transport and erect, assuming the right setting. Yet anything short of this kind of sublimity is a trivialization in my view. And our challenge nowadays is to find a truly worthy alternative garden for these dwarf plants. Reginald Farrer's advice in his wonderful book *My Rock Garden* – 'have an idea and stick to it. Let your rock garden set out to be something definite, not a mere agglomeration of stones' – is no longer sufficient. Though I hasten to add that his book remains in its other details one of the great early inspirations, enthusing a beginner yet refreshing an expert.

Various candidates for the rock garden have been tried. The most frequent, still, is the fake diminutive rock garden, electric with labels but affecting to be a natural outcrop in some lawned area. It is usually an unfortunate event from any but the plantsman's point of view. Indeed, it is safe for once to risk the generalization that all such attempts are bound to go wrong: they could always be faulted on style, but now their concept has dated so badly too. We live in a habitat-conscious age, and plants put into such transparently unlikely environments affecting a natural presence are little better than zoo subjects.

Our formal modern alternatives are much more successful. Retaining walls on sloping terraced ground, troughs, or constructed raised beds – all these can be engaging ways of displaying these small treasures as well as sensible methods of satisfying the plants' needs for good drainage and open sunlight. But they all have some drawback: retaining walls will not provide homes for the choicest plants; troughs are peripheral garden ornament, the equivalent of vases or pots; and free-floating raised beds remind me of showcases in a jeweller's. They are all garden features rather than homogeneous gardens, which are the real goal I am trying to pursue here.

There are two modern options, however, which can fairly be called gardens in themselves. They represent two extremes, the one informal, the other its grand architectural opposite, and neither approach makes use of rocks as such. The first of these two options is a garden composed of dwarf rock plants used as carpets. Such plants are often used in paving, but the only setting where you can achieve wall-to-wall alpine carpeting (save for access points) is on gravel or stone chippings. Here, you can make a garden that is practical as well as beautiful, for the plants can be harnessed to do a ground-cover job as well. Such a garden is very different in mood from the sort described in Chapter I, for it carries connotations of the scree (mountain slopes which are covered with rock and pulverized stone chippings) rather than the maquis or the sub-tropics. However, such gravel gardens look far more suitable in the average garden than the contrived scree imitation, which is usually pimpled rather than massed with plants, and one wonders if labels and stones rather than flowers are the real starlets.

The range of plants you can grow in these gravelled conditions is enormous, for when you are dealing with small plants, on flat areas, you can make pockets of peaty soil for plants which like acid conditions, and pockets of limy or alkaline soil-mix for plants with different needs. (Most of the plants will be more than happy with an ordinary free-draining and friable loam.) All the soil should be cleared of weeds and then covered with a 2in/5cm layer of gravel. You now have a garden where you can grow plants that range from sempervivums which need little more than grit and dust, to those like roscoeas which want a rich, deep yet well-drained soil. There are only two kinds of plants you may have to forswear. The first category includes those that are vulnerable to winter wet rotting their hearts and which are therefore best planted sideways in a vertical wall-crevice to prevent rain gathering in their crown. (You can only keep these on the flat by covering them with a pane of glass in winter.) And the other kind of subject includes those which have blooms or a habit shown to most brilliant effect when drifting down from a wall – *Saxifraga* 'Tumbling Waters' for one, or the trailing silvery *Androsace lanuginosa* for another. (You could of course include both trailers and vertical-crevice growers if you had your carpet on a plateau retained by a low stone wall which would ensure good drainage and accommodate both types of plants.) In a country garden, I would also eschew those plants whose leaves are just like the weeds that are forever breaking and entering: sadly, a ban therefore on the charming cobalt-blue flowered *Parochetus communis* with its rampant look-alike clover foliage, and on *Crepis aurea* with gold dandelion flowers and dandelion leaves.

46. A raised bed for alpines and rock plants reflects the movement of the serpentine wall behind it.

Bulbs, though, are at their best here, for (unless they need a summer baking so must not be covered) they look much prettier thrusting through mats of thyme, aubrieta, acaena, sedums etc. than in bare earth. But you do have to guard against their leaves dying at the precise time when the carpeting plant is going to be in full glory. Miniature daffodils (whether species like *Narcissus bulbocodium* or *N. triandrus albus*, or the sweetest of the hybrids like 'Minnow' or 'Hawera') or April-flowering tulips (such as the graceful coral and white *Tulipa clusiana* or the tawny orange *T. orphanidea*) are therefore better planted near sedums blooming in late summer than the much earlier-flowering *Phlox douglasii* or *P. subulata* forms. Similarly the dwarf blue *Allium beesianum* is more suitable with a blue-grey acaena than the trailing long-flowering lemon *Asarina procumbens*.

The other point to remember is to work up a varied tapestry of foliage colour and texture. You have at hand the silvery fur of *Artemisia schmidtiana* 'Nana' and the hard green rosettes of *Bolax* (syn. *Azorella*) *glebaria*; woolly thyme (*Thymus lanuginosus*) and the oak-leafed carpet of *Dryas octopetala*; the hard, encrusted, silver mounds of the Kabschia saxifrages, the porcupine grey or green cushions of dianthus, the symmetrical rosettes of *Androsace sarmentosa* or the smaller 'Chumbyi', the tight silver cover of *Raoulia australis* or the looser white-powdered succulence of *Sedum* 'Capa Blanca'; tiny-leafed autumn-colouring cotoneasters like *C. adpressus*, the flat close-knit green cover of the invasive *Campanula cochlearifolia* and the golden moss of *Sagina glabra aurea*.

All this amounts to gardening around your ankles, but it won't look absurd if you are careful about the way you introduce height. I have no fondness, for example, for dwarf conifers in such a setting: they are almost always employed here and always, to my eyes, reduce the carpet to Lilliput land and you to Gulliver. Better by far to have real height around those edges where it won't block light or sun from all the plants, yet will give shade to those that like it, such as hepaticas, primulas from the easy 'Wanda' forms, to the floriferous lilac *P. sieboldii* or *P. nutans* with its pale blue pagoda heads, or *Chiastophyllum oppositifolium* with its golden tassels in early summer. *Acer japonicum* and *A. palmatum* in variety are lovely in such situations (Fortescue Gardens Trust in Devon have a fine choice), at their best perhaps when they outgrow the position once allotted to them and become large bushes or short, spreading trees (Plate 47). Tall subjects like these put a carpet into perspective; if you have dwarf shrubs only for height, you are giving a false compressed scale here that you would resist in other parts of your garden. What is more, tall shrubs will help to enclose it, transforming it into a garden.

My other point concerns the flowering of such gardens. With alpine/rock plants, one has to push even harder than with other plants to contrive flowers later in the year. There is a big spring and early summer burst, but then little unless one plans. To secure a late-season performance, you can include some of the following: *Gentiana septemfida*, the temperamental *G. farreri, G. sino-ornata, Platycodon grandiflorum*, sedums, *Silene schafta, Tunica saxifraga* (irresistable in its pink powder-puff double form), penstemons, *Lapeirousia cruenta* (syn. *Anomatheca cruenta*), *Nierembergia rivularis, Myrtus nummularia* (a creeping mat with pinkish pea-like fruits), dwarf polygonum species, *Saxifraga fortunei, Zephyranthes candida, Zauschneria californica* and the succulent *Sempervivella alba*. Stalwarts which will flower most of the summer include: *Geranium* 'Ballerina' with lilac dark-zoned flowers, the soft mauve *Pratia pedunculata*, the white *Linum salsoloides, Linum narbonense* with its airy host of blue-butterfly flowers and the white, violet or blue forms of *Viola cornuta*.

The temptation to all alpine enthusiasts who become increasingly obsessed with the inexhaustible supply of treasures is to squeeze their pint-pot with just one of every plant. In the interests of a good garden rather than a collector's museum, one should back off. Stringent selection of the best performers and repeat use of them and bulk quantities of certain background carpeting numbers will probably achieve a better effect. Having rock-plant rug-fringes rather than a carpet, I have for example a group of three *Daphne cneorum* 'Eximia', three *Acaena* 'Blue Haze', twelve armeria and twenty-four variable but shameless *Dianthus gratianopolitanus*. A specialist would accuse me of profligate waste of space which would otherwise support a variety of different species. But I would argue that my approach makes an impact which is both more dramatic yet soothing to the eye than the restless minutiae which is customary in most rock plant areas. And it is one, moreover, which still allows me to have the odd treasure singly so that it will stand out, such as *Penstemon scouleri* 'Albus' with its milky tubular blossoms or the exotic *Roscoea purpurea*.

There is, however, another bolder and admittedly much more expensive and ambitious method of display for these small plants which I rank above all. It makes no concession to the miniaturism of its inmates, nor to the wildness of some of their origins, nor to their natural landscape. A formal garden in itself, it is highly architectural, self-contained yet designed to exist within the rest of the garden. As I write, I have in mind the best example I have seen and one which is innovative in its style. Whilst I am strongly opposed to imitation (it leads to the dullness of all replicas), it is nonetheless a garden which could serve as a stimulus for other late twentieth-century gardens at a time when the revival of interest in alpine and dwarf plants is substantial – yet there is no satisfactory garden in which to grow them.

The garden is owned by Sophie and Michael Hughes at Kingstone Cottage in Herefordshire from where they work as garden designers. Here Mrs Hughes has the National Collection of pinks (shared with an Oxfordshire garden as a safeguard against loss), and the impetus for an individual garden arose directly out of her specialist nursery of old dianthus. This nursery is not merely of local interest, but a mail order concern making phenomenal demands on its owners, for the Hughes supplied recently from two

47. *Acer palmatum* varieties are still among the loveliest subjects for giving height to rock plants.

cold frames no less than twelve thousand plants to fulfil orders arising from a single source.

The garden where many of these enchanting antique pinks thrive can be seen in Colour Plate III and Plates 48-50. It sprang to life almost overnight in 1984 when Michael Hughes asked his wife whether she would like a larger display area for her collection than the beds in the symmetrically curved retaining walls behind the terrace could afford. Within a day, he had pegged out the area on one side of the house to make a rough rectangular arena (42ft × 48ft/13m × 15m) and over a period of some months, completed the digging with spade and rotavator – a job, he admits, better achieved with a mechanical digger, given an entry point for the machine.

His first aim was to collect local stone from derelict walls to build retaining walls around the sunken centre which would be surfaced with bricks and gravel, laid over polythene as a weed barrier. A centre point for the scheme was also vital and Michael Hughes decided in favour of a calm focus amidst the tiers of beds which would be busy with plants. He opted for a small, straight-sided pool. The worry here was the danger it posed to their two very young children. Chicken wire would be inappropriate, so he designed and made a protective wooden framework from roof timbers and mahogany which now fits as a cage over the water. (It has already proved its worth on several occasions when saving the children.) This he left free of preservative, lest it lose its comfortable aged appearance. The pool itself was formed out of a hole, lined with breeze blocks, filled with concrete poured over scrap blocks laid on their side, and rendered within with cement. A drain-pipe leads from the pool. The whole works well, save for slight leaking caused by the after-effects of ice pressing against the walls – which can be a problem with straight-sided pools, for the ice cannot slide up as it would in a funnel-shaped area. The Hughes repair any damage during its annual cleaning, but a permanent cure would be provided by the use of a polythene liner to the pool.

So much for the how-to. The pool now contains fish, zantedeschias, *Iris laevigata* and

85

48. *(above)* At Kingstone Cottage, tiers of beds around the arena give scope for growing trailers as well as plants on the flat. Note the huge variety of pinks.

49. *(below left)* The pool at the centre skirted by bricks and stone in the gravel. Its lovely and ingenious wooden canopy through which plants spray is a child-proofing device.

50. *(below right)* Even the paths at Kingstone Cottage are integrated with the stone-walled beds, for they are cushioned with plants like the violas and strawberries here.

the tall, striped *Scirpus tabernaemontani* 'Zebrinus' which rises high above its wooden canopy. Around the pool, clusters the arrangement of ground-level beds which are kerbed with bricks, tiered beds to the south of the rectangle, and a single, retained large border to the north. There are steps in the middle and at either end, two steps lead (in one case up, in the other case down) to different areas of the rest of the garden.

There is no planting-scheme here, according to Sophie Hughes. With the proviso that she tries to avoid too much yellow and orange in high summer, she simply puts things in, but in this case she can rely on a good, instinctive eye. It is a help, too, that she makes repeated use of certain plants like the golden *Lysimachia nummularia*, acaenas, the silver *Tanacetum densum* 'Amanum' (syn. *Chrysanthemum haradjani*), dwarf hebes, vincas in different flowering forms, thymes, the blue grass *Festuca glauca*, bronze fennels, *Iris pumila* and *I. pallida* 'Variegata', *Artemisia schmidtiana* 'Nana', *Campanula cochlearifolia* (both white and blue form and also the double-flowered 'Elizabeth Oliver'), veronicas in great variety, all of which help to co-ordinate the separate beds.

So, too, do the dianthus of course. In June their massed display – never monotonous thanks to the contribution of such a wide variety of other plants – is the prettiest I have seen. There are so many forms here (Sophie Hughes has about sixty on her mail-order list which details and dates if possible their origins) that I can do no more than mention a very few, including the laced pinks that originated in the eighteenth century. You will find here the semi-double 'London Brocade', laced dark red on pale pink; the long-flowering 'Fair Folley', a single flower with two white flashes on each raspberry petal; 'Paisley Gem', raised in 1789, laced purple on white; 'Charles Musgrave' with green-centred single white frilled blooms; 'Queen of Sheba', a sixteenth-century pink with ivory on magenta feathered markings. Indeed you will find some one hundred and fifty varieties that she grows in her garden.

But the display here is not confined to a high summer feast, nor to the monomania that can be the Achilles heel of collections. Mrs Hughes grows large herbaceous plants in these beds and also full-size shrubs as backstops to the north. The amount of evergreen carpeters – acaenas, sedums, vincas — keeps the beds furnished in winter and the stony surrounds under control in the off-season of the year. And the actual flower display begins in spring with white pulmonarias, and daphnes, the pink-flowered *Lamium* 'Beacon Silver', drifts of muscari, groups of *Pulsatilla vulgaris*, golden doronicums, self-seeding clumps of *Viola rosea* and *V. tricolor*, *Euphorbia wulfenii*. And it is prolonged past the June burst until late summer by the use of herbaceous plants like *Penstemon heterophyllus* 'Blue Springs', by *Salvia haematodes*, by the deep carmine-purple wild antirrhinum species and pink lavenders, and also by the fact that the backcloth to this architectural area is the rest of the garden on raised ground beyond, with its long-flowering bed of shrubs and herbaceous plants.

It is rare in my experience to come across a new architectural setting that does not diminish the vitality of the plants it supports, but enhances them. The abundance of plants here, where even the crevices of the paths (Plate 50) are encrusted with self-sowers or spreaders like the double form of wild strawberry, with violets, purple-leafed clovers and chamomile, ensures that this is the case. But, more important, the design of this garden has not been allowed to get out of hand. It is bold, simple and, being made predominantly of the same materials as the stone house and anchored as it is near the building, entirely appropriate to its surroundings. In short, here is a rock/dwarf plant garden which combines the grower's skill with the artist's flair.

VIII. Garden Features
Pergolas, Arches, Tree Tunnels, Colour Borders and Gardens

THE TEST of a good garden – indeed, of a painting, a book or any art form – is whether it succeeds as a synthesis. Disparate ideas, images, plants (the equivalent of characters in a novel) come from different sources and from everywhere, for a living art absorbs what is around it. All these ingredients, whether the raw material or imported set-pieces, have to be blended into a whole creation. The successful integration of these very different ingredients is the hardest thing of all to achieve when making a garden; and it follows that the number of gardens which pass this exacting test is miniscule.

The reason for a garden's failure can be basic, as when the whole layout is wrong. In this case, a total re-working is the only possible cure. (I speak from uncomfortable experience. Having designed one portion of our garden on labour-saving grounds, I enjoyed it for two weeks before, braving the truth, I admitted it to be wrong. We moved two hundred plants and began all over again.) But there is a less dramatic cause of failure, in my opinion. Namely, the enthusiastic misuse of garden features. It is so common that I feel bound to start this chapter with a caution against them. The trouble lies in the fact that, though charming ideas in themselves, they are rarely integrated into a garden, but erupt without reason first in one place and then another. This, alas, makes them look what they doubtless are: pretty tricks borrowed straight from another's garden without being understood or digested on the way.

Pergolas

Pergolas are especially likely subjects for misuse. When decked out in full finery, they are so tempting that the onlooker wants his/her very own sample, regardless of its appropriateness to the garden. And a pergola that fails to fit in is a very noisy intrusion indeed. The fault usually stems from the fact that the pergola is mispositioned. This is very easy to do if you don't grasp the concept behind this kind of garden feature. It arose in Italy as a shady and protective covering to a path and evolved into an important decoration in a formal garden. It therefore justified itself through its purpose and its site, a necessity with any main building. In consequence, the purist (me, in this case) argues that you cannot include a pergola in your garden without, firstly, a formal path or paved area which it will

51. 'Only when you walk beneath a long pergola can you appreciate the rhythmic shafts of alternating light and shade.'

cover; without starting- and finishing-points of importance (a house, say, and another garden building); and without a large enough formal area to absorb it. It should be wide enough to enable two or three people to walk abreast within; and I would add my own personal preference for it to be anchored on one side to a wall where its crossbeams and uprights (the equivalent of the builder's joists and timbers) are truly at home. In all honesty, these requirements are so exacting that, if met, the pergola population would soon die out. Nonetheless, the first three points seem indispensable to me and, where they cannot be satisfied, it would be far better to exclude the pergola from the garden. As a consolation prize, there may be a case for the slightly less formal tree-tunnel, but more of that later.

Given, however, the precise conditions it needs, a pergola can be the most magnificent of garden buildings. If one has a choice, dependent on one's purse and the site, then length of run will truly exploit its best characteristics. Only when you walk beneath a long pergola can you appreciate the rhythmic shafts of alternating light and shade. Or the telescopic illusion as you look towards the far end, especially noticeable in Colour Plate VIII. Neither of these pleasures is in store if the pergola is either too short – or, in fact, too narrow.

To avoid this latter fault, you need to keep opposite uprights not less than 8ft/2.4m apart. By the time they are festooned with climbers which will take up quite a lot of space themselves, this will be none too wide. And if you intend to plant in a ribbon bed on either side of the path within the pergola, then the spacing may need to be further still. These uprights, whether wood or stone or brick, need to be plunged firmly into the ground, ideally in 18in or 2ft/45 or 60cm concrete footings, leaving about 8ft/2.4m above the ground. The crosspieces overhead, usually of wood, complete the frame; and to avoid messiness, crosspiece and upright look best if neither projects beyond their join. A pergola of this nature will be open enough to produce rhythmic bursts of light and shade in its interior; but you can turn it into a consistently shady tunnel if you add longitudinal battens of wood overhead, or cover it with cross-slats (at least 2in/5cm thick to prevent sagging). Either will give extra support to climbers, of course.

The materials you use depend on the context. In Italy, stone was customary, and made ornate and important pergolas. In Britain, the great exponent of this type of corridor has been Sir Edwin Lutyens, though he was typically innovative on an old theme. At Hestercombe, for example, he alternated round with square uprights, thus helping to break the monotony of the very long run of 240ft/72m. Elsewhere he used another variation which was to alternate brick with stone pillars. At Marsh Court, his *chef d'oeuvre*, he erected pillars of wide-jointed tiles on edge and keyed the concave cross-beams overhead into the house wall. Miss Jekyll favoured this use of concave cross-beams, particularly when partnered with a further refinement, a concave brace supporting the join between upright and cross-beam.

These monuments were devised at a time when architects dominated the garden; and they make such substantial masses that they can only be accommodated in the kind of powerfully architectural and formal environment that spawned them – one large enough, moreover, to take the reduction in space from this run of furniture. In other contexts, the light effect of a wooden pergola will probably be rather more suitable. For these, softwood poles are normally used, though they have to be pressure-treated with preservative for durability, and even then, are sometimes sunk in drainpipes in concrete (sealed at the top

52. A pergola built against a wall and festooned with wistaria makes a summerhouse at Trewithen, Cornwall. The eagles guarding the steps are a family emblem.

53. An elegant structure made of 4in/10cm concrete drainpipes crossed with dead elm battens at The Priory, Worcestershire. The planting includes vines and *Clematis viticella purpurea plena elegans*.

to prevent rain penetrating between pole and pipe). For a rustic air, the Edwardians favoured larchwood with the bark left on, but barked wood can look so amateurish that, if one can afford it, squared beams are the better option. They have a far more substantial appearance, especially if they are given 'feet', the planted or constructed equivalent of plinths for piers. These will give visual stability to any upright, whether brick, stone or wood.

I have seen in several gardens, however, ingenious substitutes for the old materials: in one case, defunct electricity poles (which were bought from maintenance engineers working in the area) still warm from dismantling, no doubt. And Plate 53 shows the elegant structure at The Priory, Kemerton, of 4in/10cm concrete drainpipes crossed with dead elm battens. Architectural salvage merchants would also be another possible source for columns: these could be suitable so long as they don't evoke the Parthenon. But in any case, avoid improvising a structure in a country garden which will look hideously modern when exposed in winter.

The quality of the material and design must inevitably affect the choice and quantity of the plants the pergola supports. No one would want to obscure completely structures which are innately ornamental, whereas many wooden erections look much the better for a full-blooded smothering. But whatever the context, my own preference is for simplicity and consistency in the planting, whether in foliage or in colour. Plants with weeping fruit and flowers are the best suited to exploit their opportunity here. Vines, the original pergola covering, are still amongst the loveliest and the most useful whether for vigour of growth, density of coverage or controllability. The effect they provide from within (and the interior is at least as important as the outside) is enchanting, sunlight irradiating the intensely green leaves and the burgundy or golden jewelled bunches of fruit. Gourds were also shown over a larch pergola in Jekyll and Weaver's *Gardens for Small Country Houses*; they make a dazzling exoticism, yet this round, turbanned kind of fruit is well suited to so artificial a form of display. Wistaria remains unequalled, especially *W. floribunda* 'Macrobotrys', for its grace and mass of leaf and trailing tresses. But other possibilities include *Campsis* x *tagliabuana* 'Madame Galen' (for hot areas where flowering will be more reliable), *Jasminum officinale, Solanum crispum* 'Glasnevin'; and for shadier spots, clematis, especially the *C. viticella* varieties, and honeysuckles. *Aristolochia durior* (syn. *A. sipho, A. macrophylla*) would do a complete foliage-blanket job. All are easier to train if you enclose the upright of the pergola with wide-gauge wire to which the plant stems can be tied – an eyesore admittedly out of season or if insufficiently covered by foliage.

It is difficult when using a variety of plants as cover for one pergola to avoid incoherence. Though you will get colour and eventfulness throughout the season, you will also invite messiness unless you are clever. One solution is to keep to a single colour as in the pergola at Lower Hall (detailed on page 180) which is wondrously festooned from April through to autumn with white-flowered plants – clematis, roses and the large-leafed milky *Wistaria venusta*.

Roses have not lost their popularity, yet, to my eyes, they are not the most suitable sole covering for a pergola. Few have good leaves as well as flowers (the best such as *R. brunonii* or *R. sinowilsonii* being either too big, or, in cold climates, reluctant flowerers) which is essential for a plant candidate here. And in any case, a whole run of roses, artificially trained as they are in this position, is to me cloying in its sweetness; it is not surprising they were a Victorian favourite with that era's fondness for over-sugaring the cake. They also have

VIII. Only when you walk beneath a long pergola, can you appreciate the telescopic illusion as you look towards the far end.

IX. *(right)* Miss Jekyll thought that white-painted furniture was 'tyrannical': here, for example, the seat is the prime focus and the doorway takes on a secondary role beside it.

X. *(overleaf)* Lower Hall (Chapter XVI): the raised red, purple and pink border is brilliantly impacted against the green gravel enclosure glimpsed through the open door in the main walled garden.

XI. 'Lavender Pinocchio': a floribunda (or cluster-flowered) rose which starts life as tan, pinks up and then matures into lavender. A lovely subject for a subtly shaded colour border.

XII. At The Priory, Worcestershire, the pink and violet border harnesses as a backstop the large yew which actually belongs to the red border beside it.

54. The rose arch spans the box hedges which converge in a long perspective on the seat.

other disadvantages: many short pillar roses which will clothe the uprights effectively instead of overshooting the mark like some ramblers, have an unyielding habit of growth. And the flowering season of most roses is either brief and without weeping fruit to follow; or it is usually intermittent, few beautiful cultivars equalling their first flush. For roses which are assets, however, see below.

Arches

Roses seem to be rather better suited instead to the simple arch. This, taking up relatively little space, needs to be less of a rent-payer than the pergola; secondly, its effects are to be viewed from without (rather than within) which is where the rose scores. Even the arch, however, is subject to misuse and needs intelligent positioning if it is not to be yet another toy littering the ground. It can play several roles to attractive effect. Like the pergola it needs a path beneath it, but this time it is an architrave around an imaginary door between one area and the next, actually telling you there is a proper transition here, or a start, or a finish to a walk. Or you could use it as a frame to a focus beyond, as in Plate 54 which shows the rose 'Adelaide d'Orléans' cradling the view of a distant seat at Mottisfont. But, equally important, this picture demonstrates how much is gained from the tight links between the lines here. The rose arch spans the box hedges which, in turn, converge in a long perspective on the seat, the focus which the arch frames. No loose ends here, so everything looks satisfyingly predestined, not thoughtless and random.

Weak-stemmed roses are no disadvantage over an arch, for their nodding blooms will look towards you. Of them all 'Adelaide d'Orléans' is the perfect choice for this position with her weeping creamy-blush flower-heads which Graham Stuart Thomas likened to cherry-blossom. But the later-flowering white 'Aimée Vibert', the white pompon 'Félicité et Perpétue' (though a bit large for other than a very big arch), the recurrent cluster-flowered 'Sander's White Rambler', 'Bleu Magenta' with her double purplish flower-trusses, the pale pink miniature-flowered 'Cécile Brunner', 'Princess Marie' with its sprays of miniature double pink shells (again, a large grower), the recurrent silvery-pink 'New Dawn', and 'Débutante' with late-flowering showers of double pink blooms are all very lovely. 'Parkdirektor Riggers' is recurrent and the richness of even a few of its crimson velvet blooms against the leaves is valuable. The blush 'Madame Alfred Carrière' which sometimes produces a splendid second flush of blossoms in autumn, needs a large arch to take her vigour.

If you don't build or commission an arch, then most garden-centres sell self-assembly kits. They vary from wood to metal to PVC-coated. Black is better than green, and anything is better than faux-bamboo, which will give the garden a bout of fallen arches. In any case, they should be stout and wide enough (say 3ft/90cm) to enable you to fan your plant shoots against their support, not bunch them together like a rocket. These arches need to be plunged firmly in the ground for, when top-heavy with foliage, they can be vulnerable to wind.

Tree Tunnels

The same is true of single-railed arches which can be assembled in a run to form pleached alleys. Though these are less formal than the masonry pergola, they still demand very careful placing – over a path, from Somewhere to Somewhere, anchored at one end at least to a starting-point, and preferably at the other — and never, never, just left to free-float in the middle of an area. They are most commonly used as a base over which to grow *Laburnum* x *watereri* 'Vossii' which will weep its long golden trails within; though in this case, the arches need to be very wide to ensure the maximum 'weeping' in their interior. At Bodnant Garden in North Wales, for example, the laburnum tunnel is 15ft/4.6m wide, the supporting arches spaced at 12ft/3.7m (linked by longitudinal rails) – and it is also about 80yd/74m long. The last measurement has little application to gardens nowadays, but the first two are important; they guarantee a rich, flamboyant and potent effect.

Bodnant's tunnel has often been copied and, of the many examples I have seen, I know one which was planted as a golden wedding anniversary present – a commemorative idea for those celestial couples who can plant together without quarrelling. But such tunnels have been formed with many different plants since their Tudor forbears, which carried vines. The kind of plant you choose will affect where you plant your tunnel (and vice versa, of course), for its grouped presence is a dominant one. Austere yew tunnels – at the opposite extreme from the razzmatazz of laburnum – might be suitable near an old formal house, in an Italianate garden, or even as a transition between formal garden and a wilder, densely wooded area where yews might grow naturally. In comparison with other tunnels, they are slow-growing but I value their ageing effect upon a garden and love their severity which saves them, whatever the context, from becoming clichés.

But to my mind, the most covetable of all tunnels, and relatively quick-growing too, is made of magnolias. I mentioned in Chapter VI the wonderful *Magnolia* x *soulangiana* 'Lennei' tunnel at Lanhydrock in Cornwall. This came into existence as the result of an inspirational idea by Peter Borlase, the head gardener at this National Trust property, and its origins are well worth recording. On his arrival at Lanhydrock in 1966, no tunnel existed, but simply several magnolias positioned beside a path. The taller of these had a wooden prop supporting its main stem and taking its branches across the path; whereas the lower magnolia had been cut back from the path each year. Mr Borlase recognized the potential for a tunnel and begged some iron rose arches which he had helped to dismantle when working in his last job (at another National Trust garden). He thus established the magnolia framework by tying every available shoot and branch over and along the arches and planted some four further magnolias to fill in the gaps between the existing two. Over the years, the coverage from six trees trained over eight iron arches has grown sumptuous and complete. The arches are spaced 2yd/1.8m from each other, and the length of the tunnel is about 20yd/18m with a gentle turn in its direction so that you proceed somewhat mysteriously, being unable to see through to the end. It is a unique and elysian experience for the visitor.

Despite its luxurious display, the magnolia tunnel is economical for the planter (six trees over eight arches for a long run), but the same cannot be said of the apple or pear tunnel. These are the most plant-intensive of structures, as they are usually formed by planting cordon fruit trees on semi-dwarfing MM.106 rootstock at the foot of each rail, spaced at about 2½ft/75cm apart. They are also the most labour-intensive of all tunnels requiring systematic attention if they are to fruit well. *The Fruit Garden Displayed*, the Royal Horticultural Society's handbook, gives details of the method; but, very briefly, each new cordon will need notching in late spring to produce side shoots on the bare upper reaches and pruning of all shoots every summer to keep the trees productive. Mature laterals are reduced to three leaves beyond the basal cluster and those arising from existing side shoots or spurs are taken back to one leaf.

This system is certainly a demanding way of growing fruit, but a very decorative method so long as, yet again, the fruit tunnel is as sensitively placed as a pergola. It shouldn't free-float, erupt in the middle of a path or end for no reason half-way through it. Unless you have a conveniently short path between a departure and a destination, you risk creating the kind of example built at Lilleshall in Shropshire which simply couldn't end. At 570ft/175m long, this apple tunnel was thought to be the longest in England and is illustrated in *Gardens Old and New*, a handsome book published by Country Life in 1903. In this case the arches were widely spaced, so the fruit trees (one per either side of the arch) were not cordoned but grown to form informal fans, their branches spaced over the battens that ran between the arches to form a huge enclosed tunnel. In flower and, even more, in ripened fruit, it must have made a thrilling showcase.

Colour Borders and Gardens

The term 'garden features' is usually reserved for structures. But I am tucking colour borders under this umbrella, as they share the same solidity and look-at-me impact as other features in this chapter. They are, however, rather more difficult to create, requiring not only skill in handling different colour values, but also a very sure knowledge of the simultaneous flowerings of a huge range of herbaceous and shrubby plants. This is the kind of knowledge only to be acquired by long observation in different seasons. But, for my part, I am exceedingly grateful to rely also on Graham Stuart Thomas's lists of simultaneous flowering plants in his book *The Art of Planting*. This compilation is amongst the most helpful crutches a gardener could lean on.

Even were you omniscient, however, the creation of a colour border must still present a challenge. To begin at the beginning, where should you position it? This is crucial for it is much less flexible than the more casual mixed border and has only four months real flower power to its elbow, since it usually relies so heavily on herbaceous (and half-hardy annual) plants. Should it, for example, go against a wall or in an enclosure; or out in the open as in the case of twin beds lining an open-ground path?

There is no doubt that the first proposition is the easier option. If you position the border against a wall or limit its arena of impact by screening trees or dark hedges, you are excluding other visual disruptions to its colour impact. If you don't do this, you have the more difficult job of making it blend into its surroundings – or trying to harness them (though the latter is achieved in Colour Plate XII where a pink and violet colour border has as its backdrop a large clipped yew which actually belongs to the red border beside it). There is also another incentive for fully or partially enclosing a colour border: namely, that an island bed or border is notoriously difficult to create since it must be equally presentable and varied to view on all four sides, quite a challenge with a limited palette. None of these problems occurs, of course, in an enclosure as at Sissinghurst with its coloured compartments. Nor in the red garden at Hidcote Manor which presents its material in the most ideal surroundings, for the plants are not only given their own hedged compartment, but the borders are enfiladed and their colour thus concentrated yet shown in perspective. All of which makes for a very high-powered microcosm.

Positioning is actually all-important. Where you choose affects also what colour you want. This cannot be imposed entirely at your will. Rather, it should arise not only from the mood of the setting, but from its backcloth (e.g. will the colour harmonize with the bricks, paint, fields near it?). For remember that a colour can be heightened or destroyed by its surroundings. Consider too the time of day when you are likely to see the colours at their best. This is especially true with white or silver borders. In her book *Gardens of the great Mughals* (1913), Mrs. Villiers Stuart described the luminous Indian gardens – whitely flowered with favourite Hindu blossoms like poppies, tuberose, datura, petunia, stephanotis, magnolias, gardenias, designed to be seen and smelt at their sweetest by nightlight, when they would gleam like phosphorescence under the moon. And it is true, even in cold northern climates, that the worst time for a white or silver border is at mid-day when the overhead light bleaches it of all subtlety. Reserve this colour, then, for further-flung areas which can be appreciated in the evening; it is not for placing in front of the house unless you are away all day. (For beautiful examples of this type of garden, see Plates 55, 56 and 94, the latter taken in a garden described on page 162.)

Blue borders, in contrast, are the truer for a good light, for blue is a recessive colour, fading quickly at dusk. This characteristic can be exploited to give the illusory effect of distance if blue is planted towards the far end of a border. Miss Jekyll was very stringent in her taste for blues and did not like mixing blues with purples, indeed preferring to keep all pure blues on their own (delphinium, anchusa, salvia, the blue cape daisy [*Agathaea coelestis*, syn. *Felicia pappei*] and lobelia); and only when the main mass of blue in her great Munstead Wood border was over, could she enjoy the presence of *Campanula lactiflora* or the herbaceous *Clematis davidiana* (*C. heracleifolia* 'Davidiana').

Of the other main colour subjects, yellow borders are like white in that the colour advances and will carry a considerable distance; its mood though is quite different, being buoyant and unromantic. Red borders are more dramatic and can cause such disturbance that they are best for the cooling contrasts of green before or after them.

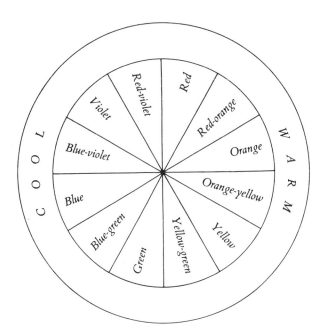

Fig 2. Chevreul's colour circle: his statements on colour harmony became the principles and laws of colour training thereafter, although nowadays most artists take a far freer approach. Chevreul believed that:

i) tints and shades of the same hue make combinations of monochromatic harmony;

ii) neighbouring colours on the pure colour scale (the colour circle) are agreeable and he called this the harmony of adjacents;

iii) all colours gain in brilliance and purity by the proximity of grey (though he thought that grey and rose were a little dull, thereby rejecting a most cherished combination in today's gardens);

iv) triad combinations, such as black (a gardener would substitute for this very dark yew green), red and yellow were successful;

v) the proximity of complementary colours (i.e. the opposites on the colour circle such as blue and orange) was successful;

also of split-complementary groups (i.e. the combination of a hue, not with its exact complementary, but with the two neighbouring colours that flank its complementary on the colour circle);

vi) if two colours combined badly, they could be separated by white, grey or, less relevantly to the gardener, black: this would make a neutral interval.

55 & 56. *(above right and below)* Two different white and silver borders demonstrate how necessary dark hedges and background walls are as a foil to this kind of garden.

The latter is by implication one of the issues explored in Michel Chevreul's great nineteenth-century treatise *The Principles of Harmony and Contrast of Colours and their Application to the Arts*, which was published in 1854 (edited by Faber Birren and re-issued in 1967). Fig. 2 illustrates his colour circle and related theories, but here I want to concentrate on one of his topics: the power of the after-image. His contention was as follows: if you look at a blue square on a white ground, then fix your eye on the white, it will see orange. His explanation for this was that the retina, fatigued by blue, was disposed to receive a stronger impression of blue's complementary colour, orange. Now, in the same way, you look for green after red.

With this in mind, remember the red borders at Hidcote, to take the most famous example. You will recall that they are preceded by the green stage and followed by the green hornbeam alley. The power of this sequence, the sum for once being greater than its fine parts, which is very difficult to achieve in a garden, convinces me there is truth in the hunger of the eye for a complementary colour as an antidote. It is a factor which has been brilliantly exploited in the garden detailed on page 177 and shown in Colour Plate X. Here the red, purple and pink border (unusual not only in its colour blend, but in the fact that it is shrubby, not herbaceous) is shown against the backcloth of a carefully composed green garden.

The conclusion of all this is that sequence of colour matters, so here is another factor to affect the successful positioning of your colour border. Miss Jekyll herself had strong opinions about this and detailed them in *Colour Schemes for the Flower Garden*. Here, she advised you to enter a gold garden from a shrub or tree plantation, sunshine after shade. The grey garden would be best reached through orange borders. From the grey garden, you go to the yellow, and thence to the blue garden (she was strict that only true blues should be used, save a couple of exceptions). And from the blue garden, one progressed to the green, with its smattering of white flowers. To speak for myself, I should be worn out from so many changes of gear.

So much for the theory and positioning. What of the composition of the border or garden itelf? The least successful colour schemes are those that seem like an exercise, scales or arpeggios in red or whatever, excluding other harmonies. The most successful are those which interpret the colour liberally and imaginatively. They use not only pale and deep tints of one hue, but other colours from the spectrum as well to reinforce the effects. And if the border is enfiladed, the colour can progress from, say, oranges to reds, to purples, to violets, to take the warm harmonious side of the colour circle – though no such sequence will work satisfactorily if you see it broadside, like a tableau. Foliage colour, too, plays a key part and sometimes the central role, for whole colour borders and gardens can be composed of foliage which is green, grey, gold, lemon, purple, ruby, and saffron and scarlet in autumn, making a far more prolonged spectacle than its flowered counterpart. Plant habit, too, is equally crucial. For, if this is ignored, you will end up with a solid wall of colour without texture or perspective – the border's equivalent of carpet-bedding, whereby flowers are reduced to one dimension only. Such a display has nothing to offer after its first glimpse, for colour is useless without good form too.

Perhaps the simplest approach to designing a colour bed is to make a list of all the good favourite shrubs and herbaceous plants in the range of colours you are including – whether blue and yellow; or red, purple and orange; or silver, pink and claret (one of the easiest because long-lasting foliage gives you your continuous base); or green and limes (ditto).

Assemble the plants into lists of simultaneous flowers. Star those which you want to feature in predominant groups (for when you are combining colours, you can't give equal weight to each colour, but should allow one to predominate, the rest to accent and flatter). Tick plants which are extra shapely. If you don't have enough with fine foliage or distinctive habit, add plants like plumy grasses which can provide just that (very useful suppliers as their leaves can be bright green, silver-variegated, blue, purplish or yellow. Eliminate the surplus and inferior plants. And then arrange your scheme as for a normal border, taking account of different heights and groupings, remembering that the latter will give you distinct monochrome masses and should be scaled to context and partly intergrouped to prevent too solid colour blocks. The whole procedure can be summarized as merge, purge and splurge.

Planning, however, can only do so much. For you are dealing not only with unpredictable plants, some of which will surely die on you in the cold country, but even unpredictable colours. Many organic colours are neither light- nor weather-proof. Some will bleach in hot sun, some brown in frost (Neil Treseder, the camellia specialist, found that the dark red flowers on camellias were undamaged by an air frost of 14°F/−10°C which harmed their white-blossomed sisters.) And colour will be changed not only by sun, shade and weather, but by a flower's own cycle of life too. *Rosa chinensis* 'Mutabilis' is one of the best-known examples, with flaming buds, pale copper opening flowers which become pink and then soft crimson in maturity. The floribunda (now called cluster-flowered) rose 'Lavender Pinocchio' (Colour Plate XI) is another most beautiful example. She is a perfect subject for a pink and silver border, or for a pink, claret and bronze one (you need to spray her lest black-spot becomes one of the colour-effects too), yet she starts life as tan, pinks up, then goes lavender as the petal matures. Subtleties such as these serve to enhance a colour border in my eyes. Stasis and predictability are the worst aspects of all garden features.

But I should hate to end this chapter on a less positive note, when an incomparable garden like Kiftsgate Court in Gloucestershire exists to show its unique combination of splendour and subtlety in the use of colour. Its magnificence, however, arises partly from an unusually wide, sometimes even deviant, palette of colour from which it draws. Thus, the yellow border is made up of dark gold and sulphur flowers, from bronze, mahogany, purple, green and grey foliage, from blue and purple flowers. The 'four-squares' area before the house portico has purples, blue and silver, and pink and red roses, chosen for their blue suffusion. The wide border is a composition of crimson, pink, mauve, purple, blue, creamy and white flowers and silver and green foliage. One can only marvel at the detailed plant knowledge and mature judgement that lie behind these memorable glories; but, for a few pence, one can also buy a copy of the plant lists that compose them and, thus armed, try to do a fraction as well on a tenth of the scale.

IX. Garden Ornament
Birds, Pots and Plants, Seats, Statues

IN THE COUNTRY, the loveliest of all garden ornament is alive and mobile. The earliest peacock butterflies, goldfinches in late summer, a little owl sitting on a gatepost in snow — seasonal visitors like these unfailingly lift the spirit. But if these are not enough, you can also cultivate your own domestic colony of ornamental birds. Dependent creatures, many to an even greater extent than the waterfowl described in Chapter V, they will make demands on you and you cannot keep them unless you will feed them regularly and give them (most, at any rate) protection against predators.

Assuming this to be the case, you can choose from quail, exotic bantams, ducks, geese, ornamental pheasants, peafowl and the free-flyers which scarcely seem to come to ground like certain doves and their relatives. If you are not predisposed towards one kind of bird, your choice could turn on whether you want eggs — and not only bantams, ducks and geese will be useful in this respect, but quail too. It will also depend on the accommodation you can give the birds. Some need simply a fox-proof shed, others such as doves a barn or a proper dovecote, an ornamental structure in itself, and yet others, like bantams, quarters furnished with perches and some sort of nest box. There are some fowl, however, like Old English Game bantams and guineafowl which are easy on the stockman and can be left to roost in trees in fox-free areas. (Elsewhere they too may need night quarters for they can fly down early in the morning and into the jaws of the enemy.)

You should also be influenced by the effect these birds have upon the garden. In some cases, with peafowl for one example, their depredations can be devastating. I have always yearned to keep these dazzling birds, whether white, plain Indian or its black-shouldered mutant. Their fantastic appearance and melancholy cries (incessantly grating to some) are magnetic to me. But they are also notorious for decapitating every flower and vegetable in the garden – the neighbour's too, perhaps – and I cannot afford the ruin this leaves. These glorious creatures are best fitted to neighbourless gardens of bare lawn and mature trees and they suit such a landscape to perfection.

Peafowl are not the only ones to spoil a garden. Even the humble chicken will scratch up the earth with its feet and very possibly your plants too. With all this in mind, I have opted to keep booted bantams. These exotic miniature fowl sport huge, stiff feathers on their legs and feet. Less likely to tear up the earth than the bare-shanked varieties, they are good birds for the gardener. My own are Belgian Millefleurs (Barbu d'Uccles), charming characters with a high-stepping gait and chestnut plumage spangled with black and silver

57. Though the most glorious of all ornaments, the habits of peacocks make them best fitted to neighbourless gardens of bare lawns and mature trees.

eyes. But there are other booted bantams you might consider, such as Brahmas, Cochins, Croad Langshans and, not least, the very pretty lavender Pekins, though these are too much fluff and nonsense to win me over. Birds such as these can do little more than levitate, so they do need absolute fox-protection at night and their quarters must be infallibly secure. I once had a fox break in through an entry-point I would not have credited, and it is a heart-breaking experience.

Ornamental pheasants are another very beautiful possibility, though read on for the flip side. The breeds which are usually kept are the Golden, the Silver, Lady Amherst's Pheasant which is white, deep blue and green, scarlet and gold, and the Reeves's Pheasant with barred black, yellow, chestnut and white markings and a wondrously long tail of some five feet. (Descriptions apply to the cock only, the hen being a comparatively dowdy creature.) Rarer birds include the magnificent Siamese Fire-back (with the loveliest of all hen pheasants) and the Swinhoe's Pheasant. A read of Sir Sacheverell Sitwell's *The Hunters and the Hunted* with descriptions of others will fire you with acquisitiveness. The trouble comes with the way you must keep them. Excepting tame or wing-clipped specimens, most (even the easy and commoner species) are usually kept in netted cages with plants for cover within. I find it uncongenial to keep strictly imprisoned creatures in the garden which is why I don't advocate aviary birds here. I therefore opted to keep my own golden pheasants free-range in the day-time, a not uncommon choice with relatively tame birds of this species. This didn't work either. The cock, a bird of great splendour with a gilded nuchal cape (puffed out in his courtship display), scarlet and gold plumage and sweeping tail feathers, proved harmless in the garden but a major pest to humans, pecking incessantly at our feet and legs. Yet worse, he so savaged his mates in the style common to many pheasants, that they left the homestead, flying off to the woodland and refusing to return. In the end, I gave the remaining cock back to the breeder and chose not to repeat the experience.

What of doves and their relatives? A flock of white doves on an old tiled roof or in pale whirring flight against green trees is one of the most beautiful sights in a garden. An even more dramatic variant is to keep a different form such as the Spanish Nun, named for its black head and white body. But there may be potential difficulties here, too. The dovecote needs careful siting for a start. It may sound obvious, but don't put it near the vegetable garden, for example. In the walled kitchen garden of Felbrigg Hall, a National Trust property in Norfolk, the huge colony of doves used to ransack the produce. This is taking account of your own interests, but you have to consider theirs also. Site their quarters as near the house as you can to deter predators. In really rural areas, even this does not always work. One owner in Powys, who built the charming little dovecote in Plate 58 for her pairs of doves, placed it on a wall bordering her house terrace and found that even this was insufficient to deter sparrowhawks from picking off her doves one by one. They killed the lot.

It is therefore a slightly uncertain business. Even the birds may let you down by breeding with rough trade, such as wood pigeons, in which case you will have grey offspring. I should therefore be chary of spending much money on a dovecote, unless you are sure the venture will have a satisfactory outcome. Build your own rather, like the above owner, whose little cote with its ivy dressing is as delightful as can be. Otherwise, if you want to buy, you can get free-standing dovecotes from the reconstituted stone merchants at vast prices, and free-standing and wall fixtures (still expensive) from suppliers of wooden cotes.

106

58, 59 & 60. Three different ways of accommodating doves in the garden.

One firm will also supply birds, food etc. (see Appendix). In all cases, the doves must be confined to their quarters for at least the first three weeks otherwise they are liable to abandon you. And in some cases, where the hapless birds have had their feathers dyed to match their master's whims, who can blame them?

Pots and Plants

Potted plants are rather a tame attraction after such animated birds but at least they are living adornment, of a kind moreover which can be re-positioned each year to vary the display and scaled to suit the surroundings.

Their usefulness is multiform. You can make them assert the style of their area; urns, for example, are a quick and sometimes trite means of gentrification, whereas ali-baba jars give a meridional air. Or you can place your pots so that they have a specific function; a pair of large potted plants will reinforce features – a gateway, a seat, steps – or invest less balanced items like a creeper-covered arbour, with tranquil symmetry. One large pot on its own will give form where it is in short supply, as in a fluffy herbaceous border. Or you can use it to jazz up a dreary corner with dark-leafed shrubs. Best of all, however, you can plan your pots to make a bravura show on a hardware surface like a terrace or pool surround where colour and leaf are inadequate. This you can do in three good ways.

Firstly, you can use plants which have an exotic, dramatic appearance, but need winter housing if they are to be permanent occupants of the place. Such an example is *Datura* 'Grand Marnier', a stunning pale apricot form of the scented *D. suaveolens*, shown in Plate 62. Given a sheltered position, a rich soil in a large tub and adequate moisture to keep red spider at bay (the major pest of daturas in my experience), this is just the kind of attention-arresting subject that truly justifies the extra work that potting plants entails. Tender succulents are another good example of this category and are far less demanding about water and care. There are many, such as the yellow-margined *Agave americana* 'Variegata' (it is spiny so needs a safe position where children or dogs are in the garden), aloes, crassulas, echeverias or trailing lampranthus hybrids festooning the sides of a pot, all of which will give an almost heraldic look to the setting in return for a once-a-week watering.

The second successful method of using pot plants is to present them with special panache. In this case, you can use perfectly ordinary plants, easy-going about watering and feeding, but their impact comes from their setting. Look, for example, at Plate 63 where an urn of white geraniums is given a special alcove of clipped yew. It is not, admittedly, an effect to be achieved overnight, and an easier possibility is to be seen in Plate 61 where a harmonious grouping of potted plants is arranged on a short flight of semi-circular steps. Steps are particularly good means of giving a variety of heights to pots and plants which are of fairly uniform size.

Such a grouping can be equally effective if it is bold and linear – pots placed at intervals along a path, say. Or at Mawley Hall in Shropshire, Mrs. Galliers-Pratt has five large hostas in a line-up of terracotta pots by a shady entrance. They represent to her entirely trouble-free gardening, for she has had them for thirty years and changed two inmates just once! They are as vigorous and healthy as any grown in an open garden, and, equally important, potted hostas are more easily protected against slugs than open-ground plants.

The third method of giving pot-plants impact is arguably the most difficult, for it depends on plant associations within the containers. A large holder may need a group of

61. *(above)* Grouping pots on steps is a way of giving a variety of heights to the plants.

62. *(below left)* Daturas, scented, pendulous and trained as standards, make stunning pot plants.

63. *(below right)* An alcove of clipped yew for an urn of white geraniums.

at least four plants, typically one of which is vertical, one or more falling down, one or two bushing on the level, all of which must harmonize in colour and leaf, in their taste for aspect and soil, and in their competing growth rates. Some of the most successful large-scale combinations I have seen include standard fuchsias, the grey *Santolina neapolitana* and trailing hot-pink *Verbena* 'Sissinghurst'; standard fuchsias, *Ballota pseudodictamnus* with velvety pale green leaves falling bushily over the sides, and purple heliotrope; *Helichrysum petiolatum*, the long-flowering pink *Diascia rigescens*, the trailing blue *Convolvulus sabatius* (syn. *mauritanicus*) and the trailing grey-leafed *Lotus bertholotti*. *Helichrysum petiolatum* is the plant most consistently included in pots, whether in the grey-leafed form of the type, or in its variegated or yellow-foliaged ('Limelight') forms. *H.* 'Microphyllum' (now called *Plectostachys serpyllifolia*) with very small silvery leaves is less common. The virtues of helichrysum lie in its speed of growth, a root-spread which is small in relation to its reach above ground, and its adaptability, for it can be grown to arch over the sides of a pot, or staked to rise as the main vertical. It is, however, tender.

What you are assembling with all these potted associations is the equivalent of a vase of flowers and the container contributes as much to the effect as its plants. The whole, if well-matched, becomes expressive. In many cases, what is expressed is a large dollop of Gracious Living, for certain pots can never shake off their indoor associations. The more genteel they are, the truer this proves. The apotheosis of Gracious Living is the reconstituted stone urn, which is redolent of the hostess with the mostest. This is fine in suitable surroundings, but I have also caught this message in highly improbable settings. Here, it is better by far to choose an unpretentious pot which looks as if it is intended for outdoor life only. The best are made of wood, stone (or reconstituted, which is still expensive) in a sturdy shape, or terracotta which is not always frost-proof. Pots of the latter are often imported from Spain or Italy (clay from Spain is usually the yellower of the two) and the range of styles and prices is wide. Strawberry pots are often used for herbs or sempervivums, the great bell pots for large shrubs or trees, and the ali-baba jars are lovely with a wide-spraying, rushy plant (narrow-stemmed so that it won't be strangled by the narrow mouth) such as agapanthus or cordyline – but don't let them stay for longer than a season or two, or they can break their clay surrounds.

Awful pots or ones such as wooden tubs which are decaying in old age can be given an extended life if you conceal them behind permanent plants in the terrace. These plants then take on a fresh role as part of the pot's associations. I have done this by using purple-leafed sage as a foreground plant, its leaves hiding an old tub, its blue flowers harmonizing with the tub's trailing blue lobelia, silver *Centaurea gymnocarpa* and a spraying vertical of a tall rosy fuchsia.

In all cases good drainage is vital and if you don't buy a decent-sized hole with your pot, you have to drill it. Crock the hole and top it with a thin layer of gravel or broken brick. I then add farmyard manure (other options are compost or peat) and fill in with ordinary garden soil, well-laced in my case with peat as it is on the heavy side. Grit or Perlite can also be added to keep the soil open. Those who are using pots as their only means of growing ericaceous plants which won't thrive in their open ground will have to buy or make up the appropriate compost. (The formula for your own is 7 parts by bulk of turfy acid loam, 3 parts of granulated sedge peat, 2 parts of gritty lime-free sand, and to each bushel add 42gm [1½oz] of bonemeal and 42gm [1½oz] of coarse hoof and horn mixture.) I also sometimes top mine with a small layer of rotted farmyard manure tucked below the leaves where it won't show. This has its uses not only as a quick-acting feed but as a mulch preventing surface drought, for a pot in a sunny position dries out almost as soon as it is watered. Indeed, it is the watering which is the most wearisome aspect of pot-gardens and, to the busy owner, here is another argument for grouping containers. You can douse the lot together.

Garden Seats

Gardens are for the peace of body and mind, and seats are the means to supply it. They invite you to give up working and enjoy the fruits of your labour. All are functional, some are comfortable, a few beautiful, and the best are all three, contributing to that mix of peace and plenty that is the real enchantment of a garden.

Only certain kinds of seats measure up to this ideal. For a start, they should look permanent if they are to offer the promise of eternal repose. So out go director's chairs, deck-chairs, upholstered hammocks or cushioned plastic for lightly-clad popsies; all are useless in this respect. Wood, stone, iron (which needs to be painted or it will rust) and to a lesser extent, galvanised steel or painted metal are more likely to help establish a feeling of permanence.

Not all of these will deliver the comfort that they promise. Stone and most iron and metal seats may supply only mortification of the flesh. This is not, however, reason to reject a beautiful old example, but simply to reconsider its site. Place it where it will be looked at rather than from; beside a path rather than at a staging-post; where a perch instead of an afternoon's leisure will be all that's required. Remember that the appearance of any seat suggests comfort and that the eye is quite happy to be deceived unless the

64. A curved white seat offers a companionable invitation.

65. A Lutyens seat at Great Dixter, Sussex, is snugly flanked by yews.

66. A yew-backed stone bench: 'it melds into comfort its man-made and living parts'.

bottom tells it otherwise. This is often the case with ornate Victorian fernleaf and fruit ironwork which is agonizing to sit on, but restful and luscious to see. Where this presents a problem, it can be solved as at Grey's Court in Henley; here a wooden slatted seat has been set into a most beautiful iron framework of moulded nasturtium leaves which form the back and sides of the seat.

Wood remains the most comfortable of all materials, and is also among the loveliest, now that some of the most elegant designs of the past are widely reproduced and accessible. Some are simple settles for a verandah, others styled in a more complicated lattice-work or Chinese Chippendale, and the grandest is Sir Edwin Lutyens' 'breaking wave' seat, though it is only suitable for the most substantial settings.

The great virtue of wood, too, is that it can be made up easily to your own design. Your local museum may have an old pattern which their craftsman can be commissioned to copy. Or a carpenter may be able to make you a 'couture' seat, patterned and angled to fit into a particular position. Tree-seats are the most frequently seen example of this category, permitting a 360° view of the garden. But they soon get dirty. Nor are they suited to easy conversation between sitters, unlike the sociable Lutyens' seats at Great Dixter (one shown in Plate 65) which are snugly ensconced in clipped yew recesses. A curved seat like that in Plate 64 offers a similarly companionable invitation.

Wood is usually painted white, a colour Miss Jekyll thought 'tyrannical'. For myself, I prefer a natural unvarnished mouse, and the fading of new wood can be hastened to match this if you keep the offending piece under tree-drip for a month in winter. White has its use as a focal point, however, at the far end of a long garden where the distance needs shortening. Or where you want to draw attention to a flowering plant.

The fashion is also to paint iron and other metals white. But Wade Blue (a deep blue-green popularized from Snowshill, the National Trust property at Broadway, whose former owner Charles Paget Wade asserted that 'Turquoise is a foil to grass and foliage') is now as good as a freemason's handshake in the local counties. You will find it – or near versions – at Kiftsgate, Hidcote, Barnsley House, the Badminton Estate, all in Gloucestershire, and it has probably oozed all over the place by now. It is sombre, subtle and arty. However, pale grey-green, a shade between lavender leaves and the deeper-hued artemisias can also look lovely.

Stone seats, and nowadays reconstituted stone seats, are very rarely comfortable and the ubiquitous benches on ornamental supports make no pretence as such. But they are a lovely foil to a dark-leafed background, whether free-growing shrubs, a clipped hedge, or their own topiary back. For an apt suggestion of permanence and snugness, nothing could exceed the charming yew-backed stone bench at Rodmarton Manor in Plate 66. It is a blend of contrasts – in texture as well as colour, and what is nicest of all, in the way it melds into comfort its man-made and living parts, and that is exactly what a garden is about.

Figures in a Garden

I cannot truly appreciate statues in a garden, be they lions or cupids or us, for too few places seem to benefit from their presence. It has been said that the best garden ornament should grow out of its home, epitomizing its surrounds. Yet most statues and sculpture to be seen nowadays have never heard of this rule.

My opinion on this matter is clearly at odds with the market, and, more embarrassingly, with almost all the garden owners I have ever met. In the last few years, the trade for reproduction figures has revived on a huge scale. The antique side of the business is yet more lucrative. Michael Crowther, owner of one of the main London dealers in garden furniture, has stated: 'People are spending more on their gardens. Antique pieces are from £500, the sky's the limit ... Identifiable figures are popular, Roman emperors, gods. Venus is very common. Animals sell well, dogs and eagles especially. *Putti, amorini* ... they all go. The English are the main buyers, but there is a healthy trade with America. When the Arabs buy, it's usually to furnish the gardens of their newly-bought stately homes in the country.'

To me, alas, this is not gardening, but shopping for pop-up gardens. An investment it may be, but it is one whereby a garden can shrink whilst the portfolio might grow. The weakness of statues in most gardens nowadays lies in the fact that their powers of suggestion are irrelevant to their site. They are attention-getters without logic behind them. And without logic, the intelligence and with it the beauty of a garden can collapse.

This is not true of all statues in all gardens. In formal town gardens, which are man-made landscapes cocooned within huge man-made units it is the norm to rely on implausible artifice rather than living diversions. In conservatories, the same reasoning can hold true. But in most twentieth-century country landscapes, I cannot find a convincing argument for choosing fake figures or animals, rather than using a formal tree, say, to stop the eye, or, better still, topiary, that most traditional of garden sculpture. Indeed, my own view is that there are only two types of garden where statues are a logical population and sculpture a logical ornament. The first is the period garden which is a faithful reconstruction, presenting the conventions of the past. (The most obvious example of this category is the early eighteenth-century landscape garden where buildings and statuary were chosen and deployed to evoke a series of reflections on the part of the observer, indeed a whole philosophical outlook.) The second type is the formal Italianate garden, like a green room of a house, with even its plants subject to formal clipping.

Of these two categories, it is the Italianate garden which provides the easiest means of incorporating statues in a garden. It is manageable, often small, and enclosed so that it can be cordoned-off as a formal compartment in a country garden. More to the point, it has the virtue of reason behind it so that it still makes sense today. Not only does it straddle the line between the natural and artificial world, thus making statues an appropriate addition, but, being evergreen, it always gives clothing to figures which are often so lightly dressed or nude that they look frozen in winter. Sheltered by conifers, the statues will provide a permanent garden which will keep its form, its points of interest and its colour, the pale tones of the figures relieving the sombre greens or blues. You can also interpret the formal garden quite liberally in a country setting and it will still work, as in Plate 67 of Newby Hall in Yorkshire, where pretty figures step out from free-growing yews beside a path.

The early eighteenth-century landscape garden is impossible to create with success now on even a tiny scale. Nowadays, it can never be more than a glib pastiche, for we live in a nihilistic age, at variance with the godly, organized and classically cultured Augustan world which was its source and which composed landscapes to support its ethos. They could evoke because they believed; we cannot because we don't. Our modern equivalent is the relatively unplanted garden with a few modern sculptures. Half-evolved shapes,

67. Pretty figures step out from free-growing yews.

though sometimes recognizably human or animal, which are meant to link Nature and Art, they are strewn on the scene in artistic relation to each other and to the buildings. They are reminiscent of that most self-conscious of outdoor offerings, a sculpture show rather than a garden.

More reticent garden-owners tend to hide their statues or sculptures. Sometimes there is reason for this. Inchoate modern sculpture is not a polite art for civilized surroundings and will find an apter home in wilder, shady surroundings – the equivalent in gardens of the Collective Unconscious. But sometimes, I rather think, the garden-owner hides his statues out of embarrassment, for he knows that ghosts do not usually come so substantial or expensive. Thus Hermes pokes out of ivy or the Marble Maiden is pushed against a tree-trunk in the fashion of Sissinghurst's Vestal Virgin. It is an admission that statues and sculpture sometimes seem pretentious and are therefore hard to place. That perhaps they shouldn't be there at all.

The late Russell Page, one of the greatest of twentieth-century garden makers, used to talk about planting sculpture. This often came down to simple trial and error and in his final project, PepsiCo in Purchase, New York, a stage for a great number of sculptures, a full-scale mock-up of a newly commissioned piece would be made and tested out in different positions, facing different aspects, before the final site was chosen.

68. Sculpture of copper and bronze in a formal setting, depicting most aptly an architectural flower.

So, if you really do pine for a statue or sculpture and cannot be dissuaded, here, then, is a course of action which might help get the matter right. Firstly, you decide on a design, test it for appropriateness with a false model, establish its setting, then commission your Work of Art which I shall call WOA for short. In all this, you bear in mind that the WOA should be simple, unpretentious, to scale, shapely and apt. Most WOAs are anything but; yet the elegant sculpture in Plate 68 shows such criteria can sometimes be met. This emblematic flower of copper and bronze adorns a small formal garden in Great Rissington Manor in the Cotswolds. It is a model in more than one sense of avoiding the pitfalls of a difficult subject.

It seems unfortunate to me that, in the last resort, it is usually left to temperament and taste to be the final arbiters on garden ornament. After all, there are two rules worth following. The first is Pugin's axiom which can well be applied to a garden: that 'all ornament should consist of enrichment of the essential construction of the building' (*True Principles of Pointed or Christian Architecture*).

The second rule is simpler and one that I have implied throughout this chapter: that pretentiousness remains the worst sin in the countryside. Nature can be punishing to it. I can only end with a cautionary tale:

> Sarah-Jane and Joshua
> Were rather keen to build and own
> A garden that was poshua
> And of the most superior tone.

No modern heaths of vulgar hue
Dared ever raise their common head
And only flowers that Jekyll grew
Were used and planted in their stead.

Yet Sarah-Jane was in a huff,
And showed a sorry discontent,
Her garden was not grand enough
To put her in her element.

A pair of Vanbrugh balls alone
Could satisfy her upstart craving,
They'd top the pillars made of stone
That flanked the formal courtyard paving.

Accordingly the eager wife
Sent in an order for the spheres,
Not thinking it would change her life
Or that the venture would bring tears.

On Friday of the following week
The snooty Vanbrugh balls appeared,
And Sarah-Jane refused to speak
To watching neighbours who just jeered.

With care Josh lifted each in turn
and pressed it in its special place,
Atop the post beside an urn,
Pushing each firmly on its base.

Within an hour a wind arose
So Josh went out to check his balls.
No worse a moment husband chose,
For at that second there came squalls.

One ball flew off and hit the man,
The second followed in its wake
And struck sad Sarah-Jane who ran
From where she stood with spade and rake.

Oh, sorry pair that wouldn't be
Content with mediocrity
But spurned their own fraternity
And middle-class paternity.

There they lie annihilate,
Humbled by each Vanbrugh ball,
Felled by hope of Pomp and State,
Their pride preceding each ball's fall.

X. Topiary
Its Style, Positioning, Plants, Training and Formal Hedges

OUR ROMANTIC SENSIBILITY is newly revived. It is a bit uncertain of its direction, being inebriated with the future as well as the past, but it promises to make a large impact on our gardens, not least in the shape of topiary. It will take a while before our freshly planted bushes can be assessed, for the training is a slow business, but they will probably be sufficiently developed around the year 2000 AD. Will this awesome date be met with a fresh load of green crockery, with teapots and jugs? Or is our second millenium going to get the majestic topiary it deserves?

Those who seek inspiration from the past will find a dangerously large number of topiary styles to imitate. For, of all living ornaments, topiary is the most subject to fashion, falling victim to the whims and tastes of its period. Its history, even in Britain, is bumpy. Of antique source originally, it furnished our gardens with their most outstanding feature for a period of one hundred and fifty years. This golden age lasted until the early eighteenth century when its fortunes plunged with unprecedented speed, after Alexander Pope mocked its forms in his phoney 'catalogue of greens':

> Adam and Eve in yew; Adam a little shattered by
> the fall of the tree of knowlege in the great storm;
> Eve and the serpent very flourishing.
>
> The tower of Babel, not yet finished.
>
> St. George in box; his arm scarce long enough, but will be
> in a condition to stick the dragon next April ...
>
> A quickset hog, shot up into a porcupine,
> by its being forgot a week in rainy weather.

People's amour-propre was even more vulnerable in the eighteenth century where their gardens were concerned than it is now. Smarting under contemporary ridicule, most chose to destroy their topiary gardens rather than look silly. With a slow gathering of momentum, axe and spade hewed and dug across the country. The pride of ownership had finally been punctured.

69. Levens Hall, Cumbria, still possesses the largest and most fantastic topiary in Britain.

But by Miss Jekyll's time, a revival of the craft had taken place on one of those waves of yearning which convert the ornaments of the past into the symbols of a golden age. The fondness of Miss Jekyll and other garden designers for clipped evergreens helped their reinstatement, but no amount of literary support could have equalled the impact of topiary's unsung but real hero – the deliciously named Mr. Herbert Cutbush. As so often happens, his name was to prove his destiny. Visiting Holland (the chief source of topiary for hundreds of years) and winkling out large specimens from farmers, cottagers and specialist nurserymen called *boomkmeckers*, he transferred them to England for resale. Here, not being one to beat about his personal bushes, he advertised them as 'Cutbush's cut bushes'.

By the end of the nineteenth century, Mr. Cutbush in particular and other nurserymen (notably, Messrs. Cheal & Sons of Crawley) had begun to give a remarkable service to a gardening public who was not prepared to wait the years required to train a subject. Yet, it is worth emphasizing that, despite the huge range available, the topiary specimens and hedges commended in the Jekyll and Weaver *Gardens for Small Country Houses* were mostly very simple. The photographs in this book showed chiefly non-representational shapes, the exceptions being corner birds on yew hedges at Mathern (a garden in Monmouthshire owned by the writer and architect H.A. Tipping). In short, once again, despite a proliferation of fancy toys that were generally available, Miss Jekyll arbited in favour of simplicity. She responded to those gardens where the topiary underlined not only orderliness but symmetry.

In our own time when topiary is once more enjoying its latest revival after many decades of economic squeeze, I think there is still an argument for the simple and dignified approach.

Topiary has the special potential to become the most distinctive feature of any garden for a period of centuries. It is a green sculptured heirloom which should increase with stature and not diminish. Formed now, it is not impossible that it should endure from our second millenium for another four hundred years, so it has to be dignified and timeless. Items which are amusing fancies soon pall, especially when you see them every day and cut them back to their witty limits every year. Admittedly, the odd drollery is a great leavener amongst a preponderance of more substantial topiary – as with the coffee-pots at Great Dixter (Plate 71) – but if you only have space for a couple of pieces, then I would play it sober.

This approach applies equally to groups as to specimens. In fact the most haunting and noble ensembles are not exact representations of daily objects – and often not even likenesses at all, but non-figurative groups whose numinous identity you must imagine. They might be called apostles, as at Packwood House, or at Malleny House near Edinburgh (where only a nucleus of four out of the original twelve remain). These have the symbolic quality of ritual groups. Or they could be called troops, as in the walled garden of Airlie Castle in Angus. Groups like these will never become identikit objects, for they bring to their surroundings an element of make-believe. Or the groups might not have a tag at all. Those yews that once clustered round Owlpen Manor in Gloucestershire (most of the originals have gone, though the owners have since planted some thirty replacements) had so forceful a corporate presence that they rendered unforgettable the romantic stone house that they guarded.

Little of the topiary in these ensembles is sculptured into more than a symmetrical mass

70. *(above)* One of the topiary gardens by the Elizabethan house of Beckley Park, Oxfordshire.

71. *(below)* Coffee pots or their fun equivalent can relieve the sombreness of substantial topiary.

or occasional geometric shape. But where the country house is a distinct example of its period, there is a sound case for crafting topiary designs which are consonant with its date without being tied to it. Such is the case at Beckley Park, an enchanting pink brick Elizabethan house in Oxfordshire. Here there are two topiary gardens. Both are dominated by geometric shapes, yet each has a touch of eccentricity which lifts them out of the standard repertoire and makes them not only precious but Elizabethan. The first garden, which was planted initially in 1921, is small, about 50ft x 30ft/16m x 10m. In fact, it is its very smallness that makes the large yew specimens especially impressive. There are fourteen topiary yews in all, 10ft/3m high and 8ft/2.4m apart. They include simple cones,

72. Haseley Court, Oxfordshire: the chess garden. Topiary on this scale is very time-consuming to clip.

obelisks and pedestals, spirals, a mighty peacock, and, an Elizabethan touch, a giant bear at rest on its haunches – the whole ensemble surrounded by an even taller yew hedge, pedimented at one end.

The neighbouring enclosure differs in being somewhat larger and made chiefly of box, its spicy scent the more intense for its confinement here. In contrast to the yew garden, the box designs are limited to a height of a few feet. Planted to form separate compartments, the box has been trimmed into crowns and peaks of different sizes. Within each 'crown', flowers can be grown.

Though each garden is different, each harmonizes with the ancient house yet will never date.

To take this question of appropriate style further, a seventeenth-century house might make use of yew obelisks planted at intervals in its formal garden, a device shown (albeit on a huge scale) in the gardens of Kip's engravings and one which emphasized the effect of spaciousness. By contrast, an eighteenth-century house might have a planting of yew screens near it – a magnificent version of a hedge.

All these examples show how topiary can be chosen which is allusive to a period yet never rigidly dated – timeless in short, but impressive.

They also illustrate how simple shapes can be made distinctive. Another method is to rely not so much on the outline of the trimmed bush as on indented design. In this case, the bush is not only trimmed, but also incised. Remarkable examples in *Cupressus arizonica* are at Tulcan in Mexico where the hedges and free-standing specimens have been carved in relief. The only example I know here is a Dickensian figure, unworthy in comparison,

122

outside a village inn, and the yews at Clipsham Hall in Rutland. But something of the sort might be tried on large yew blocks, converting them into an identity which shares the god-like qualities of the great Easter Island stones.

These are all possibilities, inspirations from the past which do not counter our present, or presumably our future, code of behaviour. In re-creating these echoes, we are choosing shapes which still mean something to us. This is important, for to copy the concerns of the past, with their mainspring gone, is a hollow exercise. It is filling a garden with reproduction furniture.

Aesthetic ideals apart, there is also a strictly practical reason for keeping shapes simple. Large-scale topiary involving complicated outlines is appallingly time-consuming in the season of clipping. Imagine the demands made by even a fraction of the great chess garden at Haseley Court in Oxfordshire (see Plate 72), an interesting example, incidentally, of the Victorian home-sweet-home passion for transferring the interior interests of the house into the garden. Or feel the pain in the heartfelt comment of Mr. W. Gibson, head gardener at Levens Hall, Cumbria (which still possesses the largest and most fantastic collection of old topiary in this country). Writing in 1903, this enthusiast gave his readers a shock-landing on the last page of his book on topiary, when he summarized his feelings: 'There is one thing to remember about the Topiary garden, it is all work.'

So it was and is on the scale and in the form practised at Levens Hall. Temper your appetite for topiary with caution, therefore. There are certain cardinal rules to remember in this respect.

Firstly, eschew low-growing parterres or knot-gardens unless you or your gardener/s have a good back now and forever and are able to clip patterns so close to the ground. The one exception to this might be simple box rows (*Buxus sempervirens* 'Suffruticosa'). But even these are usually clipped twice a year.

They therefore flout the second rule which is to limit your choice of plants to those which require only one clipping a year, bearing in mind that the actual process is demanding on two counts – firstly, the clipping itself, and also gathering the scattered shoots thereafter. Additionally, choose only those plants which are suitable for powered clippers, rather than hand shears, or, worse still, secateurs.

Limit your number of subjects to those you can manage. If you want a larger collection, the clipping can be contracted out, but bear in mind costs and also the ability of the hired man. A good design can be ruined by a clipper who is either unskilled or, worse, careless.

Fourthly, in choosing a shape, take account of the fact that a height much above about 6ft/1.8m will start involving you eventually in clipping from a ladder or using trestles – or even scaffolding, if much, much larger.

Fifthly, choose rounded or curved shapes which are easier for the inexperienced to clip successfully than squares or right-angles.

And lastly but of equal importance, it is a justifiable alternative to seek topiary substitutes in the form of evergreen trees which are naturally emphatic and formal in outline. Many of these will not require any clipping on your part, yet will give to a garden a drama which is equivalent to the real thing if they are assembled with panache. Such trees include the pencil cypresses of Italy or Spain (*Cupressus sempervirens*), tender when young but thereafter hardy, at least in the milder areas of cool temperate climates. Arrange these in curving boundary lines, or quincunx clusters or as colonnades, all of these being completely artificial dispositions. Pinnacled junipers like *Juniperus virginiana* 'Sky Rocket'

73. *Chamaecyparis lawsoniana* 'Pottenii' looks like a clipped specimen with its corseted bottom and free-growing top.

can be used in the same way. They have, however, four snags: they are shorter, they can burn in bad winters and fail to recover, they are a fairly recent introduction so their long-term behaviour is unproven, and they are becoming so ubiquitous that they will soon cease to confer any distinction on the garden they inhabit. You may find better options among the denser-growing *Chamaecyparis lawsoniana* cultivars such as the blue-grey 'Allumii', or the dark green 'Kilmacurragh', which is very resistant to snow-damage. The same cannot be said of 'Pottenii', which, though often used for its handsome vertical effect (see Plate 73), needs a cord truss or mesh-netting corset to prevent its growth splaying under snowfall, as it grows older. Of the other species, *Cupressus glabra* 'Pyramidalis' makes a good blue cone. But the Irish yew, *Taxus baccata* 'Fastigiata' is less suitable, being only columnar when young and spreading in middle-age unless clipped annually to slimness.

Mix these columnar conifers with, for example, the hardy, mushroom-shaped stone pines of the Mediterranean (*Pinus pinea*) which poets once called 'anchored clouds'; or with the very slow-growing monstrous hummocks of *Tsuga canadensis* 'Pendula'. The effect for future gardeners will be one of some grandeur and a lot less burdensome than topiary. But it has to be said that the look will also be one of borrowed foreign adornment, landscape tricks taken from a pattern book and, as such, a lot further from the heart than the native ornament of topiary.

Positioning Topiary

This exploration of topiary design is only part of the whole, for the positioning of topiary is of even greater importance. Rather more than untrained plants, it dictates its own terms. It needs, for example, sun and shelter. A perfect, clipped shrub will not grow evenly in part-shade. It will also risk injury if exposed to scourging wind and cold. Remember that it has lost its outer coat of wind-filtering and cold-protecting shoots. Indeed, Mr. Gibson of Levens Hall argued powerfully that only a sunny, *sunken* area of land within the garden would give the specimens the requisite degree of shelter. (Mr. Gibson of the 'remember the Topiary garden is all work' approach, advised digging a terrace as a start.)

However, the practical needs of the plants are not the only factors. A group of topiary makes artistic demands. A collection of, let us say, more than four items, becomes a microcosm. The larger the group, the more it deserves its own enclosure. An alien invader of the outside world (topiary is, after all, a defiance of Nature, albeit in the interests of Art), it must exclude its wilder aspects. An enfolding hedge of its own species is therefore an advantage if there exists no natural enclosure. A site near the house is usual for such architectural items which bridge the gulf between the natural and subdued world; but where the enclosure may be far from the house (as is often the case in the larger gardens of Scotland) or hidden and sheltered like the Italian *giardano segreto*, these are probably better.

But many owners of small gardens would be reluctant or unable to devote a separate area to this form of gardening. Other options therefore include planting a row parallel to the house, or leading to the house beside a path (straight lines being its complement). Or a quartet forming a feature as in Plate 74, or a pair flanking an entrance may be preferable. At Westwell Manor in Oxfordshire, for example, a pair of assymetrical spire-tipped spirals was trained to guard its rear entrance.

74. A quartet of yews forms a symmetrical feature.

In very rare instances, where a garden has a magnificent long view straight from the house or terrace, then simple topiary shapes can be given a relationship to the distance by acting as a gallery of foregrounds – rather like figureheads on a promontory.

But whatever the circumstances, the crucial point to remember about topiary is its formality; it is a grand horticultural performance, so suit it accordingly. And unless an item is large and architectural in outline (like an arbour, a porch, a tunnel, a cone), one item is rarely on. It has a self-consciousness that can only be dispelled by the company of more. So avoid the single ambitious piece, unless you want it addressed in future years as 'the cottager's pride'.

Plants for Topiary

In theory you can choose from a wide selection of plants for topiary, but in practice, forget this. The Romans to whom we owe the perfected skill of topiary, used only evergreens and this is a golden rule which we break in error of seeking versatility for its own sake and none other. One main joy of topiary is the charge it can give to a garden in the long, fallow season, nullified if the plants are, for example, beech, hornbeam, hawthorn etc. all of which I have seen used.

Yew is unquestionably the best of the lot on the grounds of colour, velvety texture, endurance, tradition, adaptability to different soils and climates (except coastal regions). But farms or farm-neighbouring gardens should be wary of its place, because cows, horses and even turkeys have been poisoned by the plant.

Box is not so hardy, is more invasive, but has a deliciously spicy scent. Holly lacks that fine plush, surface texture, but compensates in polish. Holm oak (*Quercus ilex*) is grand but can get scorched to death in severe winters. *Cupressus arizonica* (often planted under the name *C. glabra*) looks splendid in milder climates when clipped, but has not to my knowledge withstood the test of time in harsher conditions. *Cupressus macrocarpa*, a favourite in maritime climates, has furnished fine topiary in, for example, its area of origin (as at the Northern Californian garden of Cypress Grove) but, again, will die in poor winters inland if clipped. Feeble endurers like rosemary or even bay (except in mild areas) are out.

Groundwork

Preparation of the gound for topiary is important, a fact I know from the considerable difference in rates of growth between those yews I grow in richly cultivated ground and others in unprepared soil. This proves especially true when you consider the interminable period over which you expect the shrub to prosper. Dig a hole 3ft/90cm wide and 2ft/60cm deep if possible and mix into the earth some compost, decayed farmyard manure or bonemeal. (Mr. Gibson affirmed there was nothing so good for this purpose as a barrowful of coarse bones amongst the loads of loam.)

Plant container-grown subjects if possible, though bushy, bare-rooted yews under 3ft/90cm should get going at once if planted in spring and mulched and kept moist. Make sure that seedling plants will not vary in rates of growth. Uniformity of growth and performance is important. Finish the planting by adding a mulch of compost or decayed manure. Take care that the shrub gets enough water in its season of establishment. Renew

75. *(above left)* A fine example of a tapestry hedge composed of yew, holly, beech and Lawson's cypress. Different rates of growth can sometimes make such a hedge difficult to trim.

76. *(above right)* Lines of mature pleached limes flank a drive and cradle the gateway in the foreground.

77. *(below)* In youth, they might have looked like this. Pleached trees are trained on wires or bamboo; lime is admirable for this purpose because it is so flexible.

the mulch annually, keeping the ground weed-free around the bush. In sun, shelter and soil such as this, growth will be surprisingly rapid.

Training

Depending on the ultimate shape you have in mind, you can start clipping the sides lightly as soon as it begins to spread enthusiastically, bearing in mind that, even when fully grown to the desired height and reach, the bush must continue to expand by the extra 1½-2in/3-5cm of shoots which you should leave on the bush when clipping to maintain final shape. But when training, never clip the leader or any other shoots you intend to use for your design. Clip yews in August to mid-September at the absolute latest, holly at the end of May or beginning of June, and box in June, but only after the last frosts are past.

When training a young bush towards its ultimate shape, tarred string is often used (it will last as long as the shoot takes to intermesh). Otherwise wire can be used on strong branches, provided that there is no risk of it cutting into the wood. Bamboo is another option, and occasionally wooden frames are built. A temporary material for tying in is raffia, but it has to be renewed annually. Curves and ovals can usually be gauged by eye and clipped, but if you find yourself facing a perfect square, it is easier by far to employ a right-angle.

Attention to the finished specimen consists of clipping the new growth back to within 1½-2in/3-5cm of their beginning. This means that the bush expands upwards and onwards by this amount every year. The disputatious mathematician might point out that a bush would therefore expand by 16ft/5m over a period of fifty years. To prevent this monstrous increase (if it isn't desired), it will occasionally be necessary to cut back into the hard wood. Yew endures this with good temper, refurbishing itself with new shoots; holly must be treated a little more gently; and box should be reduced slowly and gently.

The clipping apart, give the bushes an annual mulch to nourish them and conserve moisture, a necessity as the growth can be so dense that even heavy rain may not penetrate to the roots. And in winter, remove as a matter of urgency heavy falls of snow which can injure the bush or its design.

Formal Hedges

So far I have only looked at topiary as self-justifying ornament, but it can be put to practical use in the form of decorative hedges. Nowadays in the country, we need such barriers to serve something of the same purpose for which they were once intended – to act as fortresses. They are defensive structures, not against a troubled world, but against one which is all too often ugly. We can no longer always, alas, sympathize with Horace Walpole writing in 1770: 'How rich, how gay, how picturesque the face of the country!'

On a large scale, screening trees are much more useful for this purpose (see page 201), requiring scant attention. But in a microcosm by a house, trimmed screens or an enclosure of hedges have an attraction which earns their owner's patient attention.

We undervalue hedges. For decades, we have regarded them as self-effacing workhorses in the garden, dividers, shelters and barriers of inferior ornamental value in themselves. Because they have genuine functions – keeping out stock and intruders, securing privacy, saying this land belongs to *me*, defining areas of separate interest – we have forgotten to

XIII. The temple at Lower Hall (Chapter XVI), hemmed with a triplet of *Erica arborea alpina* and tucked into trees at the edge of the woodland garden.

XIV. An ali-baba pot is framed between staddle stones at Rodmarton Manor. The composition makes an ornamental plinth for the airy foliage that shades them.

XV. One of our own borders plunges into the larger context of the countryside around when viewed from this angle; this means that foliage must play a main part in helping it harmonize. Trees will eventually grow in its background and will help to 'catch' it.

XVI. Colour-controlled planting of rhododendrons in woodland: a carpet of the violet *R. rupicola*, *R. impeditum*, pink *R. tsangpoense*, mauve *R. telmateium drumonium*. *R. campylogynum* is at the front and the pink *R. davidsonianum* 'Ruth Lyons' is in the middle of the foreground group.

XVII. A hellebore carpet in part-shade, an idea deriving from the dominant floor layers in woodland.

XVIII. Looking inwards: Bradley Court rose garden (Chapter XIII) includes the striped 'Rosa Mundi' and 'Camaieux', the maroon 'Tuscany Superb', the rose-pink 'Comte de Chambord' and the pompon 'De Meaux'.

XIX. Looking outwards: in a sea-cliff garden like Headland (Chapter XIV) the views out are as important as those within the grounds. *Pinus radiata* and *Cupressus macrocarpa* frame them to perfection.

make that obvious link between topiary and hedges, though both are formally trimmed trees and shrubs, and both can be big set-pieces. We ignore the dramatic possibilities of the green screens at which the seventeenth-century gardeners excelled. The Dutch had a green stage at Westerwyk with a proscenium made of hornbeam arranged in a big arch with wings composed of hedges. Near Siena in Tuscany, Villa Sergadi and Villa Gori with its wings of clipped cypress had similar green stage gardens. And the astounding topiary garden of Hartwell House in Buckinghamshire had a panoply of theatrical green architecture with its exedra, allées, arcades, a stage and shutters. Such glories are almost unattainable now, because the great heights of the hedges would certainly require trestles, almost scaffolding, to clip them. But even simple hedges of suitable plants have a value in themselves. 'Hedges of yews with turf alone,' wrote Miss Jekyll in *Gardens for Small Country Houses* 'have an extraordinary quality of repose – inspiring a sentiment of refreshing contentment.' To this, our own century might add the supportive noise that it can reduce gardening to the wielding of hedge clippers and the riding of sit-on mowers.

Given these mechanical assets of ours, there is a case for restoring the Italianate garden, that component of the Edwardian garden. A close but for its entrance and exit, its high walls were made of hedges; mown turf lay underfoot, or gravel, or sometimes a formal pool reflecting the sky and the enclosing green curtains of clipped trees.

But even this risks being merely a romantic daydream if the wrong kind of hedge is chosen, proving a labour-intensive burden. For, although in theory the range of possible hedges is huge (as with topiary), when considered from certain viewpoints – saving time and effort, resistance to disease, endurance, ease of supply and elegance – the number of candidates shrinks to a few. Having explored the subject in some detail in my previous books, I don't want to repeat myself here. My own choice, however, is for yew, holly or box among the evergreens and hornbeam as the best of the deciduous varieties. All these need cutting only once a year and are not subject to disease. Admittedly, all will also expand beyond their station and will need cutting back (a treatment to be applied slowly and cautiously to box). Smaller gardens with room for only a narrow hedge might consider *Thuja plicata* and *Cotoneaster franchetii* as better long-term options.

The right sort of hedge will only live up to its status if given the right treatment. The way it is clipped is important. It is usually visible for its entire length so its smoothness, symmetry matter; so, too, does its batter, that inwards slope which ensures that light and air reach the lower branches keeping them well furnished with shoots. Batter affects not just health but appearance too, for different angles alter impressions, the rounded top bringing a homely comfort to an old-fashioned garden, the square top a chiselled formality.

Your treatment of hedges, in fact, can give your garden some pretensions to importance. This last is a chilling phrase, but anyone who includes a pleached hedge, for example, might as well enjoy the fact that status is a by-product of its existence — even if it is only used for the practical purpose of heightening a wall.

And the same point can be true of a topiary topping for a hedge, a decoration easily achieved if you allow the shoots to grow on in the required place until they are long enough to train. Scenes of frozen animation are common in this position (one cliché is a hunting frieze), but preferable by far is a topiary topping or extension which is integral to the design of the hedge – like green, sculptured 'gate piers', or buttresses for flowers and seats, or a frame to a path. The topiary topping to a hedge is its hat which it will sport for years to come.

XI. Garden-Houses and Conservatories
Their Management and Plants

THOUGH THE CULT of the country-house garden had been refined to perfection by the turn of this century, the conservatory was not part of it. Its fashion had already started to wane. Originating at the very end of the eighteenth century, its heyday had come in the 1870s when it was taken to its zenith by the Victorians with their passion for indoor life and their faith in the products of human engineering. But Queen Victoria was not yet dead before its charms were beginning to lose out to the garden-house which implied an altogether different aesthetic. It was one which favoured the simple, out-of-doors life and encouraged garden buildings which were open to the fresh air.

Today we do not take an either/or view of the conservatory/garden-house but appreciate that they fulfil complementary functions, providing in opposite extremes of weather a temperate halfway stage. These buildings offer shelter on a small, intimate scale, the garden-house from summer heat and glare, the conservatory from winter roughness. Both can be charming additions to the life of a garden, not only extending the way it is used but enhancing its appearance.

Garden-Houses

A good garden-house, especially, appeals to the gnome in all of us. However dignified, it ought to make us want to up sticks and move into it immediately. It has a long and almost universal history, suggesting not only its usefulness but this special appeal to some odd, inner need. It was to be found in Egypt, in Ancient Rome and Pompeii, in the Far East and Persia and the countries of Mogul culture where the shade afforded by these small buildings was so necessary in a hot landscape. Further north, examples in the gardens of the Italian Renaissance gave rise to numerous imitations elsewhere in Europe. In England, they served a less practical purpose, sun being harder to come by than shade, but their ornamental potential was explored to the last detail and various foreign idioms exploited.

Here, these small garden buildings reached a peak of elegance and sometimes of whimsy in the eighteenth and early nineteenth centuries. The fashion in all its idiosyncrasy reached Scotland, too, where in 1761 an unknown architect built a garden retreat near Stirling in the shape of a beautiful but bizarre 45ft/14m high pineapple. In this era of pattern-book publishing, titles were devoted to temples and other garden buildings, one of the most notable written by Thomas Collins Overton and published in 1766. Gothic designs were

78. Eighteenth-century tree-house with a Gothic interior at Pitchford Hall.

especially fashionable and numerous delectable examples of eighteenth-century models still exist, including the little gazebo at Marston Hall in Lincolnshire. This was restored in the 1960s and its interior decorated with bird motifs.

Buildings like this are mostly too ambitious in scope to be reproduced nowadays, for the essence of a gazebo is that it is built on two floors and designed not only as an ornament but as a high viewpoint over the surrounding landscape. For this reason, the true gazebo is only suited to a large garden with ample space around. The same point might be made of any other type of garden-house in a raised site, the most extreme form of which is the enchanting timbered tree-house at Pitchford Hall in Shropshire (Plate 78) with its Gothic interior of 1760; or of the little summerhouse, a flimsy construction which would be easy to imitate, placed on a mount at Nymans in Sussex. No such building could ever be suitable in a small country garden, where a garden-house must be kept to bungaloid levels. Commanding a view of a neighbour's plot could be fraught with embarrassment.

Siting is of crucial importance for a garden-house anyway. It affects not only its outlook, but your very choice of building. For, if the garden-house is in view of the main house, it is its architectural satellite and must conform. The eye knows by instinct that garden architecture in all its parts must gel, whether this applies to shape, materials or scale. A fine garden can only result from a coherent vision and disparate items in view of each other are horridly worrying. Forget, then, those temptations in the form of treillage summerhouses, stone pavilions with pointed roofs, Etruscan temples, rustic and thatched what-nots or pattern books with plans to be bought — forget all these if they are not perfect partners to the house.

You can of course tuck them away in the nether quarters of a very large garden where they will be happily unrelated to other structures. But, even then, they ought to be relevant and deserve the right 'ecological' site. If they were living, breathing organisms, would they thrive there? Are they appropriate or have they just dropped from some builder's yard in the sky? Even if they feel right, are they in the best position? As a suggestion, consider placing them beside or beyond water if you have it, so that they are tied to their shimmering reflection. Or anchor their face quietly amidst the greenery of a group of trees. Here they can appear almost spectral, conjured from the existing scenery.

In a more formal position, where the small building is near the house, contrive to find it an equally apt resting-place. A classic shape can close a vista, for example, as in Plate 79. The Victorian writer, Shirley Hibberd, called such cases 'tasteful termini', a phrase to make one squirm though one knows what is meant. Alternatively, attach the small house to a garden wall, if you have one and if it conforms in material; place it either in the corner, or at the centre or at a point where it commands a long prospect. Otherwise, you can give the building stability by flanking it with hedges. An apron of paving etc. or a path around and to it will also act as a stabilizer, give it space around it, and will prevent its floor being muddied with footmarks.

Windows and doors will keep the weather out, but the former will probably give you extra cleaning work. And, unless you have them open at all times, they will also nullify that airy, fresh feeling that the Edwardians so enjoyed. You need a protective roof which is deep enough to allow shade and to block drifting rain. But good light is vital and sun at times an advantage. To achieve this in a garden-house with windows on one side only, place it to face the sun. You can make the most of this if you have chosen a structure that is wider than deep, so that slanting rays in the cooler part of the day will penetrate from

79. The Victorian writer, Shirley Hibberd, would have called this an example of a 'tasteful terminus'.

front to back throughout. A multi-sided garden-house (hexagonal or octagonal) with windows on each face will be lit from every quarter, however, unless blocked.

This pursuit of sun can be taken to excess. In the 1920s and 30s, summerhouses were designed to revolve facing the sun and carpentered versions are still widely available. But even the quality examples with solid floors and reliable rotating gear have the hideousness of all furniture when function is pursued regardless of looks. Indeed, most of our post-war garden-houses have resembled 'lumberjacks' concoctions. Wooden wendy-houses were seemingly our lot until the recent revival of some of the lovelier, simpler designs of the past.

Conservatories

We have done a much better job with conservatories. In fact, at the top end of the market, we have been extremely clever, copying the prettiest models of the last century and earlier, embellishing them to new heights, yet devising buildings that are highly effective at their job. They are also far easier to run than their stove prototypes, yet can be almost as snug.

Imagine that it is December. The sun is shining, but it is very cold and an earlier fall of snow has completely covered the ground. The countryside invites admiration yet repels entry. But a step away from the sitting-room and one becomes part of that glittering outside world whilst feeling clothed in equatorial warmth. Here the sun alone, unaided by another form of heat, has warmed the air to 70°F/21°C and flowers still bloom in semi-tropical rapture; the carmine passion-flower (*Passiflora antioquensis*) trails from the spandril and a purple *Tibouchina semidecandra* and a magenta geranium are entwined in mutual embrace.

This scenario would be impossible were the conservatory detached from the house, a point scarcely worth making, were it not that many purchasers use a high garden wall rather than a house as a peg on which to hang their glass room. In such a case, the conservatory becomes a glorified greenhouse with its usefulness severely reduced; one is far better off with a simple garden-house here, for summer rather than winter shelter.

A position against the house is therefore crucial for a conservatory, so that it forms a sort of vestibule or ante-chamber. Probably the ideal is to place it against a free house wall of warm aspect, for in winter you will derive the most benefit from sunlight in this position, and heating will cost you less. But in summer, a south-facing conservatory is subjected to extremes of temperature, forcing you to pay constant attention to the plants. Donkey-work of this nature is eased in the north- or east-facing conservatory. It also permits you to grow shade-loving plants.

The site itself should be level, well-drained and well-lit, but adjacent large shrubs or even trees on one side need not deter so long as they don't block light (nor their foliage the gutters); the shade they cast in part of the sunny conservatory can actually be used for growing plants that need cooler conditions.

What of appearance? If you can, position the conservatory so that it is not an excrescence on the house, but a natural continuation of its lines, an extension of its movement. Conservatories are all too often slapped like false noses onto the middle of a house's face. You can integrate it yet further if you match the material of its plinth (stone, brick etc.) to the façade of the wall that it joins.

Consider not only the appearance but the view out, too. My own conservatory, for example, is placed to take advantage of a landscape which falls away from it in all directions, allowing it to command immediate as well as long-distance views. Perched on a terrace, it looks down from a height of 16ft/5m to the gardens below and its views in the other direction run for some 8 miles across the valley to the hills beyond. (It is not a place for contemplating one's own navel.) This combination was circumstantial luck, but it did involve knocking a door in the house wall for access, and it was tempting at the time to choose the easier option of placing the conservatory around an existing garden-door at a lower level, thus losing the views. I have never regretted the extra nuisance and expense, and would urge you, too, to choose a view if you have one, for, unlike the rooms in a house, one can indeed look onwards and upwards in a conservatory.

Having established a suitable site, you can then choose the conservatory. Order brochures from as many manufacturers as possible to compare variations in style, price and size. The latter of course has a bearing on cost and you will find that prices leapfrog alarmingly for every couple of feet increase in length. Nonetheless, go for as large a building as you can possibly afford, as most people find they like to sit and eat here (sometimes sleep here too; it is wonderful to see the stars shooting above you) as well as enfold it with plants.

Don't consider style only when you choose, but think how you will use the room. The door, for example? If you site this at the end, the structure becomes a through-passage; place it at the side, and the conservatory acquires the shape of a garden-room. The floor, too? Will you grow your plants in earth-beds along its perimeter which eats up your living-space, or will you grow them in pots which are always thirsty for water (see page

80 & 81. Two modern conservatories show the extreme contrasts which can be commissioned: the first is in Kent, an airy flight of glazing, topped with Victorian cresting and finials...

...and the second *(below)* is in Norfolk and keyed into a substantial house.

141 for more detail)? Do you want single- or double-glazing? The former is cheaper. The latter, however, minimizes condensation, retains heat and acts as a soundproofing; but check that it is sealed-unit-glazing, otherwise a build-up of dirt can occur in the internal space. Decorative glazing is also a possibility, stained or frosted glass used to obscure or delight. This may be nice for you, but if you want to grow lots of plants, keep it to a limited area where it will not block clear light from falling on them.

The options, then, are wide, and so are the price differentials. The least expensive is the modular conservatory. The price of these varies according to size, sophistication and also the way in which they are erected. Most firms which sell these conservatories are versatile in the way they run their operations. You can, for example, commission your own builder to erect the structure or you can use the supplier for the job.

Alternatively you can commission custom-built designs, the most expensive procedure, but one which opens all possiblilities to you and where the style and percentage of glass to hard materials varies according to your requirements. Plates 80 and 81 show two extremes. The latter is of a brick conservatory/orangery in Norfolk which was designed and built especially to span two walls in a building where airy flights of glazing would seem intrusive in so monumental a setting. In complete contrast, the other plate shows a dazzlingly glazed rococo conservatory in Kent which was designed by its owner, constructed by a local firm and topped with Victorian crests and finials.

A far cheaper way to have an individual conservatory is to choose your own design and subcontract so that an architect provides the outline drawings, a builder deals with the foundations and solid walls and drainage, and a carpenter cuts and prepares frames and astragals. You then erect it. Planning permission is necessary in this as in every other case.

We straddled these options, ordering a modular conservatory as a kit from a supplier and commissioning a builder to erect the foundations for it. But my husband assembled and glazed the conservatory itself, a tedious but not difficult job, he says, so long as one can read instructions in builderspeak. All measurements must be punctiliously obeyed, whether you or your builder does the work; one inch out where you start to build will mean a compounded inconsistency throughout the conservatory and none of the glazing will fit. Even tiny gaps anywhere are unacceptable. They allow rain, snow, draughts to force an entry, and like a leaky ship, they seem to continue leaking no matter how often they are plugged.

All parts of a wooden conservatory are more easily painted before they are assembled, advisedly with a long-life microporous paint. White is the usual choice, though a pale green-tinged grey or grey-blue can look lovely. You can alternatively treat the wood with a preservative and stain or varnish, though the structure will not look as decorative.

Blinds are an essential you must buy before you get plants. Without them, the plants will frizzle in summer. They can be manually operated or automatic, the latter triggered by light intensity and the temperature reached in the conservatory. The nicest looking blinds are composed of bamboo slats but these tend to rot in time and at least one firm has abandoned them in favour of perforated white plastic which looks horrible throughout its long life. Expensive but very good alternatives are automatic, external cedar-lath blinds. External blinds will control heat as well as light within the building; internal blinds regulate light only. Conservatories with an octagonal or fan-shaped roof make the use of blinds tricky and it is hard to rig up a do-it-yourself system for them. I have shade cast by trees at the fan-shaped end of my conservatory, but those who don't will probably have to buy specially shaped blinds from the firm who supplied the conservatory.

Living with Plants

Right at the beginning, you must decide who takes precedence here – you or your plants, for you are usually incompatible. The reason is the plants' need for moisture. If you are going to use the room primarily for sitting etc. you will yearn for the comfort of soft furnishings. These cannot be subjected to the constant watering-down that most plants need from spring to autumn. (Without this constant moisture, all but certain succulents will suffer from excess heat and drought, and most of these benefit from a daily spraying too.) These priority requirements of plants dictate your furnishings and comfort. Upholstery and rugs are for garden-rooms with a minimum of plants. A plant-filled conservatory can only co-exist healthily with wicker or ironwork chairs, and paving, gravel or water-resistant tiles underfoot.

There is no truly satisfactory meeting-point between these two extremes that I can recommend, though I have run for six years a mid-way system in which we sit in some comfort surrounded by massed plants. I cannot recommend this to anyone outside that lunatic fringe like myself who is willing to take on the extra work of removing cushions etc. before watering twice a day. Nor can I give a quick hose down, since a jet would be too damaging to other human comforts the conservatory houses. I have to syringe with the kind of knapsack spray which one normally reserves for pesticide applications.

From any rational point of view, the gardener is foolish to add the slightest extra effort to the tyrannical work-load which any conservatory lays on its keeper. Under glass, plants need care like infants, like pets; they must be fed, watered and potted, kept in trim (you are always collecting a debris of dead leaves and flowers) protected from pests and cured of illness. The battle against red spider, in particular, must be constant. I have fought this virulent pest which thrives in hot, dry conditions with derris, malathion, the predator *Phytoseiulus persimilis* and frequent wetting of the plants' foliage; and am now in no doubt that the latter is the most effective of all, though it involves you in a yet more intensive watering-regime. It also ultimately means more work on the fabric of the conservatory itself, for that constant spraying of the foliage will leave a deposit on the windows. The glazing may grow a faint crust of lime in hard-water areas. In other conservatories, green slime will build up for the same reason. Both symptoms demand an annual scrub, the slime with something like Algofen or Jeyes' fluid. In short, there are times when the conservatory is a paradise for everyone but its disgruntled keeper.

You can ease some of this work-load in several ways. Reduce the watering by growing main plants in a perimeter earth-bed or pockets in the ground with a brick or raised edging to prevent the soil spilling onto the floor. These will withstand less watering than potted plants and large plants will in any case thrive far, far better with their feet in the ground (you will need to fight their vigour by pruning). Where you do have pots, confine yourself to larger plants growing in large pots, which will dry out more slowly than small pots. Stand these pots in saucers filled with gravel which is then kept moist.

Secondly, keep to a policy of ruthless elimination. Banish any plant which has a tendency to uncertain health. I have stopped growing daturas which are prone to red spider, fuchsias which get whitefly and a lemon tree which needed regular sponging of its leaves to make it happy. Reducing the work-load is not the sole reason for banishing ailers. A conservatory is not a hospital and I do not care to spray pesticides and fungicides in a room that is part of a house, however safe a chemical is alleged to be. And even derris, one of the least toxic to human beings, smells pungently for long after its application.

Thirdly, go automatic where you can. Heating, ventilating and watering are the three main areas. In fact, I only take advantage of automatic heating, and use a thermostatically controlled electric fan-heater. I don't have automatic ventilation because my roof vents are a heavy weight for the ventilators to cope with, and I have heard from too many quarters that they tend to pack up after a time with the strain. Moreover, they can open the vents when it's warm *and wet*, which is not what you may want. Nor do I use any automatic watering device, as I don't like the appearance of the kind of staging which supports a capillary system. Nor do I like the look of trickle and drip systems. Both, nevertheless, are undeniably useful if you are going away for any length of time.

These three preceding paragraphs contain defensive points. They do not in the slightest negate the intense pleasure that a conservatory can give. For some it derives simply from having a garden in all weathers and at all seasons within the house. For me, an additonal excitement is the sensational burst into overdrive in the range of plants I can grow. Natives from Brazil, Peru and Argentina, from Madeira and Africa, from the warmer regions of China keep me company, all tolerating just-frost-free conditions.

Plants, however, don't make a conservatory any more than these individual ingredients make a garden. And assuming you are not using a conservatory for certain monocultures, there are three essentials to remember in the stylish presentation of assorted plants under glass. Firstly, they need grouping in their natural layers, with creepers canopying above and around, mini-trees and shrubs bushing high, and spraying ground-cover plants below in patches. Secondly, foliage plants are of key importance; it is these that give the illusion

82. Cymbidiums, very long in flower, are amongst the loveliest subjects for a cool house.

83. A conservatory planted for fragrance as well as colour, with lemony *Lippia citriodora* and heliotrope.

that the garden has penetrated the house. Finally, a colour scheme is vital, ensuring that blossoms are mutually harmonious in their season. Given the prolonged flowering-period of many plants under glass, this third point may mean that you have to abjure certain colours entirely from your palette. Your aim in subscribing to all these rules is to capture a total effect, not a spotty incoherent impression.

What you grow in your conservatory depends too on its orientation (and therefore light and warmth); on the minimum winter-heat requirements you are able to provide; on whether you intend to use the conservatory throughout the year or only in certain seasons; and on whether you have a 'feeder' cold frame or greenhouse. This last enables you to sow and bring on annuals and biennials, hiding their drab juvenile dress in the working greenhouse, and only transferring them to the conservatory when they are in full flowering display. (One of the more demanding aspects of the conservatory tradition is that it resembles a florist's shop, with all its inmates at peak point. It is not supposed to be engine-room and potting-shed.)

Scent may be another wonderful extra you seek. The conservatory in Plate 83, for example, is geared not only to summer display but to fragrance too. A great central pillar of heliotrope fills the house with its warm smell, and a bush of *Lippia citriodora* beside the door reminds you to press it for its lemony astringence whenever you enter. Texture, too, is valuable in a conservatory for you are close to these plants and the more responsive to the feel of feathery foliage or waxen flowers or needle-like spines furring a stem.

The selection of plants that follow is based on my own choice and experience, some being common and others unaccountably less so. This hard core that I have found to be both beautiful and easy, is suitable for a conservatory run as a cold house, with a winter base of 40°F/5°C. A higher base will enable you to grow a greater range, but the costs in a prolonged freezing spell rise considerably if you lift this base to a mere 45°F/7°C. I should add that my own range of semi-tropical plants has shown no sign of suffering from this low winter base, despite the fact that higher base levels are usually recommended.

143

Climbers for Walls or Pillars

Hoya carnosa The well-known wax flower is a succulent climber which will grow in a bright as well as sunless part of the conservatory, so long as its roots are shaded. Its pendulous clusters of scented, flesh-pink flowers in summer drop a sticky nectar, however, so don't let its flowering trails overhang chairs etc. Appreciates an ericaceous compost in a pot or soil border. Keep dryish in winter if the temperature is based on 40°F/5°C.

Ivy (Hedera in variety) Valuable for north-facing conservatories. Choose the less rampant and most decoratively leafed cultivars such as the lacy, dark green 'Ivalace', the similar but bushy 'Meagheri', the trailing 'Telecurl' with light green, slightly ruffled leaves, or the familiar silvery 'Glacier'.

Jasminum polyanthum We take this graceful creeper for granted though it was not introduced into England until 1931 and then by Lawrence Johnston, the creator of Hidcote Manor Gardens (though seeds had been sent before to Kew). It is an essential plant for the overwhelming fragrance of its pink-budded, starry, white flowers in spring and for its ferny leaves. I grow two plants twining round wires on either side of the conservatory, but have seen it effectively used around a central pillar. Keep a watch for scale insect and scrape off before it becomes a problem. Large pot or soil border.

Lapageria rosea The type form with large, pendulous rosy-crimson, waxen bells in autumn is lovelier than the white variety. There are especially valuable named forms, too, like 'Nashcourt' though they are hard to track down. In any case, grow this climber only in shaded quarters and in a fibrous, peaty, acid compost. Give it moisture in summer but perfect drainage. Its cord-like stems can grow leggy so conceal its lower quarters with another plant. Soil border better than pots. Protect against slugs.

Mandevilla suaveolens Very sweetly scented, large, white flowers in summer star this climber profusely once it is established. Lends itself readily to pillars and overhead training, but can be rampant. It will endure a pot for the first few years but it is then happier in the soil border.

Oxypetalum caeruleum (syn. *Tweedia caerulea*) A charmer, classified as a climber but can be grown as a shorter, slim, lanky shrub needing some support. Lovely, large corymbs of small starry flowers changing from turquoise to near-lilac, giving prolific summer display. Small, cordate, hairy, glaucous leaves. Give it leaf-mould compost and keep it well-watered in summer. Easily raised from seed, in which case, keep four or five plants and group them together.

Passiflora in variety. The scarlet *P. racemosa-purpurea* and the palest lilac *P. quadrangularis* with its prominent corona and purple and blue banded wavy filaments are both beautiful, but my own choice is *P. antioquensis*, a very vigorous grower with three-lobed leaves and 4in/10cm wide carmine blooms in late summer to winter at the end of trailing shoots. I have also grown *P. mollissima* with ravishing 5in/12.5cm crystalline pink petals around a long central tube (the latter forming a mini-'banana'), but the habit of the plant is leggy and its flowering season shorter and later than the above. Both can be raised easily from seed, if they cannot be bought. Prune trailing side-shoots to two or three eyes in winter. For soil border culture rather than pots.

Plumbago capensis A shrub rather than a climber though its long, flexible shoots can be trained high and wide over a framework. Valuable for its prolific clusters of phlox-like, pale blue flowers in summer, though of little winter use for it is inclined to be deciduous, at such low winter temperatures. It is easily raised form seed and will bloom in it s first season if started early enough in the year. Prone to red spider mite so keep syringed in summer. For large pots or the soil border.

Rhodochiton atrosanguineum Elegant climber with small ivy-shaped leaves and two-tier blooms composed of a reddish-purple calyx making an umbrella over a long pendent corolla of blackest-purple. This Mexican will flower all summer into autumn and its trailing blooms are best displayed if permitted to hang down from its main stems. Pots or soil border.

Solanum jasminoides 'Album' A rapid-growing, semi-evergreen twiner massed with clusters of small, white, long-stalked and starry flowers with staminal yellow beaks in summer to autumn. A bit prone to greenfly but otherwise easy. Better in the soil border than in pots.

Sollya heterophylla Very endearing, slender, twining climber with oval evergreen leaves and nodding clusters of tiny, bell-shaped, deep blue flowers in spring and summer. Give it a peaty soil with good drainage and keep moist in summer. Happy in a large pot.

Shrubs or Trees

Abutilon The 'Bella' forms can be raised easily from seed to flower within six months in a colour range of pink, crimson or cream. Their bell-shaped blooms face outwards. Named forms are also available ('Ashford Red', the yellow 'Canary Bird' or 'Cerise Queen') and there is a hideous variegated-leafed species, *A. thompsonii*. All have a long flowering-season. Grow in a peaty soil in large pots, giving ample water but good drainage in summer. Stop the leading shoot to keep them bushy and watch out for red spider mite.

Acacia in variety. The mimosas are a joy for their early flowers and fragrance, but the choice of species depends greatly on the space available in the conservatory. Large buildings can accommodate the robust *A. dealbata* with its ferny grey-green leaves and tiny balls of yellow blossom; or *A. riceana* with similar flowers but thin, linear leaves. But these are less suitable for smaller houses than the compact, rigid-growing *A. armata* with flower-balls along its stems, or *A. verticillata* with stiff, dark green needles and yellow cylindrical spikes of blossom produced freely even when young. *A. pravissisima* is exceptional with thick, grey saw-edged leaves. Give lots of air and, if grown in pots, put out in summer but don't let the roots dry out.

Buddleja asiatica may be too large for most houses, though useful for its scented, long, thin, drooping panicles of milky-white flowers in winter. Smaller houses could take *B. auriculata* instead, with similar flowers but leaves with a white felt on the underside. Better in soil borders than pots, though firm pruning is vital.

Callistemon citrinus 'Splendens' One of the most glamorous of the Australians with intensely crimson bottle-brush flowers produced in early summer and linear evergreen leaves. It endures excellently in a large pot, but should not be allowed to dry out. One of the most faithful and rewarding of all subjects to grow.

Cassia corymbosa Evergreen pinnate leaves, folding at night, and pea-flowers of egg-yolk yellow produced in abundance in later summer. Happy in a large pot and very easy-going, but its colouring makes it difficult to place against most flowering neighbours at this time of the year.

Clianthus puniceus Only easy if you can provide a watering sytem which keeps the ferny foliage almost continuously moist in summer; if not, it will be one of the first to go down to red spider mite. For this reason, I grow my own plant outside, but must still commend it for its gorgeous red 'lobster-claw' flowers in spring under glass. There is also a white form, and a very rare pink form. All are beautiful so long as you can keep the leaves healthy. Large pot or soil border.

Camellia Evergreens for maximum winter delight in shady houses only. They can make magnificent specimens under glass as London readers may know if they peer into the Chiswick House display in early spring. They require attention, however; the roots must never dry out or bud-drop will occur and not only the leaves should be syringed but the flowers too when they appear, and twice a day if possible. Many cultivars will flower profusely in even a small pot, one criterion for choosing them; but it is also sensible to select those forms which produce finer flowers in still air under glass than they do in the turbulence outside. These include the scented, red, peony-flowered 'Kramer's Supreme' and the huge, red 'Grand Prix' or 'Drama Girl'. Both the latter are very flashy and you might prefer the peachy formal double 'Souvenir de Bahuaud Litou' or the smaller-flowered, compact 'Mrs Bell', a formal double white. I have also grown under glass the modern rose-striped pink 'Galaxie' (an American *williamsii* hybrid) and the sugar-pink, anemone form 'Elsie Jury', the latter tolerating a warm position as she is a cultivar needing sun to ripen her buds.

Cupressus cashmeriana Loveliest of conifers with weeping branchlets of glaucous foliage for the shadier conservatory. Best in peaty soil, either in a very large pot or in the border. If the former, put outdoors in summer in a shaded position and keep moist. Spray foliage freely in warm weather under glass.

Echium fastuosum This neat shrub from Madeira grows to about 3ft/90cm. It produces branching stems which grow woody as they age, giving the plant a gnarled look early in life. Each of its stems bears thick rosettes of long, linear, downy, grey-green leaves. Dense 4in/10cm long cylindrical spikes of small, intensely blue flowers erupt from the centres of the leaf-rosettes in early summer and a well-branched, well-spiked plant will be dazzling then. Best in a peaty, well-drained compost in a large pot or soil border. Never let it dry out or bake in summer or it will get woody and stunted. Very easy from seed.

Geranium (Pelargonium) The zonal and ivy-leafed forms are so widely grown that I need say little here, except to remind you of their value as winter-flowers; this timing is easily managed if you raise some from spring cuttings but disbud them in summer and feed and water them regularly in autumn and winter. The scented-leafed geraniums are less often grown, though a huge range of species and hybrids can be bought with a range of smells from attar of roses (and thus she is called), to lemon (*P. capitatum*, *P. citriodorum*, *P.* 'Citronella' etc.) orange ('Prince of Orange', *P. graveolens* etc.) camphor (several but try 'Lilian Pottinger'), cedar ('Clorinda'), balsam (lots including *P. denticulatum*), lavender (*P. dichondraefolium* is delicious), apple (*P. odoratissimum*) and peppermint (*P. tomentosum*), the latter additionally welcome for its large, emerald, velvety foliage. Many of these make a wonderful addition to pot-pourri.

Grevillea in variety. *G. robusta* makes a highly ornamental foliage plant with 9in/22cm long, dark green, fern-like leaves with a covering of silky, silvery hairs beneath. It forms a very quick growing pyramid, best in a large pot or soil border. *G. rosmarinifolia* has glaucous leaves (like rosemary, of course) with whorled pink, carmine or claret flowers in different named forms over a long season. *G. sulphurea*, the hardiest, is yellow. Lime-free compost essential and all will rapidly show their displeasure if allowed to dry out at the root.

Nerium oleander   This plant is so poisonous in all its parts that with dogs (that is, potential leaf-chewers) in the house, I have refrained from growing it. There are a number of forms with waxy white, pink or deep red single or double flowers that look like small roses against their background of deep grey-green leaves. The bush needs pruning to keep it in shape, by taking the young shoots back to a couple of eyes from the old stems a few weeks after flowering. Pot or soil border.

Tibouchina semidecandra   Magnificent evergreen from Brazil with downy leaves and up to 4in/10cm wide, blue-violet flowers that glow like huge jewels in later summer to winter. It enjoys a peaty, well-drained compost which should be kept rather dry in winter, but moist in summer. Its flowering capacity is affected by root space, so it is best in a very large pot, or ideally the soil border. If it gets straggly, you can prune it immediately after flowering or in early spring. Alternatively, you can make use of its lankiness by training it as a climber on the walls. It will still need pruning in this position.

Perennials, including Bulbs, Corms etc.

Billbergia nutans   This easy-going bromeliad produces 12in/30cm arching stems in spring with pendent bells of pink, violet and green. It tolerates endless neglect, but its chief virtue lies in the fact that it clumps up quickly, lending itself to enough divisions to form a grouped arrangement for a green and spiky-leafed theme. Old, flowering rosettes die, so make sure that there is enough room in the pot for new shoots to develop in abundance. Keep it in shade and give it a peaty compost.

Ferns   These are best grouped and in a shady, humid conservatory make the most graceful of all foliage plants. Compact growers for ground-level masses include *Cyrtomium falcatum* with dark green, deeply notched pinnae which resemble holly; *Adiantum pedatum*, a shorter fern up to 12in/30cm with horizontal, fan-like blades held at the top of each stem; and as a front-row subject, the Maidenhair Fern, *Adiantum capillus-veneris* with its frothy, dense mounds of pale green leaves. *Nephrolepis exaltata* is the long-suffering Ladder Fern, but in a low winter temperature it will tend to be deciduous. Of the tree-ferns, *Dicksonia antarctica* makes a magnificent specimen plant, when established, with long arching dark green fronds topping its thick rufous trunk. But you will lose it fast unless you keep not only the fronds but the trunk well sprayed from spring to summer. All need a leaf-mouldy soil, which doesn't dry out.

Hedychium gardnerianum   There are now a number of named forms of half-hardy to fairly hardy hedychiums, but assuming these prove difficult to obtain, this variety is easily raised from seed. The rhizomes should be kept dry throughout winter, but will start to produce tall, broad-bladed leaves in early summer, a few weeks after you begin to water and feed them. Its 4ft/1.2m spikes of yellow and white, heavily scented flowers blossom in late summer to autumn, followed by scarlet seed pods. I have found them indifferent as to soil, but demanding on water throughout the summer. Dry off after the flowering spikes have died down. Will clump up in a large pot and spread rapidly in the soil border.

Rehmannia angulata   A lovely subject for grouping with 4ft/1.2m spikes in summer of drooping, purplish-pink, foxglove-like flowers. Easily raised from seed or kept young and strong by division of the old growths in spring. The new shoots should then be

146

replanted. Feed and water them well in summer but keep them dryish in winter.

Sarracenia flava One of the easiest and most stunning of the carnivorous plants, with 18in/45cm tall erect, cool yellow pitchers in summer, dying back in winter to a few flat leaves. 'Maxima' is the finest clone, a vigorous giant to 3ft/90cm. No carnivorous plant can honestly be called easy, but their bizarre appearance and fascinating mechanisms for attracting and digesting insects put them into that category of plants which are worth a bit of effort on the part of their keeper. Console yourself with the fact that it is claimed that one large pitcher can eat several thousand household flies, wasps and bluebottles. A few rules on their management can be given here; if you have propane, natural gas or a paraffin heater in winter, you must ventilate the conservatory on even the coldest night. The compost should be six parts moss peat, two parts perlite and one part horticultural sand. Never apply fertilizers. Stand the pot in about 1in/2.5cm of water throughout the growing season and use rainwater for this purpose. (Hard alkaline water is poison to these plants.) When the pitcher starts to die down, it is important to keep the dead portion trimmed off in stages, leaving the live part on the plant.

Strelitzia reginae The Crane Flowers are the finest treasures I have in the conservatory. This plant was introduced into England during the reign of George III and the thrill of its first flowering at Kew inspired Sir Joseph Banks to name it after the Queen. It has a magnificent and complicated blue and orange flower, the broadened base of the bloom forming a landing-stage for the sun-birds which pollinate it. Its clumps of leathery, broad but pointed leaves increase rapidly to 3 or 4ft/90cm or 1.2m high and wide, so the plant is at its finest if given room in the soil border. It will, however, bloom well in a large pot until it grows too big. Give it a well-drained but light, peaty soil and keep it moist in summer.

Zantedeschia aethiopica The white Arum Lily is tolerant of a wide range of temperatures in the sunniest part of the conservatory so long as it is kept standing in a saucer of water throughout the summer months. The type produces its furled, white trumpets in spring over a long period, though it can be induced into winter blooms in a warm greenhouse if it is dried off in May, kept dry on its side until August, re-potted and stood outside in a rich but well-drained compost and brought under glass before frosts begin.

I grow two different forms, the first 'Green Goddess', a native of Madeira where it grows in the mountains above the frost line. This form keeps its trumpet furled for several days, remaining green until it spreads open into a white and green spathe. The other is a particularly handsome Victorian called 'White Sail' with a long-lasting white spathe which curves backwards. Both reach about 2ft/60cm tall.

Succulents

All enjoy a daily spray and watering in summer heat.

Agave americana A large-growing agave with grey-green leaves, viciously spined along the edges as well as at the tip. Slow-growing if kept cramped in a pot, but if planted out, will spread at least 4ft/1.2m high and wide. Keep it well-watered in summer and give it a well-drained compost.

Aloe arborescens One of the 'tree-aloes' with rosettes of light green, serrated leaves, a suckering habit and sprays of pendulous, scarlet flowers in spring. Its rapidly-growing roots get huge and too cramped in any but a deep pot; but if you have room to plant it out, it will make lusty clumps and offsets. Good in a gritty, sandy, peaty soil. Keep well watered in summer.

Echeveria Varieties with highly decorative carpeting rosettes were great favourites of the Victorians and have now sunk to the status of municipal bedding-plants. Their clustered rosettes can be near-black, pale blue, red-tipped green, or mealy white and make stylized undergrowth for taller succulents or spiky-leafed plants. Most flower in spring or early summer, though their flowers play second fiddle to their leaves. Give them a light, quite rich and gritty compost, well-watered in summer and never entirely dry in winter or the leaves will drop off.

Sempervivum Hardy for the most part but very useful for potting in the conservatory as they cascade around the container, the rosettes swarming down the sides to the ground and their flowering toadstool stems topped with pink stars in early summer. All will outgrow their pot rapidly. Nice ones include the cobweb houseleek (*S. arachnoideum*) with small hairy rosettes, or the forms with larger rosettes for wide, shallow containers such as the maroon *S. schlehanii rubrifolium*, *S. tectorum atropurpureum*, 'Royal Ruby', or 'Blood Tip', green with upturned, red tips.

84. A spendthrift example of pre-war brilliance in the woodland garden: the days of massed cardiocrinums among rhododendrons are over, but the idea might be imitated on a much smaller scale.

XII. Wild Meadow, Copse and Woodland
Plants, Mowing and Grazing Regimes, Native and Exotic Treatments

IN THE EIGHTEENTH CENTURY, landscapers worked with water, grass and trees alone, consulting the *genius loci* in their choice. Alas, the twentieth-century genius of the countryside has lost most of his untamed origins: his wet lands have been drained, many of his trees felled, 125,000 miles of his billowing hedgerows and 95% of his lowland hay meadows have disappeared — and all this since 1949. In most places this genius has been corked firmly back inside his bottle, and the countryside that should be his is either gentrified or turned into one vast food or timber factory.

In defiance of this, some of our gardens have become in parts a contrived sanctuary for the wild flora (and fauna) that are missing from the featureless countryside itself. In my own garden, for example, I have encouraged wild daffodils, green hellebores, cowslips, ladies' smock, primroses, bugle, the rampant lesser celandine, dog and sweet violets, early purple orchids and wild scabious – most are here in abundance, fugitives to my isolated niche from a more hostile world outside. Some of these I have fostered by scattering seed or planting bulbs that friends have given me. Nearly all, however, have seized their opportunity and spread by themselves, quick to colonize a hospitable land.

Evangelical conservationists sometimes discount the other side to this picture. In the country, a hospitable site to pretty things is equally enticing to the unattractive and aggressive. Nettles, docks, ground elder and thistles arrive not singly but in rampaging hordes, some mildewing as the season ages, others harbouring aphids and disease. How does our ecologist-gardener react now? Rarely, I think, in a non-interventionist way. He begins a selection process on his wild plants, killing those that displease him – at which point you must forget about the wild aspect. The reality is that a 'perfect' wild garden tends to be a suburban concept; for it is far easier to cultivate in an area which is not subject to the continuous mass invasion of 'weeds' from outside into your arbitrary inside. In the country, on the other hand, a wild garden of more than a season old, must be firmly maintained, certainly to a laxer degree than the garden proper, but it will still involve you in care and quite heavy effort. Otherwise the reversion to natural scrub will begin with a dynamism which will shock those whose closest approach to the countryside has been through the medium of gardening-fantasists.

There are, however, grades of care required in wild gardening and one of the easier forms is the meadow-garden, where flowers are naturalized in grass. (A lovely and accessible example with fritillaries and autumn crocuses is at The Courts, Holt, in Wiltshire, a small National Trust property.) To see a wild flower reserve in spring is to realize that this form of gardening is perhaps the closest we can come to recapturing that world of innocence which we have most certainly lost; and, although the dynamic of meadow-gardening in this century has been conservationist, it has proved equally an outlet for nostalgia.

I ought to stress, though, that its only beautiful, as opposed to interesting, season is in spring and early summer, when the flowers are so close to the ground that they seem embroidered on the surface. As the season advances, and the plants grow tall and tatty, the gardener finds that reality is diverging greatly from his inspiration. The lesson to be learnt here is that, unless you will tolerate the browning chaos around you later in the year, settle for half-measure meadow-gardening and keep the area under control from late June-July onwards.

There are other desirables too. Space is one important factor. My own feeling is that meadow gardening is unsatisfactory unless one has a large garden and can turn a considerable area into 'field', well beyond the gardened environment of the house. Little strips of meadow, near a house and measured in feet rather than acres, have some of the pathos to me of caged animals.

The earth is another consideration. To support the widest variety of flowers, you should have poor soil, for nutrient-rich earth encourages the overgrowth of coarse plants at the expense of less vigorous and more vulnerable flowers. Without this natural soil control, you could only redress the pecking-order by weeding out every couple of years the more rampant in favour of the less competitive plants. The third factor is that the site should be open and sunny. And, lastly from your point of view, it should also be flat and come with a hefty man or woman. The reason for this is that in a fully established area, the grass is mown when long, a heavy job requiring a powerful mower. This is punishing on anything more extreme than a gentle slope. Worse still, all the grass or hay-clippings must be picked up. Dead litter lying on the ground at any time of the year will ruin your flowery mead. Now you see why the meadow may be a surburban ideal – admirable for people with flat gardens and energy fuelled by feelings of rural deprivation.

All this notwithstanding, given a suitable space and the will to begin, where does one start? By planting, I would suggest, a background of suitable native shrubs and trees, of naturally different heights, in harmony with the region and, of preference, all to be left unpruned. If you do have to hedge them for reasons of space, nature conservationists advise you to keep the tops tapered (do not square them off as usual); this shape is more valuable to wild life and permits bottom cover and the re-growth of saplings. Hawthorns, white and frothy in early summer and rosy when fruiting, hazels and dog roses are suitable, and, if there is lots of space, perhaps wild crab apples and willows for catkins. Given a harmonious background of this kind, one's small meadow will be less likely to look like borrowed clothing.

The next step is to eliminate all coarse weeds in the area to be meadowed, but this is a piece of advice to adapt as you choose. In my own case, I have killed docks, nettles and thistles where possible with glyphosate. Coarse grasses I have left, despite received wisdom, and in the years when we have not mown at all till autumn, there has still been an abundance of wild flowers. Remember, after all, that one is not striving to include every

150

suitable wild flower. No need to strain to achieve the flower count of untreated chalk turf which can possess up to forty species to the square metre plus a dozen liverworts and mosses. Indeed, you will ruin your pleasure in this kind of garden if you are fanatical about it. One of its main purposes is to release you from the programme of *constant* endeavour which can spoil your enjoyment of other parts of the garden. The work-load here is only very occasional, albeit extremely heavy at the time.

With relatively weed-free grass, you can now start adding the flowers. Wild flower mixtures can be bought from seedsmen (see Appendix), but do buy those that are not only appropriate for your soil (whether wet, dry, calcareous or acidic) but suitable for your region. If you buy a foreign mix, this may upset the balance of native flora to the extent that the latter will be crowded out. (This does not apply, of course, to annual exotics which will die out over winter.) Your local conservation group should be able to advise you.

Minute flower-seed is best mixed with an equal part of silver sand and broadcast over small patches of earth which have been cleared of turf and raked to a responsive tilth. Ideally sow in autumn for fresh seed will be more viable then, but if you sow in spring, top the grass with a mower or brush-cutter to about 4in/10cm as it grows. This will give the seedlings less competition.

If you are starting the grass in the whole area from scratch, again ensure that the earth is free of weeds, and then sow a mix of short grasses. A recommended selection from a Royal Horticultural Society specialist is 60% chewings fescue, 20% browntop bent and 20% creeping red fescue; a grass seedsman may make this up for you. Alternatively, Thompson and Morgan seedsmen (and others) have marketed a dwarf grass seed and advise that you sow 10oz/280gm of this with 1oz/28gm of their wild flower seed selections, thus compressing two operations into one. Again, mow this flower lawn when it is about 4in/10cm high and continue through the first season, before settling into your chosen mowing regime. The seedlings will be sturdier as a result.

Another method is to establish wild flowers as you would for a herbaceous border, by raising seedlings in a separate plot, growing them on and planting them out in wandering drifts and large patches in areas clear of turf. The advantage of this is twofold. Firstly, the plants are stronger, they will establish themselves vigorously and, if you scarify the turf around and put down a peat cloth, they will mostly seed themselves into colonies and renew their numbers. The second advantage is aesthetic and is too often neglected by the conservationist with tunnel-vision. You can control the density and mix of the colours you introduce. By limiting your palette, as nature quite often does, you can increase the impact of colours and produce powerful effects of astonishing richness. Near here, for example, unclipped verges in high summer are a glorious mix of just two colours, cream and intense violet-blue, the first from packed drifts of meadow-sweet (*Filipendula ulmaria*), the second from field geranium (*G. pratense*).

This is the main reason why I have chosen not to supplement my own wild, native flowers with purchased, mixed flower-seed; have preferred, instead, to increase existing colonies of cowslips, primroses etc. from their own seed or transplant native plants from one part of the garden to another when they are in flower (the time when they are most adaptable, I have found). It is not purist scruples which underly my choice, but an appreciation of the given colour harmony. The spring colours, especially, of my wild flowers are consistently fresh and harmonious – cream, lemon, violet, blue – and the

85. Blue *Camassia esculenta* flowering in grass in May; they will flourish in heavy soil.

reiteration of the same species gives the wilder parts of the garden an artistic unity that one changes at one's peril.

Bear colour in mind, too, if you introduce bulbs, for wild gardening is anything but a Liberty Hall permit. Discordant introductions destroy the deceptive simplicity which you are trying to create. With spring bulbs (excepting many tulips) you can scarcely err in colour terms. Even so, your best effect comes from simplifying, from reducing the number of varieties you include and encouraging instead a seasonal dominance by one or two species. Of the multitudes for naturalizing, choose from (for February) *Crocus tommasinianus*, snowdrops (around the shadier edges of the site unless it is fairly damp); for March, *Narcissus pseudo-narcissus* (Lent Lily or wild daffodils), *N. bulbocodium* (lemon-yellow in the form *citrinus*), *N. triandrus albus, Ornithogalum nutans*; for March to April, *Anemone apennina* and *A. nemerosa*, blue *Scilla sibirica, Chionodoxa luciliae*; for April and later, snake's-head fritillaries and *Leucojum aestivum*, both for damp places; for May, *Narcissus poeticus recurvus*, bluebells (the native *Hyacinthoides non-scriptus*) and camassias; and perhaps for June, martagon lilies which are easy in sun or shade; for August and for grass which is not mown earlier in the season, montbretias.

All these should first be scattered over the ground in broad drifts of their own kind, but threading into one another. Then you plant them where they have landed in sandy, gritty soil at the bottom of small trenches made by thrusting a spade into the ground. Push the spade 4in/10cm deep into the soil in a variety of angles, no two ever parallel. In effect the bulbs are being planted in short rows, but this will not be apparent when they grow, so long as you have been cunningly random with the angles of your spade thrusts. This method is a million times easier than using a bulb dibber.

It is the mowing regime you choose which will restrict or enlarge your range of wild

86. Daffodils have naturalized in grass and spread down the slope towards the south.

87. Inviting, clearly distinct paths mown in grass present you with a choice of destinations.

flowers. As I have implied, my own view after trial and error with different regimes is that the spring and early summer flowers give the loveliest effects. To allow these to flower and to set and disperse seed, we usually do not start mowing in certain areas until the turn of June/July. If, however, one wished to break into blossom again at the other end of the year, introducing areas of lilac, pink and white autumn-flowering crocuses and colchicums (*Colchicum autumnale, C. speciosum*, the vigorous *Crocus speciosus* and *C. kotschyanus* [syn. *C. zonatus*]) one would have to stop mowing again in August to allow the bulbs time to develop. It is usually simpler to confine these bulbs to certain areas of grass and just stop mowing in these parts. This is a sensible practice for the colchicums produce large sheafs of leaves in spring and these should not be mown down even when they are yellowing later in the year, or the plants will suffer.

There have been a few years, however, when we have chosen not to mow at all until the autumn. By then, a steady succession of meadow species has become apparent – of vetches, yarrows, knapweeds and scabious. One could supplement these with mallows, campanulas (especially the tall *C. latifolia* and the dwarf *C. rotundifolia*, the harebell), foxgloves, mulleins and evening primroses. But it is the flowering grasses which make the most dominant impression notwithstanding the flowers; and, after summer rains, these look disenchantingly messy to even the most genial eye. At this time, too, the grass is far too long to enter, so whole areas are out of bounds to you. The most you can hope to do is to keep mown throughout the year a criss-cross of inviting clearly distinct paths running through the hay.

The mowing regime is a matter for experiment. But once you have chosen a rhythm that suits your site, outlook and appetite for work, then, if your interest is partly conservation-ist, you should establish it as a regular practice. It is when farmers abandon traditional practices that a substantial loss of species can occur. The less common and adaptable kinds may not be able to cope with an unpredictable habitat. A rare plant's life-cycle or ecology may not equip it to cope with change; and if such plants die out, so might a brood of butterflies which is unable to mate or lay eggs, or a nectar-feeding beetle will search in vain to find flowers at the only time when the adults are flying.

In writing all the above, I am highly conscious that this threatens to become unhinged from reality. For it is a fact that those gardeners in the country with enough land to spare for meadow-gardening will probably wish to keep animals on that area. Are the two incompatible? Yes, obviously, as far as pigs and goats are concerned. Not necessarily with horses and sheep, so long as one can maintain a grazing regime in the same manner as a mowing regime. Horses and sheep feed differently. The former tend to pull many plants up by the roots and can therefore damage more interesting species, but they are also highly selective feeders, which can be an advantage. Conservationists would advise you, therefore, to keep just one or two horses, and to divide the paddock into small areas, so that parts can be kept ungrazed during the summer which will help flowers seed and survive. This same advice holds good for sheep too, though these are, in contrast, non-selective feeders. Of all stock, however, they will create the finest type of grass land. I have a few pet sheep (Ryelands which are like creamy, cuddly teddy bears). Moving gradually over the paddocks, reducing the vegetation gently and evenly, within five years they have changed and refined their coarse pasture to a neat, springy turf. (For those seriously interested, the local Nature Conservation Trust may well have a booklet on grazing management. Otherwise, readers in Britain could obtain *Information Leaflet No. 2*

'Lowland Grasslands of Worcestershire' by A.J.L. Fraser, Worcestershire Nature Conservation Trust Ltd.)

The Copse and Woodland Garden

The apparent counterpart of the open, sunlit expanse of flowering meadow is the woodland garden, that other form of wild gardening. They are unrelated, however, for the former can be contrived, whilst the latter is usually a 'gift', few having the patience to plant proper copses where none exists. As such the woodland garden tends to be a natural world whose wildness must be understood and respected.

Its mood is quite different too. It is a closed, self-contained landscape of cool shadows which can be manipulated to marvellous effect. There is some parallel to be drawn between the mature woodland garden and the interior of a tall, old church, a connection which ecclesiastical architects of an earlier age exploited. It is to be found in the massive and tall columns of tree trunks, the vaulting of overhead branches and the roof of leaves. Both worlds are protected from glare and heat, yet lit by unexpected, angular shafts of light. Both are quiet, and muffle the obtrusive noise of the outside world. Even their smells are not dissimilar: musty, fungoid and persistent. The feeling of age and timelessness is a shared characteristic of each, not to be forgotten when making a woodland garden.

In *Gardens for Small Country Houses*, Gertrude Jekyll and Lawrence Weaver included two gardens made in forest clearings. The first, Woodgate, Four Oaks, was set in six acres of virgin woodland, near Sutton Coldfield; the second, High Coxlease at Lyndhurst, was in the heart of the New Forest, Hampshire. The unusual charm of the former depended upon the retention of its indigenous trees – oak and holly, silver birch, mountain ash, firs and Spanish chestnut. The second, equally stolen from the wild, had also kept its trees and its abundant foliage, and grew its garden flowers out of a sea of fern.

Yet Miss Jekyll was far too experienced a gardener not to emphasize that gardens of this kind, on whatever scale, must represent some kind of trial of strength between the owner and his land. 'When shall the axe play and when shall the wielding of it be stayed?', she wrote with her customary stiffness. And, indeed, it is at this point that one begins with a woodland garden: for gardening under a canopy of trees depends not only on the type of tree, but the number one allows to remain.

When you inherit a copse or woodland you want to garden, you have to look at it critically, at first as a botanist and timber manager, and then as an artist. You need to know that woodland consists of four layers – tree layer, shrub layer, field layer (made up largely of flowers) and ground layer (chiefly mosses and liverworts). The last three depend on the tree layer. If, for example, the tree layer is composed of closely planted conifers, the shrub and field layers will disappear, killed by the lack of light and the dense accumulation of the needles which make the ground too acidic. So you cannot attempt to garden a dense conifer copse, unless you are willing to embark on a degree of tree-felling and ground-clearance; or, alternatively, will simply garden the boundaries.

Deciduous woodland is another matter, but the principle remains the same; the degree of flowers etc. depends on the type of tree and its extent. Larch and birch trees cast a light shade, for example. Oak, a medium density tree, with a high open canopy, allows up to 20% of sunlight to reach the woodland floor. Beech, by contrast, reduces this amount to 5%. The shrub and small tree layer (up to about 15ft/4.5m) also affects the extent to which light can penetrate. If this layer is coppiced, there is a burst of response from the field layer the following year; seeds stir into sudden life, dormant rootstocks send out shoots; and primroses, lesser celandines, violets, wood anemones and wood sorrels, yellow archangel may all begin to spangle the woodland floor in an enchanting pattern of soft colour.

It must have now become obvious that you will never garden your woodland satisfactorily unless you keep it under management, by periodic coppicing and sometimes by felling. It is pointless to introduce or encourage flowers unless you are willing to control your trees and shrubs too. We have learned this with our own copse of high oak, ash and an underlying shrubby layer of hazels, elders and hollies. From time to time we cut back or completely remove some hazels, the messier, scrubbier hollies and most of the elders – a job to be done with caution lest we make a wind channel. The tall canopy trees with their soaring straight trunks we leave untouched, though low branches may need to be lopped to let in light and air. These high stems make the framework within which one can design. In all this, our purpose is not only to give form to the area, but to keep a balance between the different layers, and to keep the flowers not merely alive but multiplying. One does not want a dead and silent wood on one's hands (that is the prerogative of timber merchants and the Forestry Commission), but one with flowers and butterflies and woodland bee species, bursting into life in the spring.

One also needs to know a little about the woodland cycle if one wants to garden it successfully. Spring is the main season of woodland blossom, when sunlight can reach down through the high, bare branches and stimulate growth in flowers. It is therefore spring flowers you should encourage; economical in their needs, using light through their leaves for this brief period in order to blossom and complete their cycle, these will reward your efforts most.

So much for the manager and botanist. What about the artist? He has two main options, placed at opposite extremes; both are equally inspiring, though suited to different surroundings, soils and, perhaps, temperaments.

The first option consists of accepting the quiet native spirit of the natural woodland garden and conforming to its laws exactly. In doing so, you will know that you are supporting a richer, more extensive wildlife here than in any other part of the garden; 60% of our breeding land-birds need woodland, scrub or trees, and probably more than half of the British species of butterflies and moths are also found in woodlands, visiting the native flowers. You therefore plant (or leave) only indigenous trees, and enrich the existing groundwork of woodland plants, choosing from such flowers as bluebells, celandines, martagon lilies, cow parsley, lily of the valley, wood anemones and wood forget-me-not, the dog and wood violets, *Iris foetidissima*, *Helleborus foetidus* and *H. viridis* (all these last three calcicole plants), cowslips, the native Herb Robert and its related shade-loving geraniums which are alien but established like *G. phaeum* (with plum, slate or white blossoms) and *G. punctatum* (with the strange spot on its new leaves). In the open grassy but damp rides, you can have creeping jenny and bugle; in dappled shade, foxgloves; in heavy shade, hart's tongue ferns and the garlic-smelling ramsons (*Allium ursinum*) with their snowstorm of blossom sheeting the ground in May. Wood spurge (*Euphorbia amygdaloides*), the crooks of Solomon's Seal, tall stands of the male fern (*Dryopteris filix-mas*), the catkin-flowered sedge (*Carex pendula*) and spurge laurel (*Daphne laureola*, a typically calcicole plant) give form at a higher level. A groundwork of the common small-

88. *Allium ursinum*, the garlic-smelling ramsons, will sheet dappled shade with its white starry flowers.

leafed ivy (*Hedera helix*) knits them together.

Think big and also very plain. Writing about her own wood, Miss Jekyll said: 'The preponderance of one kind of tree at a time has given a feeling of repose and dignity'. Now, this maxim is equally true of the field layer in woodland. Therefore plant or encourage self-sowing of a particular flower in great carpets or stands (see Colour Plate XVII where this ideal has been well adapted to a shady part of the garden proper). The cardinal rule of nature is that a single variety of plant tends to dominate its area in woodland, sometimes colonizing an entire floor as with wood anemones, hart's tongue fern or wild daffodils, or sometimes all the walls and ceilings of the area, as with a stand of trees from self-sown seedlings. It is this fact that helps to contribute towards the peace. You are not exhausted here by the restless variety that is commonplace in, for example, a herbaceous border or a rockery.

Timelessness is its other attribute. This means that your role is to consolidate the enduring, fashion-free elements of the one part of a garden which may still be here in its existing form in a hundred years' time. To this end, obliterate all signs of humankind, the one species that is truly alien to woodland. Make your paths lightly mown grass (if starting from scratch, you can use a shade mixture) or of natural soil – not gravel. No seats. And, emphatically, no statue of Pan peeking through fronds, affecting to be the spirit descended and not a lump of overpriced stone.

This kind of perfected native glory is at its most exquisite in spring, but a less purist form, permitting the occasional use of foreign rose species, hydrangeas and monkshood would extend its charm through till the autumn.

Another very common and more eclectic treatment is to embellish basic native plants throughout the year with harmonious aliens: Miss Jekyll, for example, made use of cistus in her clearings, but in shade you might favour instead the rose-pink suckering bramble *Rubus odoratus* with velvety leaves and flowers all summer to autumn. Herbaceous plants demand much more care from the gardener, but possibles include the North American trilliums and *Smilacena racemosa*, or the Asian *Kirengeshoma koreana* (a coarser, more upright, but very vigorous form, which is better suited to rough and tumble than its

157

89. *(left)* This nineteenth-century picture of Henry Cooke's Indian garden shows the ultimate flight from English woodland; here, workmen lift one of his banana trees in preparation for the winter.

90. *(below left)* The introduction of *Trachycarpus fortunei* and gunneras amongst the rhododendrons makes woodland exotic.

91. *(below right)* The exceedingly rare hybrid between *Lysichitum americanum* and *L. camtschatcense* grows in a shady, moist ditch.

prettier relative *K. palmata*). Add to these the Himalayan *Podophyllum emodi* with its pale flowers, red fruit and marble leaves; *Dicentra macrantha*, with ferny foliage and apricot 2in/5cm lockets in spring; *Glaucidium palmatum*, with an exquisite pale lavender bowl of petals, if you can afford a group, have peaty soil and will weed out threats. In clearings, you might use the umbelliferous yellow-green biennial *Smyrnium perfoliatum* or short-lived perennial sweet rocket (*Hesperis matronalis*). I planted over a hundred lilac and white seedlings of the latter at the edge of old trees in my former garden. At dusk they were magical, the haze of mauve and white almost luminous in the shadows around. The scent, too, was dizzying, proving how perfectly a closed area can contain every drop of fragrance within its bowl.

In this sketch, we are already beginning to move along the axis of possible styles, away from native wild gardening and towards the option which, at its most extreme, is dominated by exotics. It is for acid soils, and in its most exaggerated form, it might be called foreign jungle. It is unashamedly flamboyant, because it depends largely on rhododendrons. Here is the plant collector Frank Kingdon-Ward's description of the sight of rhododendrons among the mountains of Asia, 'blazoning the hillsides, rolling like crimson lava down the mountain gullies ... staining the landscape with royal colour'; or, again, 'thousands of rhododendrons, lit up with balls of fire, or with the golden glow of yellow lamps'.

It is this same kind of scene that has been re-created on a very small scale for the past century and a half in so many British gardens. That one can build so fantastic a foreign world in so inappropriate a setting, without (as seen in the best colour-controlled examples like Colour Plate XVI) offending the surrounding garden or countryside, is due entirely to the self-containment of the woodland garden. The very fact that it excludes the world outside allows one greater scope, and a freer hand in the introduction of colour, which is the more intense for being in a shadowed emerald setting.

In this country, this style is seen at its noblest in the great moisture-laden Cornish and western seaboard gardens, for some nine-tenths of the known species of rhododendrons grow in the wet monsoon mountain zones of Asia and need mist, a saturated atmosphere and a heavy rainfall with winter snow if they are to thrive to full potential in an adopted country. It is in these gardens too that you will find the marginally hardy banana tree (*Musa basjoo*) and tender tree ferns (*Cyathea* and *Dicksonia*). The latter remains evergreen at the coast, though it will lose its leaves inland in hard winters; at Trewithen, Cornwall, for example, I have seen it looking completely dead in the icy dell, but it puts out its first tiny green fingers in May. In many of these gardens, the arching screens of bamboos and hardy palms (*Trachycarpus fortunei*) in the clearings reinforce the tropical effect.

Nonetheless, the most extreme example I have discovered of the tropical woodland garden was paradoxically not in the sheltered wet south and west, but in the cool 500ft/140m uplands of Gloucestershire. It was here in the nineteenth century that a most extraordinary garden was created. Henry Cooke, its owner, a retired Surgeon-General in the Indian Army, described it in 1899 as the vivid realization of an earlier garden he had tended in India: 'It only wants the gorgeous colouring of the Crotons which attain to so great development in the Indian garden to complete the picture.'[1]

---

1. Details of the garden can be found in my article in January 1979 in *The Journal of The Royal Horticultural Society*. It was as a result of this that the film *The Assam Garden* was shot here in 1984.

His boast was not an empty one. Great banana trees, sparmannias and daturas all grew here; but his use of these tender exotics is of less practical interest to us now than his ideas on the permanent planting to frame them. He planted the boundaries of his ponds with *Iris kaempferi* in brown, maroon, indigo and white shades, and with the brilliant orange *Lilium pardalinum* and *L. superbum*. He filled his spaces with palms, massed clumps of senecios, eremuruses, spiraeas, azaleas, *Leycesteria formosa*, pampas grass and miscanthus at one level; and, beneath, with montbretia, hostas, blue agapanthus, pink crinum and ostrich ferns according to the sunny and shady spots. Primrose and copper day lilies flowered in summer, *Lobelia cardinalis* in autumn. *Dicentra eximia*, the little bleeding-heart, was allowed to colonize waste spaces. Nearby, *Phormium tenax* and *Gunnera manicata* increased in wet ground, as did a selection of rheums. Bamboos were a feature and companion to these was a clump of scarlet fuchsia towering 8ft/2.5m high, and shedding bark like a London plane tree.

When I found this garden nearly a hundred years later, some of the original plantings still thrived; the bamboos were like a forest, the azaleas and rhododendrons tree-like, the polygonums a rampant army and the palm trees still flourishing. All else had fallen sacrifice not only to our winters but to the loss of labour to maintain it.

With so heavily planted a garden, it was all entirely predictable, for his dream was an impossible one to endure in our century. Yet its potency affected my own tastes. Like Henry Cooke, I too felt that 'it is in the wild garden that the tropical element so naturally comes in'. The practical gardener realizes this; it is relatively wind-free, so gives protection to large-leafed plants; it minimizes the severity of frost, so shelters tender subjects. But the real reason is more nebulous. Its self-containment is such that it allows us to escape all sense of reality, if we wish it.

So I, too, have planted clumps of bamboos in the hope that they will one day join fronds, and made a walk of lace-cap hydrangeas with spreading bushes of *H.* 'Blue Wave', the white *H.* 'Libella', *H. serrata acuminata* 'Grayswood', *H. villosa, H.* 'Mariesii', *H. aspera* (check the form when buying – the quality of the flowers can vary considerably), the greenish-white mop-head *H. arborescens* 'Grandiflora' and the strange *H.* 'Ayesha', the possessor of a domed plate of waxen florets like lilacs. Rhododendrons are there, chosen for their huge leaves as well as some for their jewelled bell-flowers, hybrid forms which usually stand more sun ('Lady Chamberlain', 'Lady Rosebery', 'Caerhays John' and 'Caerhays Philip'). *Rosa filipes* 'Kiftsgate' grows over several trees, joined by its double-pink seedling 'Pink Bouquet', by 'Paul's Himalayan Musk', and the pink 'Princess Marie' (which can be seen in maturity over a great holly at Nymans Garden in Sussex). Groups of camellias edge a clearing near the pool, assorted for colour. In youth they have a stiff and ugly habit, but all promise to be beautiful, especially favourites such as 'Waterlily', a large lilac formal double, and 'Inspiration', a semi-double rich pink. Most are in their infancy, but the planting is, I trust, prudently labour-saving. I hope, too, that despite a succession of bad winters and the depredations of rabbits, it stands in part a chance of lasting for a hundred years. And also of confirming Henry Cooke's own words which he felt with such fervent intensity: 'There are few who visit me who are not impressed with the beauty and interest which a wild garden affords as compared with the ordinary garden'.

Six Gardens

The last section of this book is devoted to six gardens. A country garden is an individual and this is the one aspect these gardens have in common. But they are gathered here for two reasons. Firstly, because they are rewarding examples of the kind of approach I have outlined throughout this book. Secondly, because five in particular have sensible and realistic answers to offer within their own terms of reference (the sixth garden is *sui generis*, a miraculous and demanding achievement). All the gardens are privately owned, but I give details about those which are, at present anyway, open to the public.

92. The 1702 gazebo at Bradley Court, shown in Kip's engraving (overleaf).

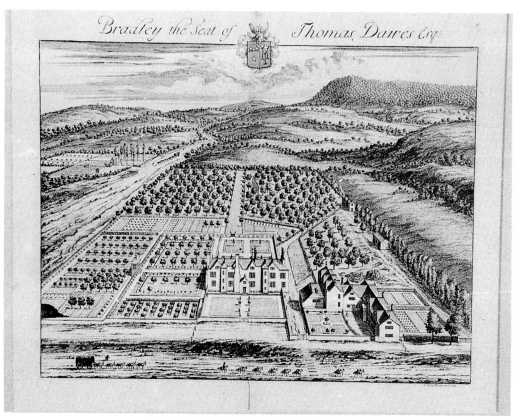

93. 1707 engraving by Kip of Bradley Court. The gazebo to the left of the house is shown in Plate 92.

XIII. A Historic Garden

BRADLEY COURT in Gloucestershire was built in 1559. Grey and gabled, with two projecting staircase towers, the whole enhanced by a touch of romantic decay, its Elizabethan front looks out towards the Severn Vale. Its eighteenth-century rear faces north over a long green view to a trio of huge Scots pines. Through their old trunks, the monument to William Tyndale (the translator of the Bible who was burnt in 1536 as a heretic) can be seen two miles away on the Cotswold Edge. It is an antique view and from an ancient garden, too, for Bradley Court is the only one in this section of the book to be listed by the Historic Buildings and Monuments Commission as 'of special historical interest by reason of its heritage'.

Thomas and Penelope Messel have owned this 12 acre garden since 1982. He is a designer and she a painter, a division of skills similarly sustained in their work on the garden, for he is the 'shape person' and his wife the 'colour person', filling in his shapes. Thomas is also the grandson of Leonard Messel, creator with his father of Nymans Garden in Sussex (now among the most beautiful of all National Trust properties) and a plantsman whose self-named camellia and magnolia are now grown throughout the world. Between them, husband and wife have therefore the understanding to develop such an old, precious place.

162

A 1707 engraving by Kip shows how much of Bradley Court and its gardens has remained intact. The south front of the house is relatively unchanged, so is the framework of the walls in the formal garden to the west and also the exquisite gazebo of 1702 with its ogee roof. The architectural inheritance, then, is rich; though not, of course, the horticultural one, for the formal disposition of plants shown in the engraving has long since died or been obliterated in the succession of different styles over the last three hundred years.

These facts mean that the challenge of owning such a garden is twofold and seemingly contradictory: one must restore it harmoniously to its period yet develop its potential. Or, in Thomas Messel's words, it is both a discipline and a liberation. Building on the success of the immediately previous owners here, the Messels have found brilliant and original solutions to restoring the garden without spoiling its romance, forfeiting its manageability or forgoing the horticultural riches of the present.

The herb parterre (Plate 95 and Fig. 3) before the Elizabethan front of the house is a wonderful example of how the Messels have played magic here with the past. What they inherited was a gravelled forecourt with a central lawn and silver birch and chestnut trees, the most recent layer in the three-hundred-year-long succession of styles and hardware they discovered as they dug beneath the surface. The inspiration to replace this with a formal herb garden had first attacked the Messels whilst the house was still under negotiation. The source of the idea came somewhat from the parterres of the Loire Valley, more particularly from the Botanic Garden of Padua University (built in 1545 and the oldest in Europe). But though the idea was compelling, its execution proved awesome. Existing earth and pathways had to be bulldozed and replaced with fresh importations of new rubble, earth and gravel. And the planting itself involved seven hundred box (*Buxus sempervirens* 'Suffruticosa') to edge the beds. These were imported from Belgium at a price that was less alarming than it would be here.

The pattern of the parterre is an original and partly asymmetrical one. It was designed to conform to the Elizabethan house and to fit the sloping, imperfect rectangle of the courtyard with its bowed front wall which the Messels have hedged with yew. As with all the most successful gardens, the parterre's design is tied to the house. Based on a cruciform path, one axis leads straight from the front door and is crossed almost mid-way by a second. Figure 3 shows how the background beds of taller herbs are symmetrical, whereas those in the foreground are made out of abstract shapes and design elements taken from within the house and 'painted' with chervil, parsley and chives, with lime-green thymes and purple clovers. In fact, the colouring of this apparently green and gravelled forecourt is entrancing, with its gold and purple sages, its lavenders, blue rues and silver helichrysum.

In contrast to the crisp formality of the centre patterns, the beds at the foot of the side walls are filled with soft, full foliage plants which drape over and narrow the path. They hold angelica, artichoke, white cistus, hostas, *Buddleja alternifolia, Carpenteria californica, Ceanothus* 'Trewithen Blue', *Abutilon vitifolium* and *Akebia quinata*.

The finishing touch here makes the link with the garden shown by Kip. Elegant, scooped-top gates next to the road were commissioned to match the shape (though not the positioning) of those in the engraving. In due course, stone ball and plinth ornaments on each pier will complete the match with precision.

To the west and in the distance, the 1702 gazebo sits framed in the view through the

94. Part of the walled rose garden with white roses, foxgloves and artemisias around the copper tub.

doorway out of the parterre garden. On two floors, the upper storey faces eastwards to the house over a large walled croquet-lawn, the lower floor on terraced ground looks west into the country, its Tudor door opening into another walled area which the Messels are planting with flowering fruit trees. Their spun-sugar confection in spring will make an enchanting view from the gazebo's upper window. Yew hedges either side of the little building (Plate 92) will be allowed to grow higher until they can be sculptured into scrolls which will frame and repeat the shape of the ogee roof that rises above them. The wide beds of limy clay either side are planted in large wedges of spikes and mounds. Purple foliage predominates (*Acer palmatum* 'Dissectum' in one of its maroon forms, *Cotinus coggyria* 'Royal Purple', *Rosa glauca*) and black irises contrast with pale lemon ones. A wall with bee-boles backs the wide south-facing bed of ceanothus, *Piptanthus laburnifolius*, pale roses and the apricot Hybrid Musk 'Buff Beauty'. An unseen relic lies beneath them in the form of an eighteenth-century path, which cannot make planting any easier.

On the other side of this bee-boled wall is the most secret of all rose gardens, its lusciousness tucked into its own enclosure, invisible from casual view. A visit here in late June is an entrancing experience, for the scents and crowding of the blossoms of the old roses especially are the more concentrated for being seen and smelt in the confinement of a small walled space. The area is divided into three. Crimson, pink and white old roses are clustered at the top end (see details in Colour Plate XVIII). The middle section consists of a lawn with a quartet of mop-head acacias (*Robinia pseudoacacia* 'Inermis') and, beside this, a paved area centered on a fine copper tub surrounded by a white garden of mounded alba roses, *Crambe cordifolia*, white foxgloves, silver artemisias and bronze fennels (Plate 94). The quartet theme is repeated with four grey cupressus trees which make this bottom, and third section of the rose garden, with two bosomy *Viburnum opulus* 'Sterile' for contrast and for flower arrangements in the house. The foliage of plants here is assertive; *Euphorbia*

95. The herb parterre, edged with 700 box plants, at the foot of the south-facing Elizabethan front of Bradley Court.

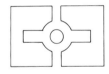

Fig. 3. Outline plan of parterre at Bradley Court reveals the clever asymmetry of its design.

wulfenii, hostas, pittosporum, *Vitis* 'Brandt'. The perpetual-blooming 'Little White Pet', a dwarf sport from the *sempervirens* rambler rose 'Félicité et Perpétue', pouffes at the front of beds.

Just outside this sumptuous enclosure lies a mount. Not an Elizabethan original from which the squire would assess the outside world, but the recent spoil shifted by bulldozers summoned to level over-high lawns to the north of the house which blocked the views both to and from the building. The mount, at present partially covered with mahonias and viburnums, has yet to receive its final planting, but its form was, like the parterre, inspired by one at Padua's Botanic Garden, where a path winds up and down in a separate trail, permitting a clandestine meeting amongst thick enclosing shrubs.

Indeed, the secrecy of many of these individually gardened areas is part of Bradley Court's fascination. It is one of its intensely romantic assets that it does not yield up all its treasures lightly. One such example, reached by a narrow, dark, evergreen-clad path, is a grotto. It adds to the strange time-switch feeling of this place, but was in fact built in 1976 by Adrian Garnett, the previous owner. It is an astonishing achievement by one man. Designed to fill the cavity left by a felled elm, it was built in local stone, like an ice-house with a funnel at the top. Its first self-supporting incarnation collapsed but its replacement, which is enduring, was fashioned by setting stones into pre-stressed concrete. Sombre and womb-like, it is lit solely by the skylight through the roof, and its pool is fed with rainwater and a spring which can be diverted here from feeding the pool which lies at the end of the long lawns nearby.

The lawns themselves are a large green lung. They are banked on the right and bordered on the left by an avenue of fastigiate hornbeams which culminates in a statue of a soldier cut from *pierra bianca di Vicenza*, a stone which is very soft when cut with shears but hardens with time. Relatively unadorned save for clipped yews near the house, the lawns are also planted with a mighty Judas tree and silver-leafed shrubs (*Pyrus salicifolia, Elaeagnus angustifolia*). But the real glory which crowns their austerity comes from the group of magnificent Scots pines at the far north end. Not as antique as the framework and buildings here, but they too are emphatically part of the heritage. Yet in a garden like this, the very long-term future has to be planned, and at the feet of these grand specimens are a trio of infant pines, at present the size of mushrooms compared with their giant forbears, but growing as replacements when the old generation must finally die away.

The only obviously twentieth-century feature in the garden is the swimming-pool but that is wisely hidden from sight and only a purposeful bather would find it. Having reached it, however, he would enter a scented enclosure with banked living walls of high climbing roses (*Rosa filipes, R. paulii, R. virginiana*, 'New Dawn' and 'Max Graf'), philadelphus and honeysuckles. This is an inspirational scheme, for their flowering coincides with the months of the year when the pool is most likely to be used.

Perhaps by now the scale of the place has become apparent. The measure is not simply one of size (though the garden is unusually large by present-day standards). Nor is it only a matter of history. It is also to do with preparation for the future. The latter is vital. The Messels, for example, have given as much importance to the planting of large enduring trees in the outlying areas as they have to ephemeral plants in domesticated parts. An avenue of London plane has been planted in a paddock of rough-cut grass and massed daffodils; *Davidia involucrata, Sorbus* species and *Cercidyphyllum japonicum* among others accompany it. In another field, a grove of *Metasequoia glyptostroboides* has been joined by Turkey oaks and holm oaks. And at different points throughout the garden, the Messels plan screens of grey willow and black poplar, the latter obtainable from the National Trust in the old, more gnarled and slower-growing form than the modern type. It is this kind of scrupulous attention to detail, to the most suitable plants for even throwaway positions, that helps to make this such a remarkable place.

To develop a garden like this, you need not only an acute sense of the past. You also need vision and large horizons if you are not to waste its potential. After all, you are not just maintaining a heritage, but making your own contribution and giving a revitalized heritage to the future. You need the practical ability to manage. Yet you also need artistic tact, knowledge and originality. In all, this is a combination of qualities that rarely go hand-in-hand though they do in the case of the Messels. This is fortunate, for the ownership of a garden like Bradley Court is a considerable responsibility. It is a place which has already been singled out by its official listing as 'special'. It is rather more than that in my opinion. It is a domain with powers of enchantment that should prove one of the most exceptional private gardens in England.

96. A composition of blue and yellow: agapanthus, potentillas, cordylines, eucalyptus, hypericums.

XIV. A Sea-Cliff Garden

HEADLAND is a garden on the edge of the world. Built into a precipitous cliff, bounded by sea breaking on three sides, it is a paradise one could not think existed outside the imagination. A garden that looks outwards to vertiginous views and inwards to secret paths and intimate nooks, its variety is of such contrasting nature that even its whereabouts in the world would be hard to place. It is, in fact, in Cornwall, and were you to sail a boat into the River Fowey, you would see the garden poised a hundred feet above your head.

The briefest of tours will show the excitement of this place. You enter on patterned paving around the house. From here a long flight of steps beside a sloping lawn leads down to an underworld of lush growth on the northern flank of the garden. Here, hydrangeas and ferns are shadowed by tall Monterey pines and cypress; and between their old branches (Colour Plate XIX) you can see the harbour with its small boats and rim of white houses and, if you open a gate in the garden wall, steps to a secluded beach for swimming.

But move away from this domestic scene and walk southwards, to where the sun is blinding on the open sea and you will find that the landscape of the garden takes on a fantastical aspect. Start climbing steps and small alleys winding against the cliff and you see giant outcrops of rock, plushy with lichen. Though monumental in size, some are draped

97. A secretive area, shadowed by the Monterey pines and cypress shown in Colour Plate XIX.

by nests of sub-tropical succulents, by agaves, crassulas, echeverias and lampranthus. On narrow plateaux, Australian and New Zealand plants thrive – acacias, eucalyptus, grevillea, cordylines, and hebes. As on some Mediterranean cliff, self-sown acanthus form a vertical sheet down to the sea, and the air is scented with the warm resinous smell of massed cistus. Yet to confound all such foreign impressions, you will also find here in spring the simple Englishness of daffodils and narcissi in grass. And hear throughout the year that other reminder of the north, the cry of the pretty oyster-catcher.

Though only one and a quarter acres, the garden seems bigger, an illusion due not only to this variety, but to different perspectives to be viewed from its many levels. Laid out as it is on a 'vertical' rather than linear plan as in a conventional garden, and open on three sides, the views from the garden not only change but grow larger or are telescoped according to your position.

Imagination, hard work and the passage of time are some of the prerequisites of such a garden. The original vision was that of a sea captain sixty-five years ago who saw the possibilities of a house in the old quarry on the headland, and, having built it, probably laid the first access paths. But the true foundations of the garden were laid post-war by the Burdett family who, with the dedicated help of a local man, Sidney Menear, brought in more stone and soil to extend the paths and enlarge the pockets for planting.

The present owners, Jean and John Hill, arriving in 1974, therefore inherited an established garden and a wonderful basis from which to begin. But the garden had by now become overgrown and was also not entirely to their taste in some respects, so their immediate goal, after clearance, was to bring out the wild beauty of the place. It was an aim that involved making the necessary constraints of paths and terraces blend with the huge unfettered outcrops of rock which form the cliff face. The result of this re-structuring is that narrow paths of stone or plateaux of mown grass now run in a successional series of levels between the dramatic framework of the rocks. Many of these paths, whether on the lines of the original ones or complementary to them, are the work of John Hill and his helpers – as are walls and an arch. Cleverly detailed, they are mostly of natural stone, though in one area Cornish shillet has been used on edge to delightful effect and good purpose since it doesn't become slippery when wet.

This problem of changing the structural features was daunting enough, but at least it was a finite challenge, albeit of long duration. The most serious challenges are rather those which are continuous, and the Hills face certain major obstacles as long as they garden this landscape. The first concerns the nature of the terrain; the second is to do with the elements, wind and salt. Take the first. Spare a thought for the sheer logistics of planting and maintaining such a garden. You are on an escarpment and, in many parts at least, dealing with what is virtually a hanging garden. Your bonfire, for example, is on a rocky outcrop perched near the edge of a cliff. No stepping back smartly to get out of the smoke. Even more constricting is the fact that some of the planting takes place above your head, so *you need a ladder to plant*. You may well need a ladder to weed, a job that keeps you busy for weeds love this fertile soil (the salt reduces the natural acidity of the earth to neutrality) and not all are as decorative as the wild scabious, sea-campion, wallflowers and sea-cabbage that Jean Hill allows to remain. Bear in mind that a few mis-directed steps or a wobble, and you and your ladder could go sailing over the edge. Consider all this and you will realize that more than simple energy and agility are required. You also have to be the bravest gardener in England to cope with this place. *Pace* Dr Johnson and his dog on hind legs, it is remarkable that such a garden exists, let alone in a form where the beauty of the planting and detailing of the stonework are achievements in their own right.

The second problem is that posed by the elements. It is one that most coastal gardeners must come to terms with. They must choose plants which will resist not only the salt spray (and the lower reaches of this garden are drenched in storms) but also the wind. At Headland, the wind-problem is rendered extreme by the rock face. The trouble here is that violent wind hits the face which acts like a dam; piling back against nearby plants, the wind forces them out of the soil and away from the cliff. Thus, even reputedly wind-hardy subjects are up-rooted if they are planted too near that worst area of turbulence immediately against the rock-face. Bulbs, in particular, need to be carefully positioned in sheltered nooks. Daffodils, for example, lose their heads if they are planted anywhere near the rock.

Persistent trial and error in both choice and positioning of the plants is the only solution, for even the advice of coastal nurserymen has proved flawed when tested in this uniquely difficult site. Indeed the behaviour of certain plants confounds all usual wisdom. Such is the case with cistus, for example. Of the massed cistus grown here, *C* x *purpureus*, *C. ladanifer*, *C. 'Sunset'* and *C* x *corbariensis*, it is the latter, always rated the hardiest, which proves the most liable to succumb. Now, when introducing any new or previously untried plant, Jean Hill makes a practice of planting it whilst still in its container in the ground and assessing its resilience to gales. Any signs of wind-burn mean that it needs to be moved elsewhere.

Wind protection, then, is vital, though the Hills have learnt to be selective in this respect. Artificial screens erected to shelter particular subjects are of little use and can actually cause extra damage by blowing against them. Natural protection is more effective, hence the planting of perimeter and internal ribbons of hedges on many of the successive levels. The most resistant of these give good shelter, but in these conditions, not all perform as they would inland. The silvery *Hippophae rhamnoides*, for example, though

98. Headland: steps up the cliff-face wind between hedges and giant, lichened outcrops of stone.

wonderfully bushy to eyes used only to craggy inland specimens, produces very few of its orange berries, because the wind blows most of the flowers off. And hawthorn gets distorted into a crouching shape, probably because gales rob the bush of buds on the outer side so that new growth is only made on the inner flank. Olearias have proved reliable, however, and these are planted as massed edgings, notably *O. haastii*, *O. macrodonta*, the grey-leafed, tender *O x scilloniensis* (all with showy white flowers) and the lovely and entirely different *O. solandrii* with its heath-like foliage. *Griselinia littoralis, Phormium tenax, Arbutus unedo* (though these last two are grown as individuals rather than massed), *Euonymus japonicus* and escallonias are also reliable, give or take some wind burn on the edges. So too are clustered bamboos, though a recent flowering (a simultaneous event throughout Cornwall, so this quirk of bamboo behaviour is not just folklore) has caused some deaths.

These shelter belts, disposed as they are between heaven and earth, make decorative ribbons in themselves, but it is the individualized areas of planting which are especially impressive. 'Wattle Alley', for example, is not simply a collection of wattles and gums, but has been assembled with a view to colour. It is a composition of blue and yellow. Blue-leafed eucalyptus, grouped agapanthus, tender echiums, prostrate ceanothus, gentians, massed *Scilla peruviana* (one of the loveliest bulbs with strap-shaped leaves and wide conical heads of deep, rich blue in May) contrast in their season with *Hypericum patulum* 'Hidcote', yellow potentillas, *Hypericum calycinum* in clefts in the cliffs, and *Acacia verticillata*, a tender spiny-foliaged evergreen with yellow tassels in spring. Here it is clipped (first by the wind, then by the Hills) into a formal mound.

In this spot, as elsewhere in the garden, Jean Hill has shown herself to be one of those very rare amateurs who can handle plants in large, bold masses rather than isolating individuals in a spotty fashion. The use of bold effects and brilliant colour is vital in this clear, southern light which can bleach those pastel displays, currently in English fashion, into insignificance. But it takes confidence and an intuitive feeling for the challenge of the surroundings to handle plants in this way.

Nowhere is this more apparent than in the 'rock garden' which has been planted with a marvellous eye to colour. Forget about a conventional alpine treatment here which would seem absurd in this landscape. Here, instead, the massive natural stone is clothed with prostrate junipers and rosemaries, brooms, the spreading *Cupressus macrocarpa horizontalis aurea, Phormium tenax*, and massed swords of scarlet autumn-flowering kniphofias. But earlier in the summer, the most brilliant area of colour is to be found in the almost frost-free pockets permitting the growth of succulents, notably agaves, echeverias, sedum, crassulas and lampranthus. The latter, some imported from Israel and Lanzarote as well as from local sources, make dazzling carpets over the rocks – though at all times of the year, the green fleshy feelers of this wind-resistant plant form a handsome pattern against the stones.

In fact, at all seasons this garden is clothed and of interest. And when the owners have taken their fill of looking inwards, they can seek shelter – for there is always some nook to be found out of the wind. Here, in peace, they can sit in one of their many seats and watch that constant entertainment of sea and sky.

The garden of Headland in Polruan-by-Fowey, Cornwall, is at present open to visitors on Wednesday afternoons in summer and on other special occasions.

99. From the drive, the house is glimpsed between 'meadow' borders of naturalized bulbs and fine trees.

XV. A Wiltshire Farmhouse

ALL THE BEST GARDENS disclose their distinction at the very first glimpse. At Kellaways, your initial view of the small stone manor house is through the trees lining the drive, indicators in themselves of the exceptionally rich and eclectic planting that is the hallmark of this garden. *Tilia mongolica* with ivy-lobed leaves, the apricot and yellow flowered *Aesculus* x *mutabilis* 'Induta' and the magnificent large-leafed *Populus lasiocarpa* are here, yet – another characteristic of this garden – they all look entirely natural and unforced. For they rub shoulders with the homelier *Malus* 'Lemoinei' and their feet are deep in 'meadow' borders of naturalized snowdrops, aconites, cardamines, fritillaries, bluebells, and martagon lilies and the lovely mauve *Geranium tuberosum* which is so little seen yet seeds itself about in the long grass here.

The owner-gardener of Kellaways (with some part-time help) is Mrs. Daphne Hoskins. She began the garden on first arrival in 1949, a challenging period for gardeners as 'we all planted our gardens on coupons then'. The only assets to be inherited from her predecessors here were the brick walled garden flanking the early seventeenth-century house, and a field beyond. This area is now a shrubbery of the most imaginative kind: and the walled garden is the planted heart of the entire one-acre garden. Open the ironwork door in its wall and you encounter an almost palpable burst of plant force from old-fashioned

172

herbaceous flowers jostling against foliage beauties of more modern appeal, and shyer rarities such as the steel blue *Mertensia asiatica* which only wise husbandry and a winter-cloche will keep alive.

But, though Kellaways exemplifies the energy of all heavily planted gardens, the degree of its organization and planning is immediately apparent. This is partly due to its arrangement into self-contained enclosures or areas, but it is also thanks to the plant controls within them. The walled garden, for example, has a calm grassed centre, broken only by formal beds of roses and pansies and by the focus of a small lead statue of Mercury which Mrs Hoskins inherited from her parents' large garden. And, even though the plants surge exuberantly in huge borders against the lawn and entirely smother the terrace, their keeper's hand is apparent in their order and their colour. At the far end, for example, two great mauve and pink lilacs, the Canadian hybrids 'Elinor' and 'Bellicent', mark each end of the wall, linked by a 40ft/12m sea of bronze and purple *Iris germanica* that run between them. The wall behind them is clothed with the chocolate-purple-flowered *Akebia quinata* and spangled by the mauve *Clematis* 'Herbert Johnson' and *Clematis montana rubens*. And the onlooker, standing on the lawn, will see impacted against this the harmonious shades of a second border before it of pink pyrethrums and geraniums.

Indeed, colour associations in this garden are far, far too numerous to mention – though Mrs Hoskins modestly disclaims any credit ('God puts them there' she says of the self-sowers). In late spring, the great east-facing border in the walled garden glows with the burgundy spathes of *Trillium sessile* amongst the blue crooks of *Mertensia virginica*, with the rosy blue-leafed *Dicentra eximia*, and the first drumsticks of the mauve *Allium aflatunense*. As the latter gets fully underway a few weeks later, their foil changes to early-flowering primrose hemerocallis. Near these, the cut-leafed pink-flowered *Paeonia veitchii* blooms before the mauve fluff of *Thalictrum aquilegifolium*, and a dusky pink oriental poppy partners a swatch of mauve sweet rockets. Their velvet carpet of self-sown generations of *Viola* 'Bowles' Black' is supplemented in high summer by an edging of pinks.

Turn to face the opposite side of this garden. Here, the great border (trimly kerbed by a striped brick and mortar edging) has one of the real jewels – the filigree-leafed *Paeonia tenuifolia* with its glistening crimson, gold-stamened bowls and, as its companion, the crimson-carmine tulip 'Captain Fryatt'. Further up, golden tulips are grown with blue polemoniums, whilst blue lupins, blue geraniums, *Asphodeline lutea* and delphiniums are yet to come on stage. Behind this border, lies the perimeter wall bed on the other side of the path, and similarly crammed with treasures. That excellent rich pink shrub, *Indigofera pseudotinctoria*, has the white *Clematis* 'Miss Bateman' and the climbing rose 'Seagull' near it; the miniature pink climbing rose 'Pompon de Paris' is associated with *Rosa glauca* and *Clematis* 'Perle d'Azur'; cream camassias with the flaming *Paeonia lobata* 'Fire King'; the velvety red *Salvia microphylla* (syn. *grahamii*) with the scarlet *Lonicera sempervirens* on the wall above it; the double mauve *Clematis* 'Countess of Lovelace' with the blush rose 'Madame Alfred Carrière'.

It is all a seeming embodiment of those fabled and extrovert herbaceous gardens that have slipped from our grasp into the past. Yet it is a great deal more, for the infiltration of the loveliest shrubs gives it ballast – of roses such as 'La Noblesse' and 'Général Kléber', the modern 'Elizabeth of Glamis' and 'Kronenbourg', of *Carpenteria californica*, hoheria and ceanothus. Such is the density of all the planting that one would suppose that only the survival of the fittest could apply, yet everyone here looks in exuberant health, thanks to

100. The west-facing border in the walled garden of Kellaways. A path runs between this and the backing wall which is festooned with the climbing rose 'Seagull' on the far left.

a selectively applied top dressing of bonemeal in autumn, to the addition of hop manure in spring (very lightweight so much more easily applied than its cumbersome farmyard equivalent) and, not least, the alkaline alluvial soil in which all grow, over free-draining Kellaways limestone rock.

A low wall separates the walled garden from the less formal shrubbery beyond, an area partly contained by a high beech hedge. The same exceptionally rich planting continues here with no opportunity lost (*Clematis spooneri*, for example, festoons a dead paulownia skeleton with its large creamy blossoms), yet the dominant note here in June is formed by the glorious collection of roses. There is an enthralling assortment here of rugosas, damasks, albas, moss roses, but eclectic again for you will find 'Oeuillet Parfait', the double yellow Scots, the modern 'Chianti', 'Fantin-Latour'. These roses provide the culmination of a month-long sweetness of scent in this part of the garden that began with the flowering of huge bushes of *Daphne* x *burkwoodii* and *Daphne pontica*, the latter so big that it crosses the path.

By now it must have become obvious that Mrs. Hoskins is not afraid of plants, unlike so many modern gardeners who dread the labour that more than a quota might involve. But it is in this part of the garden that the reason for her confidence becomes apparent. It is not simply her enormous knowledge of and affection for plants, but it is her real mastery of ground-cover planting, that reviled means of keeping weeds under control and effort to a minimum. In most gardens, both public and private, they have become a *pis-aller*, a way of coping. At Kellaways, Mrs. Hoskins has turned the use of ground-cover plants into the kind of art that convinces you they are a first choice for beauty rather than utility. She uses, for example, carpets of the self-sowing pinkish-mauve *Claytonia sibirica*, in flower for weeks, with purple and pink *Lamium maculatum*. The latter is also planted (see Colour Plate XXI) to make an enchanting spring flower-combination on one side of a grass path with the creamy plumes of *Smilacena racemosa* on the other, topped by the dark pink flowers of *Malus* 'Lemoinei', one of a group of apples including *M.* 'Neville Copeman' with pale mauve blossoms and 'Prince George' with double pink flowers. Pink *Lamium maculatum* is also partnered by Bowles' golden grass with the glowing rich rose-red of *Prunus tenella* 'Fire Hill' nearby. And it is even used as a silvery carpet for the exquisite

101. A remarkable collection of shrub roses and ground-cover plants distinguishes the less formal area.

frilled and spotted pink *Nomocharis pardenthina*, an indicator of Mrs Hoskins' skill, for it is difficult to keep outside the moist and cool regions of this country.

The blue sprays of *Brunnera macrophylla* have their own diminutive underplanting in *Mitella breweri*, a dwarf evergreen with shell-like green foliage and beaded spikes of creamy-green flowers, widely used here as the perfect reticent cover for shady places. A tall silver *Hippophae rhamnoides* is lit by a throng of variegated-leafed purple honesty beneath it. And the range of geraniums in the garden, perhaps as a group the most graceful and subtly coloured of all weed-smotherers, is extensive: the spreading *G. procurrens* (syn. *G. collinum*), *G. macrorrhizum*, *G. sanguineum lancastriense* and 'Glenluce' among others.

Euphorbia robbiae, too, has been given the most intelligent and graceful associations. In the outskirts of the shrubbery, in a difficult area under sycamores, it partners that lovely foliage plant *Stephanandra incisa* 'Crispa' with its little crinkled leaves and mounded form. And, in another self-contained shrubbery, to the other side of the house and screening farm buildings, it makes a large lime-green rug beneath the great blush-white bowls of a *Magnolia* x *soulangiana*. This tree is nearly forty years old, being the first subject to be planted in the garden. It had a bumpy start, for it was eaten to the ground by an escaped calf, then subsequently by a mare. Crushed but not vanquished, it has lived to surmount all that and now makes a great mound of some 20 × 30ft/6 × 9m.

The same gifted and imaginative combinations are to be seen on a large scale in these trees and shrubs, as amongst the herbaceous planting throughout the garden. *Pyrus salicifolia* 'Pendula' is a lovely shimmering silver beside the same white magnolia which had such a difficult childhood. Purple berberis is a foil not only for the silver pear, but on its other side, for the beautiful blush-flowered *Staphylea holocarpa*; with the variegated *Aralia elata* 'Variegata' beside that and, an echo of the same theme, *Cornus alba* 'Elegantissima' beyond. Two huge *Kolkwitzia amabilis* close the reverse side of this group with philadelphus, tree peonies and roses.

There is a tremendous amount to learn in a garden like this, not only in the wise and artistic management of a vast range of plants in a limited space, but also in the balance between calm empty spaces and crowded, eventful areas. A walled swimming-pool enclosure on the outer reaches of the garden is very simply planted, for example (though note the lovely quartered pendent blooms of *Rosa* 'Vicomtesse Pierre de Fou'). Rather, pride of place is given here to a selection of mosaics (by Bath School of Art) in the former calf-pens at one end; to the paving – a good example of a blend of diamond-laid and square-laid slabs; and, in an alcove, to the little lead statue of Diana which, like the figure of Mercury in the walled garden, was a family inheritance.

Simplicity, too, is the keynote around the facade of the house, for nothing is allowed to spoil its calm serenity. A narrow border of tulips hems its feet, lifted in early summer and replaced by, for example, an equally simple line of nicotiana.

It is a joy to explore a generous garden of this kind where living things (not only plants, but white doves, too, whippets and Jack Russells) are the main source of interest rather than the more self-conscious kind of garden sundries. It is a garden that expresses a love of life, and that, quite separately from its capacity to teach, makes it a very happy place to be in.

At the time of writing, Kellaways is open for the National Gardens Scheme once in June, and by appointment only from November to March.

102. A path flanked by pairs of fastigiate yews bissects the walled garden beside the Tudor house.

XVI. Opulent Domesticity
and Quiet Woodland

LOWER HALL in Shropshire is a modern plantsman's garden and amongst the most varied and sumptuous of its class. With four acres of walled enclosures, water and woodland, with both limy and acid soils, it has scope for a huge diversity of plants. But more distinctive still is the way these plants are assembled. Grouped as they are for colour and theme and appropriateness, it is the luxuriance of the whole which strikes you first and your botanical appreciation comes afterwards. This sequence is rarely the case with plantsmen's gardens.

Lower Hall is owned by Christopher and Donna Dumbell. It enjoys as near perfect a site as you could wish, for the garden is bounded by a charming village on one side and by open fields on the other, the whole bissected by the River Worfe. Opportunity was there for the taking and the owners have explored this potential to the full. When they arrived in 1964, there was simply a large walled orchard adjoining the house, and a paddock with beeches, willows and a boggy ditch. In the last twenty years, the Dumbells have not only revolutionized this place, but more than doubled its size as they acquired peripheral land to the east. The garden is therefore their own creation, and one could say much the same

103. The border was designed by Lanning Roper. One of its stars is *Rosa chinensis* 'Mutabilis'.

of the house, for it was only after they stripped its rendered overcoat that its 1550 timber and plaster facade was revealed. The house is now one of the glorious assets of this garden, its Tudor exuberance adding sparkle to the enclosure that flanks it. So, too, do the gables and roofs of the black and white village cottages that peer over the garden wall, for the Dumbells have wisely borrowed rather than concealed this neighbouring architecture and turned it to the garden's advantage.

It is, in fact, one of the great charms of Lower Hall's walled garden that it does not exclude the outside world. The eye is lifted above its confines to a skyline on one side of village roofs and church spire, and on the other side to the soaring trees of the garden beyond. Doors, propped open in invitation, break the length of its walls. And these views that lead both out from the garden and above it, supplement the riches of the planting around you.

This walled garden beside the house is laid out on geometric lines, but it is a complex unit of different areas and sub-divisions, each with its own separate mood and purpose. Two of its areas were designed by Lanning Roper who gave some help with planning and planting, but this garden as a whole is largely the Dumbells' own creation. It was also the first object of their attention when they arrived in 1964. One of their earliest tasks then was to re-lay the concrete paths in a basketweave pattern of old and new bricks. These now border part of the periphery as well as forming the main axis to the house. This axis breaks the garden into two halves, but is also decorative in itself, for its run is broken with a circle of brick paving, lavenders and a bronze sphinx, and its length is flanked with five pairs of fastigiate yews and, at either end, arches for the rambling roses 'Adelaide d'Orléans' and 'Albéric Barbier'.

To the west of this path, the original orchard theme of this garden has been retained, but many of the fruit trees are now canopied with roses and clematis and interspersed with lilacs and large shrub roses. More espalier fruit trees and climbing roses are trained on the sandstone walls beside them; there are white species roses (*R. brunonii*, *R. wichuriana* and

104. (*opposite*) Vertical conifers and mound-forming hostas and rodgersias near the water gardens at Lower Hall.

R. fedtschenkoana), the full-petalled coral-pink 'Dreamgirl', the wide single pink 'Meg', 'Dorothy Perkins' and the purple-maroon 'Rose-Marie Viaud'. Irises and hollyhocks grow in the border beneath them. As the black and white village gables top the wall at this point, the effect is intentionally that of a cottage garden at their feet.

To the east of this central path, both mood and style change, for the walled garden is subdivided here into yew enclosures of separate identity. There is a herb and flower area at the far end, of almost fluorescent brilliance in high summer with the magenta *Geranium psilostemon* and lime *Alchemilla mollis*. In this respect it contrasts with the softer colours in the adjacent yew enclosure which conceals a swimming-pool. Here the terrace and surrounds are planted in yellows, mauves and pinks. *Buddleja alternifolia* with its long mauve tassels in June is partnered by the yellow cones of the silvery *Cytisus battandieri* against the wall. At their feet a columnar golden Irish yew gives height to a small bed of pink lavender, *Geranium* 'Wargrave Pink', helianthemums and *Hebe rakaiensis*. And at skyline level, the whole scene is crowned by the great Scots pines in the garden outside to which the grille-topped door will lead you (shown in Plate 5).

Return along this side of the garden towards the house and you enter the shade of a pergola (its brick piers topped by wooden crossbeams) running beside a garden room which was once a stable block. The pergola is swathed in milky-coloured flowers and the black-graped vine 'Brandt'. The flowers are chosen to give a long season of bloom, starting with *Clematis armandii* and continuing through the year with *Wistaria venusta, Rosa banksia* 'Alba Plena' (a shy bloomer in the Midlands), 'Sander's White' and *Clematis flammula* with its scented froth in autumn. Their pale luminosity is a link with a white border at right angles nearby; its white tulips are followed by white irises, *Geranium sylvaticum album*, shrub and standard 'Iceberg' roses, campanulas and foxgloves, silvery cardoons, artemisias, white lavenders and, last in the sequence, Japanese anemones.

The hedge which backs this border is the reverse of a small, three-side yew enclosure planted by Lanning Roper. Simply a paved area, bordered by lavender and 'Frau Dagmar Hastrup' rugosa roses, it has a quartet of small box cones which centre on a lead fountain and pool. Lanning Roper also designed the house border opposite this garden and seen to the left of Plate 103.

But it is Mrs Dumbell's red and purple raised border further along the same path which excels in genuine glamour. It is unlike the typical red border, for she has taken it in a direction of her own and lit it with volumes of pink to wonderful effect. Mounds of dark foliage are provided by the pink-flowered *Weigela florida* 'Foliis Purpureis' and purple sage; underplanting includes bergenias, valerian, ballotas, *Fuchsia* 'Riccartonii', blue-leafed dianthus and hebes (*H. pimeleoides* 'Glaucocaerulea'). These are a foil to *Indigofera heterantha* (syn. *I. gerardiana*), *Buddleja* 'Lochinch', *Cytisus* 'Mrs Dorothy Walpole Improved', and old and modern shrub roses such as the striped gallica 'Rosa Mundi', blood-red 'Fountain', 'Stephen Langdon', 'Redcoat', and the burgundy hybrid perpetual with a white picotee edge, 'Roger Lambelin'. Two huge and brilliant 'Cerise Bouquet' dominate the border, whilst the roses on the wall are more softly shaded ('Norwich Pink' and 'Glory of Edzell', a single pink with a yellow eye). Other beauties include the pink *Robinia hispida* trained against the wall and a voluptuous shower of *Kolkwitzia amabilis* 'Pink Cloud' which backs 'Cerise Bouquet'.

This last combination is a marvellous success, the more so as a door in the wall stands open beside this partnership, allowing you a view into a small green enclosure beyond.

XX and XXI. Kellaways (Chapter XV): marvellous colour in the walled garden *(above)* and the shrubbery *(below)* with *Malus* 'Lemoinei', *Smilacena racemosa* and *Lamium maculatum*.

XXII *(previous page)* A Japanese garden in Oxfordshire (Chapter XVIII): water, stone and green foliage are used to create scenes whose precision never disturbs the tranquillity.

XXIII. *(left)* The first breathtaking view from the blind entrance to the Japanese garden.

XXIV. *(below)* Well Cottage (Chapter XVII): the front garden with *Iris sibirica,* geraniums, *Clematis* 'The President', which provide shades of violet, and *Asphodeline lutea* the golden spires. Pink *Polygonum bistorta* 'Superbum' is in the background.

This bewitching transition, with warm foreground colour impacted against background green, is shown in Colour Plate X.

This self-contained green enclosure lies at the foot of the west façade of the house. It was dug out by the Dumbells to form a sunken gravel garden, bordered by raised beds of evergreens – *Euphorbia wulfenii*, camellias, *Yucca filamentosa*, ivies and ferns, their greens enlivened in summer by the lime of alchemillas. A tiered and fluted circular stone fountain surrounded by a quartet of potted cupressus is the centrepiece. Further pots of evergreens and evergreys such as *Dorycnium hirsutum* are assembled on the semi-circular steps at the foot of the house wall (shown in Plate 61).

To enter this cool atmosphere after the exhilaration of the red border is to experience the truth of one of Chevreul's colour theories in his nineteenth-century thesis; that, due to after-image, the eye expects green after red, for example, and is satisfied to receive it. It is, in fact, the same refreshing effect to be gained at Hidcote (see page 102).

To some extent you experience a similarly calming transition as you leave the effervescence of the main walled garden and walk into the outer garden across peaceful lawns. Your destination is the water garden, but you see on your left a blue and yellow border of *Ceanothus thyrsiflorus*, campanulas, violas, hemerocallis and rues, around a white seat. And to your right is an old group of Scots pines, halesias, *Cornus kousa chinensis*, a lime tree and the scented, pink *Robinia pseudoacacia* 'Rosea' which has grown huge since its planting here in 1968.

A small stone bridge with a balustraded inset (see Plate 32), flanked by rush-leafed plants, connects the lawn with the water gardens. The lake here is about 4ft/1.2m deep: the Dumbells have since been advised that a greater depth would have freed it of surface duckweed. It has a thick margin of *Caltha* species, primulas (though there is a fight in progress against primula sickness), water-loving irises, astilbes and mimulus. But the foliage effects are quite as rich. Note the airy creamy and green masses of *Cornus alba* 'Elegantissima' at the north-facing end, topping *Darmera peltata* (syn. *Peltiphyllum peltatum*); and the rheums, gunneras, bergenias and *Arundinaria nitida*.

The waterfall in the rock garden and the lake are supplied by water from the River Worfe, raised by a hydram, a most ingenious piece of engineering which harnesses gravity, works night and day and takes no electricity (see Appendix for a supplier). The river itself pours over two widely spaced weirs (the second added later) both built of cemented bricks over concrete footings. An ornamental wooden bridge crosses the water near this point, which in winter roars and sometimes floods around it.

You have now arrived at the third stage of the garden, a highly cultivated woodland. However, when the Dumbells first acquired this long strip of land, bordered to the west by a stream, it was simply a patch of scrub, alders, brambles and nettles. They cleared it and, since this left them exposed, began to plant it in masses and glades. It now contains the most discerningly selected of coniferous and broad-leafed trees. Until the winter of 1981, it had also a wonderful collection of rhododendrons, but of the species and woodland hybrids few survived except for some hardies, *R. yakushimanum* and *R. bureauvii* (the frost-pocket proved too much for the tenderer varieties). There are abundant riches, however, from other genera. Among the magnolias, you find the rare *M. tripetala* with widely splayed creamy and sticky petals, *M. hypoleuca* (syn. *M. obovata*) with its great scented creamy bowls and dark red stamens, *M. loebneri, M. soulangiana* and the fragrant white *M. wilsonii* (*M. campbellii* did not survive the 1981 winter). Young groups of birches are here, too, to supply bark interest: *Betula ermanii* with its pink-apricot trunk, *B. nigra* with its peeling bark, *B. albosinensis septentrionalis* for its shining rufous trunk. The red-barked *Prunus serrula* and *Pinus ponderosa* with its patterned tree-trunk are assets for the same reason. Other conifers include *P. sylvestris*, *Metasequoia glyptostroboides* and also the Japanese *Sciadopitys verticillata* with·its whorled needle habit. Since the Dumbells have planted for interest here throughout the year, they have added Japanese maples, parrotias and amelanchiers for autumn colour amongst the darkness of the evergreens. And all these specimen trees rightly take their place against the quieter backcloth of native field and woodland trees: poplars, oaks, alders and maples and white birches.

The underplanting in the woodland is in part labour-saving with great swatches of *Pachysandra terminalis*, epimediums, lamiums and low-growing gaultherias; and, in part, highly demanding, for in certain areas there are virtually herbaceous beds. One of these is composed of North American woodlanders, such as *Viola cucculata*, dodecatheons, clintonias, *Podophyllum emodi* and masses of trilliums. Both these last are a reminder to Mrs. Dumbell of her American background, for they grow wild in the woodlands there.

At the end of the long glade stands a small temple (Colour Plate XIII), shaded by trees, and hemmed with a triplet of *Erica arborea alpina* with their scented white bells in spring. This point precedes the transition to the last and most recently acquired part of the garden, where the land grows noticeably softer and wilder. Here the Dumbells have rented open woodland and planted it with Tenby daffodils and fritillaries, and encouraged bluebells and ferns either side of the mown grass paths.

Within its four acres, the garden has therefore encompassed two extremes, progressing from opulent domesticity to its opposite of quiet wilderness. But the taste and knowledge of the owners shows in all its parts. It shows in the fact that the best forms of plants are used. It shows in their choice of plants for foliage interest and ease and shapeliness of habit. And it shows, of course, in their colour. This last is especially important to Mrs Dumbell who, as an American, is perhaps more careful in her use of it in England than the English themselves, seeing it with a fresher eye. In her own words, England is not a place for harsh colour: with the exception of the berrying season, our hedgerows are so softly shaded. But, unlike many of the English too, she is not afraid to experiment with colour, and the garden she and her husband have created is effervescent with fresh ideas for plant associations.

So far, I have ignored the question of maintenance. A garden of this complexity is hugely demanding, though the Dumbells keep it in the highest order through their own efforts and those of one full-time gardener. As little as possible is left to chance. The vast array of roses grown here means a large pruning programme and scrupulous attention to spraying. All tender plants and even some that are very marginally hardy are given a winter blanket of conifer brashings woven around a structure of poles. The attentions of the tree-surgeon are required every three or four years to doctor the woodland. Yet the controls that are essential to a garden of this kind never interfere with the voluptuousness of its effects, the impression of luxurious abundance. Plants are allowed to self-sow – from foxgloves to *Smilacena racemosa* to Solomon's Seals; climbers such as wistarias, roses and clematis are encouraged to envelop trees; shrubs arch unfettered to the ground. Fizzing with ideas, sensuously planted and admirably maintained, this garden should be an exemplar to other plantsmen.

Lower Hall is usually open to the public once a year under the National Gardens Scheme.

105. The embowered back of Well Cottage and its terrace.

XVII. A Designer's Cottage Garden

IN THE FAR WEST of Herefordshire there is a line of hills called Blakemere Ridge. It is ground that Kilvert walked, the last high land in England before Wales to the west. Blakemere village lines the road at the foothills, and here a garden of quality leaps out from the landscape.

It is a small, front garden before a pink plaster and timber cottage. It has cottage garden characteristics — a cornucopia of herbaceous plants, the lowness of the fronting stone wall which exposes it to view from the road — yet it clearly defies such categorization. Its mix of plants is untypical: *Iris sibirica*, geraniums, inulas and asphodels. And their colours are unusually intense and controlled: rich violet-blues, light yellow, a touch of pink, all glowing in an organized green framework which stabilizes their evanescence. In short, real beauty has been conjured, not just predictable cottage prettiness (see Colour Plate XXIV).

A closer inspection confirms the art that has gone into its making. There are none of the drawbacks that come with a traditional cottage garden, such as haphazard colours and structure, or an over-dependence on ephemeral flowers. All this has been rejected in favour of a more sophisticated compromise. Plants have been chosen to flower in continuous succession, and herbaceous subjects are balanced by evergreens of strong foliage and shape: *Euphorbia characias*, *Cotoneaster* 'Hybridus Pendulus', *Ruscus aculeatus*, x *Fatshedera lizei*.

In its sophisticated mix, this front garden proves the prelude for a cottage garden entirely in its own mould. For 'Well Cottage' is a garden with peonies, but, equally, banks of zantedeschias; *Aralia elata* 'Variegata' yet also delphiniums; a wild flower 'meadow' but phormiums too. Impossible to blend, one might suppose, but the owners, Richard and Vroni Edwards, have done it with tact, panache – and, admittedly, specialist knowledge.

At this point, I need to digress a little to explain this last comment. Gardens, which are so often discussed simply in terms of pH factors, climate and plants, are really the result of something much less discussable: namely, their owner's personality, knowledge and development. To the nursery rhyme question 'How does your garden grow?', there is but one answer: it grows as you do. In the case of the Edwards, this is especially true, for halfway through making their garden, they enrolled on a one-year certificate course in garden design at a main horticultural college. Vroni Edwards thus made the front garden and the terrace at the rear when she was a keen amateur; and she made the remainder after she had become a certificated garden designer. Both 'before' and 'after' parts are seamlessly linked, but there is a development in ambitiousness to be traced on the ground.

Before, however, exploring this in detail, more general facts are in order. The plot extends to about three-quarters of an acre, all in view of the house. In the owner's words, it is 'wedge-shaped', splaying out towards the end, with a shared right-of-way to one side and an additional area beyond that. In front is the road with, opposite, a garage and more houses. But at the back, in an arc as far as you can see on either side, are the green fields, at first flat and calm and then rising steeply to the great hills behind. Here is the true asset of this garden's site. The front garden, alone, is concealed from them; but move to the rear of the house and Blakemere Ridge forms a powerful backcloth, even from the terrace at the foot of the cottage.

This dominant view of the hills has had a twofold influence on the garden's design. Firstly, it prevented the garden from being an oasis which is unrelated to the land outside. The Edwards respected this point by rejecting conventional boundary hedging in favour of a free-growing and mixed assembly of trees and shrubs, a shelter-belt against the prevailing wind. But Blakemere Ridge affected the garden in a second way. The visible criss-cross of the fields up the foothills demanded a garden-layout which sympathized with their lines. This the owners solved by dividing the remaining length of the garden into an irregular sequence of three areas, linked by paths which curve widely from side to side. Made by Mr. Edwards from local stone roof tiles, sunk in concrete studded with local pebbles, they blend with the landscape. Moreover, they make the lines of the rear garden flow with the fields rather than fighting them; forming, as it were, a small prelude to the foothills. The planting of a Scots pine to the left of the garden is also a link with a conifer high up in the hills (the latter now takes on a role like one of William Kent's eyecatchers – though it may die if it learns of its new responsibility).

The garden was flat when the Edwards arrived. To provide additional interest, they gave it a change of height with a bulldozer. Thus a sunken terrace to the rear of the cottage now leads to a small lawned plateau (contained by retaining stone walls) which is followed by another drop in levels. The sheltered position that the terrace thereby enjoys makes it very snug and it looks it, moreover, for it is cushioned in bosomy evergreens that make its enclosure inviting even in January (see Plate 105). It is flowery, too, with *Clematis armandii*, *C.* 'Mrs. Cholmondeley' and *Rosa* 'Madame Alfred Carrière' on the pinkish house wall (the colour of local sand, so it blends into the landscape); with peonies and

106. The hills form the backcloth. Grass flows like a river from side to side between groups of plants.

scented honeysuckle to the one side of the terrace, and with *Ceanothus thyrsiflorus repens*, *Chaenomeles* 'Nivalis', *Daphne odora* 'Aureomarginata' and *Escallonia* 'Iveyii' to the other. Plants thrive in the paving, for the soakaway beneath ensures excellent drainage; rosemary, *Cistus corbariensis, Cotinus* 'Royal Purple', *Stipa calamagrostis* and prostrate creepers and cushions like purple-leafed clovers and *Dianthus deltoides*. You encounter the quirky individuality here, too, of *Fuchsia microphylla*. The majority of such plants are sufficient to give form and cover throughout the year, but they are not allowed to obscure the excellent detail of the paving itself. Heavy stone slabs (each was numbered and charted to the ½inch/12mm on a graph before being transferred to its allotted position) form a wide border around a central rectangle of brick paving (matching the bricks used inside the house – a careful link). And a clever and inventive solution was found for the manhole problem, which was disguised by a surround of diagonally laid bricks and topped with a flagstone lid.

This terrace was designed before Mrs Edwards had received her professional qualification. The remainder of the garden was, however, completed at a later stage and the owners were thus able to draw on their training to help them. Vroni Edwards's first step was to draw a scale site-survey and analysis-plan of the area, incorporating every detail that could be useful. Thus the information concerned not only soil, drainage, rainfall, land-levels, instructions on what to keep and what to banish, but also drew attention to exploitable possibilities (e.g. 'only window in cottage low enough to see out from a sitting position') and to dangers to be avoided (e.g. 'ditch-water coming from the south-west occasionally' or 'beware colour of flowers and foliage seen against house walls'). Armed thus, Mrs Edwards planned her design for the remainder of the garden.

Even if you were colour-blind, it would still be obvious that this part of the garden was the work of a trained designer. From a higher viewpoint (an upstairs window, for

189

example), the abstract pattern of the garden and the relationship between its spaces and island beds becomes evident. Other clues to a professional influence include the use of large groups of the same plant, the manipulation of drifts, links in leaf shape or in colour or in habit between plants. Thus, Mrs Edwards has controlled the leaf colour here in the large, informally shaped beds. The result is that your eye moves from dark greens on the left (*Lonicera pileata* and *Rubus tricolor* for evergreen groundcover, *Pinus sylvestris* for height, and an airy infiltration between of white-barked birches, *Betula pendula* 'Tristis', *B.p.* 'Dalecarlica' and *B. jacquemontii*); through to mid-greens in the centre bed above the terrace (predominantly *Choisya ternata*); and on to silver and grey-greens on the right. Here the eye takes in *Elaeagnus* x *ebbingei*, senecios, *Iris pallida argenteo-variegata*, *Euphorbia wulfenii*, *Hebe albicans*, *Eucalyptus niphophila* and the glorious *Aralia elata* 'Variegata', a shrubby tree with white-margined large ferny leaves and plumes of white flowers.

At the far end, beds flank juniper-dressed steps which lead down from the plateau into a second lawned area. Both beds are planted for pastel flower effects: with *Ceanothus thyrsiflorus repens, Caryopteris clandonensis* 'Kew Blue', *Potentilla* 'Abbotswood', *Buddleja alternifolia* and a large group of *Acanthus spinosus* to the left; and, to the right, *Cistus* 'Silver Pink', *Rubus Tridel* 'Benenden', *Viburnum plicatum* 'Mariesii', the lilac-pink *Magnolia* 'Leonard Messel' for height, and a drift of *Morina longifolia*. The latter with its long-lasting seed heads has been planted to form a wonderfully cut-leafed and spiry combination in summer with the later-flowering *Acanthus spinosus* in the other bed.

Beyond these borders, this second lawned area is spare and uncrowded, supporting simply a great monolith on its grass (a Christmas present – real gardeners will understand). Like a group of massive stones on the path in the previous section of the garden, it makes a comfortable seat; like that, too, it is a focal point, but not too much so. Beyond, to the left, is a dark-leafed and predominantly red planting of *Weigela florida* 'Foliis Purpureis', *Rosa* 'Parkdirektor Riggers', *Photinia* x *fraseri* 'Red Robin'; and a complementary but lighter planting to the right surrounding a damson of beautiful shape thanks to Richard Edwards' pruning.

The path which has continued to roll from side to side now leads through a 'gateway' of *Aesculus parviflora* (an admirable shrub for bold foliage and white flowers with red anthers in later summer) to the last section of the garden – a wilder area, consisting of a flower meadow and a pool. The native *Cardamine pratensis* was already here in the damp grass, but to this the Edwards added two wild flower mixes, one for damp shade and the other for open but moisture-retentive meadow. The first selection includes foxgloves, red campion, figwort, teasel, hedge parsley etc.; for the open meadow, there are ox-eye daisies, cranesbill, yarrow, cowslip, bird's foot trefoil, buttercup, vetch etc. Great mullein (*Verbascum thapsus*) and self-heal (*Prunella vulgaris*) are common to both mixes.

The pool is some 2ft/60cm deep, dug from impermeable, heavy clay subsoil by a JCB. Primulas and irises fringe its banks, but its stars are a group of nearly twenty *Zantedeschia aethiopica* planted 8in/20cm below the water's surface. Their quantity alone would make them dazzling, but it is their positioning that lifts them to perfection. Their white sculptured flowers are marvellously framed against grouped component parts of a cider mill, transported here on a forestry lorry. These stones are not only the culmination of the two large stone assemblies further back in the domestic parts of the garden, but they are also a link with the Ridge. For here, in these ancient hills, there is a neolithic monument called Arthur's stone. Thus the *genius loci* has been captured in this garden.

107. Creepers on the house integrate it into the garden, where bamboos are pruned into blocks.

XVIII. A Modern House in the Country

WHITE DOOR in a white wall opens. You pass through to a tiled porch. Baffled by a facing wall, for you have entered obliquely through the side of the porch, there is a second's confusion. A sideways turn. Then the sudden mirage of an intensely green, stone- and water-filled Japanese landscape. It seems a conjuring trick, so exotic the vision and so concentrated its loveliness. No matter how jaded your palate, the shock of a blind entry on this beauty must be a fresh experience and one which remains uneclipsed.

I have left this Oxfordshire garden till the last in this book, because it is exceptional and not only in its un-Englishness. It is also the most ambitious and the most surprising. One cannot avoid the concomitant that it is equally the most uncompromising in the degree of absolute perfection it has exacted in its creation and now in its upkeep.

The owner of the garden is Milton Grundy, Chairman of the Warwick Arts Trust, and the designer is the painter, Atroshenko. That the latter is an abstract expressionist, that he was born in Hong Kong, that he has visited the most famous of the Japanese gardens, all these are factors which are crucial to this garden's success. It could not have been created by an uneducated, untravelled or unpainterly eye – nor by an Englishman.

To begin at the beginning, the origins of the house and garden were in 1959. From the start they were intended to be interconnected, an aspiration that is difficult to fulfil

191

108. The gravel garden, indebted to but subtly changed from the garden of Ryoan-ji in Kyoto.

successfully unless you build for both (mentally if not literally) at the same time. In this case, such planning was essential as it involved the use of certain materials when constructing the house. Although it is made of traditional Cotswold stone, fibreglass and resin were incorporated into its base, as the water in the garden was designed to lap at its walls as in a moat.

The house itself is uncompromisingly modern in its form, and one realizes at once, in that first breathtaking view from the entrance, why a Japanese garden was so brilliant a choice. Here is an ideal complement to a modern stone house. It echoes its materials – its stone, sand and wood. It reinforces its reflective surfaces, matching the great glass windows with the horizontal mirrors of its own water. Its plants are trained to link house with garden, certain bamboos for example pruned into strong blocks and, contrastingly, free-growing creepers tied to the house walls. And – perhaps the most perfect example of visual harmony – from within the house, the garden appears at each floor-length window like a series of huge wall-paintings.

A marvellous choice of garden-style, then, but bear in mind that a Japanese garden is by far the hardest kind to do well. There are successful large-scale examples on the moist West Coast of America, but here, in our drier climate, there are too many examples which rely on just bits and pieces of water and hardware, random lanterns and the odd tea-house, the mispresented legacy of a short-lived cult which had its heyday in England around the turn of the century. These do not convey that coherence of Eastern vision which can only be attained by synthesizing many different ingredients so that they flow effortlessly into each other on the canvas.

In a traditional Japanese garden, this unity is achieved by a perfect sense of proportion, by a disciplined purity of style and by the symbolism that particular features carry to express a philosophy and outlook. The garden is a living landscape of mountains and rivers and seas, 'borrowed' through the inclusion of small hillocks, stones, pebbles and water. In Mr. Grundy's garden, there is wisely no such weight of foreign piety and symbolism with its complicated laws and theories. But unity *has* been created within the quarter-of-an-acre garden by the perfect proportions between stones and water and plants, between light and darkness, and space and enclosures.

These open and hidden areas are linked to each other by a sequence of stepping-stones and paths which take the visitor on a long looped circuit round the garden. His journey rewards him with the most enchanting glimpses of other spaces. He would not wish to hasten, but his progress must in any case be slow because he treads on stepping-stones, which sometimes rise and fall in different heights. This unhurried pace in itself gives a feeling of great tranquillity. Thus, in the mood it evokes of quiet meditation, this garden meets the requirements of Japanese tradition.

The central spine of this enclosed, intensely private garden is formed out of two irregularly shaped lakes. Surrounding the house, they are crossed by bridges and bordered at different points by moss, pebbles, irises and the spreading foliage canopies of shrubs. Around this water-filled core of the garden, there are certain clearly defined areas, some of which can be seen at their most spectacular from a raised platform at the head of the garden which gives a long overall view.

Some of these distinct areas owe their origin to certain famous gardens of Japan, whereas other parts are less precise, and the furthest reaches almost English wild garden. The gravel garden near the house is one example of a specific type of Japanese garden. It is indebted

109. The moss garden beneath the huge chestnut, green and empty.

to the most famous temple garden in Japan, that of Ryoan-ji in the old capital city of Kyoto. Here, stones are grouped in a bed of raked gravel within a courtyard. In the absence of any record, various interpretations have been given for this garden. One explains it as the frozen moment when the islands of Japan (the stones) were dropped into the sea (the gravel) which rippled at their impact (and is raked accordingly into a pattern of circles round the stones and straight lines in the spaces). Milton Grundy's English version has these stones and patterned gravel and also the 50 yd/46m-long varnished and canopied wall beside the garden (though in Ryoan-ji, the original thirteenth century wall is made of mud). But there is nothing stereotyped about this English imitation. There is a personal addition, for example, in the small summerhouse closing the end of this gravel garden. It is a building worth noting in itself. To comply with the owner's wish that it should seem like an old and traditional Cotswold barn, the architects set back the rear of the summerhouse by 5°, giving a consequential slant to the roof level.

Subtlety of this kind is apparent throughout the garden. Similar care has been taken with the sand garden that leads to the house entrance. Most people would make this flat. Instead, it is very shallowly pillow-shaped. Equal refinement is shown elsewhere. At some points of the garden, there are small hillocks covered in moss; steps up these banks direct your feet to a predetermined perspective on the garden.

All these are feats of design and construction, but perhaps it is the making of the moss garden that defies belief. Although moss is used at various points around the garden, the

194

main area lies beneath a huge and densely leafed horse-chestnut tree which already existed when the garden was begun. This moss garden with its lantern and stepping-stones and, above all, its emptiness is somewhat indebted to a garden in Kyoto but, whatever its origins, the establishment of this great, green, velvety carpet here has involved a continuing commitment. In the first place, moss has to be carefully gathered and pressed into the earth (a well-trodden soil with plenty of nitrogen is important for its growth, as it will not thrive in loose earth). It must then be kept free of leaves and twigs, swept like a carpet or, in the owner's words: 'One needs a Buddhist monk to brush moss as a spiritual exercise before the day begins.' Mossy problems do not end here. It needs re-positioning in places, for birds scratch it up, especially in winter and early spring in their search for insects. And at all times of the year, weeds and grass are always threatening to infiltrate its uniform green. (Bird scarers are the answer to the former and a very dilute solution of gramoxone to the latter.) But the greatest problem of all is its need for moisture. In this garden, the owner had to incorporate an irrigation system that could keep it sprinkled twice a day in dry weather.

In fact, the whole garden has been made in the teeth of a climate and soil which would have daunted lesser mortals. The soil is sufficiently alkaline here to exact continual treatment of lime-hating plants. There are, for example, a great many azaleas here, exploding with colour amongst the green of early summer, but these will only thrive on a fortnightly diet of Maxicrop and iron.

The materials of the garden have come from varied sources. The pebbles beside the water are from Eastbourne, the tall stones from Westmorland (an area which produces hard stone which, when frozen in winter, will not absorb water and split) and some of the stone ornaments were composed by a masonry firm in Battersea which rejoiced in receiving such a congenial commission compared with their stock requests for gargoyles. This quantity of stoneware has been softened, however, by the abundant leafiness throughout the garden. Birches, bamboos, azaleas, *Cotoneaster horizontalis* are planted repeatedly, but varied by cherries, lilacs, wistarias, *Corylopsis glabrescens*, precisely grown conifers, ferns in the shade and *Iris pseudacorus* beside the water. Roses and honeysuckle festoon a viewing platform. Lacy maples, a Japanese favourite, colour brilliantly in autumn. *Magnolia sieboldii* is another link with Japan, symbolizing in the briefness of its blossoms the Oriental view of the transience of life.

But at the far end of the garden, the sophistication is deliberately diluted and there is a grassy patch with the feel of an English woodland clearing. Blue, pink and white bluebells have naturalized, white potentilla and lilac give a change of height. Indeed, this abundance of enclosing foliage both here and round the rest of the garden gives the strange effect that one cannot tell where the garden stops.

It serves as well to hide the fox-proof netting that has been erected to protect a collection of ornamental waterfowl. Ducks have no part in a Japanese garden (it was storks and cranes with their formal poise which graced their gardens) but this little family of tufted ducks, European and red-crested pochards, ringed teals and even an interloping white egg-layer are a facet of this garden's absorbing personality. Together with the wild garden, they provide contradictory aspects. They prevent this lovely place from being trapped in the kind of ruthless aesthetic which cannot tolerate a carefree intrusion. They help the garden to belong here. They prevent it from being an illusion. There is a liveliness in the formal perfection.

1. Specimen Trees

CONIFERS

	Special Features	Growth, Ultimate Height and Soil	Site and Associations
Araucaria auracana (Monkey Puzzle)	Dark green, spiny leaves on rope-like branches. Open habit and domed outline when mature. Sombre and weird appearance.	Vigorous when young. Moist loam. 66ft/20m.	Extensively planted in the Victorian era.
Abies bracteata	Very dark green leaves on weeping branchlets and whiskery cones. Very beautiful fir. Pyramid outline.	Fast-growing. Best in sheltered sites. Deep moist soil. 80ft/25m.	Only for very large gardens.
Cedrus atlantica	Dark green broad-spreading tree with barrel-shaped cones. Most widely planted in its blue form, *C. a.* 'Glauca'.	Rapid when young. 116ft/35m.	Only for very large gardens. Blue form usually ill-sited.
C. libani (Cedar of Lebanon)	Dark green needles, tabular branches. Spreading outline and flat top.	Not so fast as the above. 80ft/25m.	Large gardens only. 18th century associations.
Cunninghamia lanceolata	Shiny green leaves with two silver bands on underside. Bushy when young, becoming gaunt in age. Drawback can be browning back behind shoots.	Slow at first, then rapid. Needs sheltered position to avoid damage. 30ft/9m.	Very exotic-looking tree, suited to an idiosyncratic inner area.
Gingko biloba	Deciduous conifer. Exquisite ribbed pale-green foliage yellows in autumn. Slim, conic outline when young but can get broad in age.	Fairly slow. 80ft/25m.	Suited to large inner or outer garden.
Juniperus recurva coxii (Coffin Juniper)	Dark greyish-green leaves on long, weeping branchlets. Large shrub or small tree with conic outline	Medium growth to 33ft/10m.	Very graceful tree for confined area. Give shelter.
Picea brewerana (Brewer's weeping spruce)	Hung with deep green curtains of weeping branchlets. Slim, conic outline	Slow to 50ft/15m.	Again, very graceful.
P. smithiana	Similarly drooping branchlets to the above but not quite so long. Bears purplish cones up to 7in/17.5cm long.	Quick-growing to 100ft/30m.	Needs much larger area than above.
Pinus bungeana	Patchwork bark of cream, purple, brown, green. Leaves bound in threes. Often low-branching. Very ornamental.	Slowish to 50ft/15m.	Distinctive in inner or outer garden.
P × holfordiana	Long silvery-green leaves, like *Pinus wallichiana* (see below) of which it is a hybrid. Banana-shaped cones. Wide-spreading and needs space.	Fast-growing to 80ft/25m.	Twentieth-century hybrid and one of best ornamental pines for large modern garden.
P. montezumae	Most beautiful of all pines with blue-grey needles about 8in/20cm long and equally long cones. Reddish bark. Broad, domed crown.	Not entirely hardy and ill-suited outside mild areas. 66ft/20m.	Very dramatic, almost tropical effect.
P. patula	Rich green pendulous leaves, reddish bark, conic outline.	Best in sheltered sites. Fast to 30ft/10m.	Exellent for stonework area if not cramped. Gives lush effect.
P. pinea (Stone Pine)	Umbrella-shaped conifer with dark grey-green needles in pairs. Rugged, picturesque tree with a wide spread eventually.	Slow-growing to 30ft/10m.	Mediterranean associations. Eventually needs space but good on very large terrace.
P. wallichiana (syn. *P. griffithii*, *P. excelsa*)	Up to 8in/20cm long, grey-silver-green needles in fives, long banana-shaped cones. Wide-spreading near ground.	Fast-growing to 80ft/25m.	Very handsome tree for large gardens only. Excellent for modern or Victorian settings.

Podocarpus macrophyllus	Lush-looking large shrub or small tree with long, bright green (glaucous beneath) leaves.	Vigorous but not for chalk soils. 33ft/10m. Not for cold areas.	Gives tropical effect in sheltered site.
P. salignus	Small tree or large shrub, often forking low. Long grey-green leaves.	Fairly vigorous. Best in shelter. Moist soil. 40ft/12m.	As above.
Pseudolarix amabile	Deciduous conifer with pale green leaves turning gold, then rust in autumn. Often shrubby when young, then broadly conic.	Needs lime-free soil. Slow to 40ft/12m. Hardy but prone to frost damage when young.	Very beautiful tree for a classical setting.
Sciadopitys verticillata (Umbrella Pine)	Unique appearance with long, lush leaves, arranged in dense spokes around stem. Bushy for a long time, then pyramidal.	Needs moist, lime-free soil and bears part-shade. Very slow to 45ft/13m.	Tropical, strange appearance. Looks handsome near water. Excellent in enclosed garden.
Taxodium distichum (Swamp Cypress)	Deciduous conifer whose leaves turn rust in autumn. Late into leaf in spring. In wet soil, develops 'knees', woody projections from roots.	Will grow in water-logged soil but should be 'mound-planted'. Lime-hater. Slow to 100ft/30m.	Grown beside rivers and pools. Large gardens only.
Tsuga canadensis 'Pendula'	Weeping form of Eastern Hemlock making a low mound of drooping branches.	Very slow growth indeed to about 6ft/2m by about 13ft/4m.	Bizarre, even monstrous appearance, but striking on a terrace.

BROAD-LEAFED TREES (Deciduous and evergreen)

Acer cappadocicum 'Aureum'	Maple with seven-lobed leaves, yellow when young and in autumn. Broad crown.	Fast-growing to 33ft/10m.	Fine centrepiece in golden-foliage garden or near yellow lysichitums in spring.
A. davidii	Fine snake-bark maple, grey-green striped white. Often multi-stemmed. Good autumn colour.	20ft/6m. Avoid sunbaked site.	Lovely on a terrace, in open garden or in woodland. Small garden candidate.
A. griseum	Magnificent reddish-brown flaking bark. Three-lobed leaves colouring in autumn. Outline broadens with age.	Slow to 16ft/5m. Avoid sun-baked site.	As above.
A. platanoides 'Drummondii'	Green leaves margined with creamy-white, though edges tend to brown as season advances. Broad crown. Leaves can revert to plain green.	Fast to 40ft/12m. Better in a sheltered position to delay tendency of leaves to brown.	One of the best trees for highlighting a dark background.
Arbutus × *andrachnoides*	Hybrid with marvellous red-brown bark, often multi-stemmed. Evergreen leaves, small red 'strawberry' fruit.	Quite fast to 40ft/12m.	Grand tree for a very large terrace or near a house.
Castanea sativa (Sweet or Spanish Chestnut)	Conic when young, broad-domed when old. Ornamental ridged trunk. Good yellow in autumn. Lime-green catkins in summer.	Fast-growing to 100ft/30m.	Wonderful ornamental in open outer ground of large garden.
Cercidiphyllum japonicum	Branches in regular, pendulous, horizontal and ascending arrangement. Usually fine autumn colour.	Rapid to 50ft/15m. Best in moist soil.	Elegant winter outline so plant near the house where it can be admired then.
Cercis siliquastrum (Judas Tree)	Heart-shaped leaves on bushy, shrubby tree. Massed with deep pink-lilac pea flowers in late spring/early summer.	Slow to 40ft/12m	Lovely tree for a terrace or against dark evergreen background so that flowers will show.
Cornus controversa 'Variegata'	Tiered wedding-cake arrangement of branches. Silver-variegated leaves and cream flowers in early summer.	Slow to 20ft/6m.	Must have space so that tiered habit is visible. Best against dark background.

Davidia involucrata (Handkerchief Tree)	Broad outline, but unimpressive until it is old enough (10–20 years) to produce great white bracts in early summer.	To 50ft/15m.	Only spectacular in flower so a last choice for a specimen where space is limited.
Eucalyptus gunnii	Rounded evergreen blue-grey juvenile leaves, sickle-shaped and grey-green in age. Conic when young, tall-domed when old.	Very fast to 100ft/30m.	Exotic appearance, good for associating with maquis plants in large garden.
E. niphophila	Beautifully patterned python-bark and often multi-stemmed. Grey-green evergreen leaves. Best in a sheltered but open site to prevent tendency to lean sideways.	Quite fast to 30ft/9m.	Lovely terrace tree though casts little shade; or good as a dominant plant in a white garden.
Fagus sylvatica 'Purpurea Pendula' (Weeping Copper Beech)	Mushroom habit. Glistening copper leaves.	Very slow to 24ft/7m.	For small, colour-related areas.
F. s. 'Heterophylla'	Fern-leafed beech with finely cut leaves, but branches can revert if damaged. Very ornamental.	Fairly rapid to 100ft/30m.	Only for a large garden but fine lawn specimen.
Fraxinus excelsior 'Pendula' (Weeping Ash)	Wide-speading weeping tree, late into leaf, but branch habit sufficiently exciting for winter value.	Fast-growing to 50ft/15m.	Wonderful lawn specimen given space.
F. e. 'Jaspidea'	Golden-yellow shoots and branches give good winter value. Leaves yellow in spring and autumn.	Vigorous, 50ft/15m.	Lovely boundary and open space specimen at all times of the year. Large garden.
Koelreuteria paniculata	Pinnate leaves, reddish in spring, yellow in autumn. Crowned with yellow flowers in panicles in later summer. Broad-headed tree.	Flowers best in a warm dry situation, though any soil suitable. 40ft/12m.	Useful for a small garden, but broad crown casts a lot of shade.
Liriodendron tulipifera (Tulip Tree)	Large saddle-shaped leaves, yellowing in autumn. Broad-headed outline. Orange and green-marked 'tulip' flowers in early summer when 15–25 years.	Fast to 100ft/30m.	Only for large gardens, but fine open ground or boundary specimen.
Magnolia campbellii mollicomata	Great pink flowers like waterlilies in earliest spring on bare branches when 12–18 years old.	Good, lime-free soil. 60ft/18m.	Mild area and shelter preferable to avoid damage to early flowers. Especially impressive where tree can be viewed from a higher point.
M. c. m. 'Lanarth' *M. c. m.* 'Caerhays Belle'	Magnificent, large, dark cyclamen coloured flowers. Salmon pink flowers in massed display.	As above As above	As above. As above
M. hypoleuca (syn. *M. obovata*)	Summer-flowering. 8in/20cm wide, very scented, white flowers with crimson stamens against large grey-green leaves. Bushy when young, gaunt in age.	Lime-free soil. Fairly vigorous to 25ft/7.5m.	Exotic-looking tree, well suited to site near a house.
M × loebneri 'Leonard Messel'	Starry, lilac-pink flowers (darker buds) in spring on bare branches. Shrubby when young, elongating to pyramid.	Fairly quick to 25ft/7.5m.	Charming subject for woodland or semi-wild planting as well as near a house.
M. salicifolia	Very fragrant, starry, white flowers on bare branches in spring. Elegantly pyramidal tree.	Vigorous to 25ft/7.5m.	Lovely woodlander or suited to semi-shaded corner in small garden.
M. sargentiana 'Robusta'	8in/20cm rose-pink and white waterlily flowers in spring on bare branches. Very wide-spreading shrubby tree. Flowers when about 12 years old.	Vigorous to 25ft/7.5m high and wide. Lime-hater.	Very exotic flower. If space is available stunning in sight of house.

M × soulangiana 'Alba Superba', 'Burgundy', 'Lennei', 'Rustica Rubra', 'Sundew'	Most commonly planted magnolia. Goblet flowers in spring are white and scented ('Alba Superba', early); wine-red ('Burgundy', early); pink-purple outside and white within ('Lennei', late); rosy-red ('Rustica Rubra'); very large, apricot-flushed white ('Sundew'). All are shrubby and rounded, but 'Lennei' is especially wide-spreading.	Not suited to chalk or lime. Vigorous to 16ft/5m.	First candidate for placing near a house but not suitable for training against a wall, with possible exception of 'Lennei'.
M. sprengeri 'Diva'	Magnificent pink to carmine flowers on bare branches in spring. Not a first choice only because it does not flower when young.	For lime-free soil. Usually smaller but sometimes to 40ft/12m.	Lovely tree in open woodland especially amongst evergreens.
M. × veitchii 'Peter Veitch'	White flushed mauve-pink flowers on bare branches in spring. Slimmish crown. Flowers from about 10 years old.	Lime-free soil. Vigorous to 40ft/12m and eventually much taller.	Good subject for inner or outer garden.
Myrtus apiculata (syn. M. luma)	Small evergreen leaves and beautiful peeling bark of cinnamon and cream. Often multi-stemmed. Only tree-like in mild areas.	Not reliably hardy. In mild areas, fairly quick to 20ft/6m.	Lovely subject for sheltered courtyard or in open woodland.
Paulownia tomentosa	Huge coarse leaves and purple foxglove-type flowers in early summer if not damaged by winter when in bud. Often multi-stemmed. Domed outline.	Very vigorous to 30ft/9m.	Showy, tropical-looking tree near a house or for planting of lush appearance around a pool.
Platanus orientalis (Oriental Plane)	Deeply five-lobed leaves and pinkish-brown bark. Great spreading head of branches, sometimes layering into ground. Most noble and impressive effect	Eventually to 80ft/25m but not in chalk soil which is best avoided.	One of the best subjects for large open ground planting; will dominate the area.
Prunus subhirtella 'Autumnalis'	Showers of fragile semi-double white flowers gauze bare branches from autumn to spring in mild spells, climaxing in April. Avoid forms where graft is at top of the trunk. Pink flowers ('Rosea') also available.	To 20ft/6m.	Charming subject for extended winter value near a house.
P. s. 'Pendula'	Forms wide-spreading hummock. Pendulous branches attractive all year. Blush-white flowers (pink in 'Rosea' and deep rose in 'Rubra') in spring.	Grows to 16ft/5m × 24ft/7m.	Arresting on a large terrace. Small garden may not have room for its lateral space.
Pterocarya × redherana (also P. fraxinifolia)	Pinnate leaves and very long greenish catkins in summer. Large, widely spreading and handsome multi-stemmed tree.	Best in moist loam but grows in any soil. Very quick to 33ft/10m high and wide.	Handsome open ground specimen in large areas.
Quercus ilex (Holm Oak)	Most noble evergreen (some conifers excepted) tree for large gardens. Lush dark greyish-green foliage and whitish shoots and yellow catkins in early summer. Great rounded head.	Slow-growing at first then quickens. Eventually 66ft/20m. Best in mild areas.	Very handsome open ground or boundary tree in large sheltered gardens.
Robinia pseudoacacia 'Frisia'	Bright gold pinnate leaves all summer, apricot in autumn.	Fast-growing to 40ft/12m. Avoid exposed positions.	Good for colour-related areas in sheltered site.
R. p. 'Inermis'	Green pinnate leaves on a distinctively neat round head. Non-flowering.	Vigorous to 26ft/8m.	Useful for formal surroundings.
Salix vitellina 'Pendula' (syn. S. × chrysocoma) (Weeping Willow)	The ubiquitous weeping willow with golden pendulous branchlets. Subject to scab and canker; treat with fungicide.	Vigorous to 66ft/20m. Tolerates dry as well as damp soils.	Only for large garden. Do not plant in cramped conditions. Spacious watersides only.
Sophora japonica 'Pendula'	Very picturesque with drooping contorted branches. Late into leaf; long, pinnate foliage.	To 13ft/4m high and wide.	Charming natural arbour in small garden or for terrace.
Xanthoceras sorbifolium	Shrubby and best encouraged into small tree with wide spread. Long pinnate leaves and flowers (white with dark pink eye) in erect panicles in late spring.	10ft/3m. Avoid chalk.	Extremely elegant on terrace or in a small garden.

2. Trees for Grouping

CONIFERS

Calocedrus decurrens (syn. *Libocedrus decurrens*)	Narrow, dark column with rounded apex. Rich green.	Tolerates hot, dry sites if watered when young. 80ft/25m.	Best in formal surroundings. Large gardens.
Cupressus sempervirens	Very slim, dark Mediterranean cypress with pinnacle outline. Ascending branches.	Not for cold areas. Fast when young but slowing. 40ft/12m.	In Mediterranean, often accompanies *Pinus pinea* (Stone Pine). Only for formal surroundings.
Larix × *eurolepis*	Dunkeld Larch is hybrid of two species. Narrowly conical with slightly glaucous deciduous leaves, yellowing in autumn.	Vigorous and healthy. Tolerates soil extremes better than its parents. 60ft/18m.	Graceful for large open-ground groups and late autumn colour.
Metasequoia glyptostroboides (Dawn Redwood)	Bright fresh green, deciduous conifer, shading pink and gold in autumn. Conical outline. Feathery appearance. Reddish peeling bark.	Vigorous and suited to moist but not waterlogged soil. 60ft/18m.	Very graceful large open-ground groups; exellent near water.
Pinus radiata (Monterey Pine)	Bright green needles in threes up to 6in/15cm long and cones to 5in/12.5cm. Conic outline when young, highly domed in age.	Very vigorous indeed. 100ft/30m. Best in mild areas.	Picturesque tree for large open ground Mediterranean or coastal effects. Tree of Californian origin.
Pinus sylvestris	Native Scots pine, slim when young, craggy and broad-headed when old. Pinkish-red fissured bark. Dark leaves bound in twos.	100ft/30m. Very hardy.	Picturesque subject for large open-ground planting.
Taxus baccata 'Fastigiata' (Irish Yew)	The slim form of the yew. Dark tree often planted in chuchyards, so beware funereal arrangements in the garden.	33ft/10m.	Suited to formal surroundings.

BROAD-LEAFED TREES

Acer of Snake-bark type, especially *A. davidii* (see page 197)			
A. pensylvanicum	Green bark, striped white. Three-lobed leaves, yellowing in autumn.	Quite fast to 25ft/7.5m. Not for shallow chalk.	Good for formal or informal, or for open woodland.
A. rufinerve	Green trunk striped white. Red and yellow leaf colour in autumn.	25ft/7.5m.	
Alnus incana 'Laciniata'	Alder with lacy leaves, columnar trunk.	60ft/19m; moisture.	Beautiful for groves in damp sites.
Betula (Birch) in variety *B. albo-sinensis* (and var. *septentrionalis*)	Pinkish-orange, peeling, shining bark. Leaves turn yellow in autumn. Conic outline.	Vigorous to 50ft/15m. Moist soil. Not for shallow chalk.	Lovely in open ground or woodland.
B. nigra	Pinkish-orange shaggy bark.	50ft/15m. For wet ground.	As above.
B. ermanii	Lovely creamy-pink bark; young shoots are white. Conic outline.	To 66ft/20m.	Open sheltered woodland to avoid early frosts.
B. jacquemontii	White peeling bark. Broader head than the above.	40ft/12m.	Open ground or woodland.
B. pendula (syn. *B. verrucosa*)	Native Silver Birch. White bark, graceful drooping branchlets.	Vigorous to 50ft/15m.	As above.

Cordyline australis	Cabbage palm with bunches of sword-like evergreen leaves on branches. Domed crown and much-branched in mild areas. Panicles of creamy flowers in early summer.	Not reliably hardy and only for mild areas. 16ft/5m.	Splendid sub-tropical effects when grouped in mild moist gardens. Good in formal surrounds.
Eucryphia × nymansensis 'Nymansay'	Broadly columnar tree with dark evergreen leaves. Smothered in 2½in/6cm white flowers with gold stamens in late summer	Best to avoid chalk. Very vigorous to 20ft/6m.	If space, best to group in semi-formal garden.
Prunus avium and *P. a.* 'Plena'	The wild cherry, massed with single white flowers (or double white in the form 'Plena') in spring. Small red fruits. Colours richly in autumn. Conic when young, spreading and domed in age. 'Plena' is later to flower and longer-lasting in bloom than type.	80ft/25m. Very good on clay and chalk.	Wonderful open ground or open woodland tree.
P. serrula	Grown not for its insignificant flowers, but for its shining red bark. Broad-headed.	16ft/5m.	Open ground or open woodland tree where trunks can be given prominent position.
Sorbus in variety			
S. hupehensis	Blue-green pinnate leaves and pink and white persistent fruit clusters.	16ft/5m.	Formal or open ground.
S. × kewensis	Heavily cropping orange-red berries. Broadly spreading head.	16ft/5m.	As above
S. sargentiana	Small scarlet fruits. Leaves colour red in autumn.	16ft/5m.	As above.
S. scalaris	Wide head of ferny leaves, purple and red in autumn. Small red fruits.	16ft/5m.	As above.
Trachycarpus fortunei (Chusan Palm)	Chunky fibrous trunk and long evergreen leaves in fans. Small yellow flowers in conic drooping panicles. Fairly hardy palm though leaves suffer damage in cold winters.	Slow to 25ft/7.5m.	Sub-tropical effects especially near water; or in formal garden, though too slow-growing for other than long-term value.

3. Trees for Special Functions. (i) Windbreak Trees

CONIFERS

Cupressus macrocarpa	Dense, rich bright green foliage. Columnar outline in youth, spreading and often flat-topped in age.	Fast to 100ft/30m.	Only for large gardens and best in mild maritime areas.
Pinus cembra	Deep blue-green leaves bound in fives and deep blue cones. Very decorative.	Slow to 33ft/10m.	Exellent for small gardens in groups and very hardy.
Pinus nigra	Dark stiff needles in twos and cones to 3½in/8cm. Dense, burly tree.	Eventually 100ft/30m. Good on chalk soil.	Only for large gardens and very hardy.
Pinus ponderosa	Scaly, yellow and rust-coloured bark and long dark grey-green needles in threes. Cones to 10in/25cm long. Spreading or drooping branches. Ornamental.	100ft/30m.	Only for large gardens and very hardy.
Pinus radiata (see page 200)			

BROAD-LEAFED TREES

Acer pseudoplatanus	Sycamore has deep green leaf with pale underside. Great round head.	Very quick to 100ft/30m.	Outstandingly hardy windbreak for large garden.
Alnus glutinosa Also *A. incana*	Common alder has dark green pear-shaped leaves and catkins in early spring. Spreading head. Often multi-stemmed. Young shoots and leaves grey.	Very rapid to 66ft/20m. Not for shallow chalk but good on moist soil.	Very hardy windscreen for moist position in large garden.
Cotoneaster × watereri	Semi-evergreen leaves, white flowers in spring and heavy red or orange crop of berries. Small spreading tree.	Very rapid to 13ft/4m.	Good tough subject for small garden.

Crataegus species. All thorns are tough and make bushy-headed windscreens.			All ultra-hardy windscreens for small garden.
C × prunifolia	Dark glossy green leaves reddening in autumn when it bears dark red fruit.	16ft/5m.	
Populus alba	Glaucous leaves with white undersides. Large-headed tree but airy, dainty appearance.	Rapid to 66ft/20m.	Large garden subject.
Quercus cerris (Turkey Oak)	Slender and open in youth, domed in age. Dark green leaves	Very rapid to 100ft/30m.	Only for large open ground areas. Best for maritime exposure rather than inland.
Q. robur (English Oak)	Late into leaf and yellow-green in spring, darkening to deep green. Great rounded head. Distinctive winter outline with 'elbow' branches.	To 100ft/30m and very long-lived.	Only for large open ground gardens. Very hardy to exposure.

3(ii). *Trees for Open-ground or Field Planting* (N = native and usually of value to wildlife).

All the following are broad-leafed trees. My own inclination would be to avoid conifers in this situation with the exception of our native Scots Pine (*Pinus sylvestris*: see page 200), native yew (*Taxus baccata*: see page 200) which is not a true conifer, larch (*Larix decidua*, *L. kaempferi* and *L. × eurolepis* [see page 200]) and the more decorative and fast-growing windbreak conifers given on page 201 but used in small quantities.

Acer campestre N	Field Maple with great round head when planted singly. Good autumn colour.	Vigorous to 40ft/12m.	Good isolated, clumped or used as tall hedge.
A. platanoides	Yellow flowers on bare stems in spring. Good autumn colour.	Fast to 66ft/20m.	Good as a screen.
A. pseudoplatanus N (see page 201)			
Aesculus hippocastanum (Horse Chestnut)	Noble, spreading tree, early into leaf with white 'candle' flowers in early summer and conkers. Casts heavy shade.	100ft/30m.	Use where ornamental as well as functional aspects can be appreciated. Not for roadside planting.
Alnus cordata (Alder)	Attractive pyramid shape. Glossy dark green leaves.	Rapid to 50ft/15m. Wet soil tree.	For wet areas.
A. glutinosa N (see page 201)			
Betula pendula N (see page 200)			
B. pubescens N	Graceful birch. Bark more reddish than above.	Rapid to 50ft/15m.	For northerly areas.
Castanea sativa (see page 197)			
Carpinus betulus N (Hornbeam)	Spreading crown in age and grey fluted trunk.	Good on heavy soils; avoid chalk or lime. To 66ft/20m.	Useful where heavy shade is needed.
Crataegus monogyna N (Hawthorn)	White flowers in early summer, red fruits and reddish leaves in autumn.	To 30ft/9m.	Highly adaptable for hedgerow sites.
Corylus avellana N (Hazel)	Shrubby, rather messy outline but nuts are of value to wild life.	To 30ft/9m if not coppiced.	Tolerates shade.
Fagus sylvatica N (Beech)	Wonderfully stately, very spreading tree but casts dense shade.	Best on well-drained soils, especially chalk. To 60ft/18m.	Tolerates shade.
Fraxinus excelsior N (Ash)	Airy, pinnate-leafed tree with tall domed crown. Late into leaf.	Rapid to 80ft/25m. Tolerates extremes of soil.	Has many uses and of value in a site where only light shade is needed.

Ilex aquifolium N (Holly)	Evergreen prickly foliage and red berries on pollinated females.	To 33ft/10m. Best in well-drained soils.	Tolerates heavy shade and good for woodland.
Malus sylvestris N (Crab Apple)	Lovely in flower and fruit which can be used for jelly. Spreading head.	Best on calcareous loams and clay. To 30ft/9m.	Very decorative at the edge of a plantation.
Populus alba (see page 202)			
P. canascens	Tall, open poplar, suckering in habit, with pale grey trunk and long decorative, red male catkins in winter.	Vigorous to 100ft/30m. Moist soil.	Needs sunny position and ideal for wet, but not waterlogged area.
P. nigra N	Burred trunk and heavy branches. Big bushy outline.	Rich moist soil. Fast to 100ft/30m.	As above.
P. tremula N (Aspen)	Suckering tree with trembling, dancing leaves.	For moist heavy clay. Vigorous to 66ft/20m.	As above.
Prunus avium N (see page 201)			
Quercus cerris (see page 202) *Q. ilex* (see page 199) *Q. robur* (see page 202) *Q. rubra*	Broad-headed oak with dull green leaves colouring richly in autumn before falling.	Fairly fast to 66ft/20m or more. Best on lime-free soil.	Thrives in most open sites
Salix alba N (White Willow)	Silky and hairy leaves giving silvery appearance. Slimmish, conic outline.	Fast on moist soils to 66ft/20m.	For streamsides and ponds or use as screen.
S. caprea N	Pussy Willow with furry yellow male catkins in spring. Female form has silver catkins. Rounded, sometimes shrubby outline.	Moist soil. To 30ft/9m	Decorative tree with ornamental value to site.
S. fragilis N (Crack Willow)	Narrow green leaves, rugged bark, and wide-spreading head with splaying branches which break outwards.	For moist or wet soil. Fast to 66ft/20m.	Watersides etc. but never plant where branches can break and damage buildings etc.
S. pentandra N	Ornamental tree with shining bay-like leaves and yellow (male) catkins in spring with early leaves.	Damp, rich soil. To 40ft/12m.	Worthy of planting in conspicuous site.
Sorbus aria N (Whitebeam)	Greyish-white leaves, greening early in season though remaining white beneath, colouring in autumn. Rounded head. White flower-heads, red fruit.	To 65ft/20m. For calcareous soils. Fairly fast.	Ornamental tree, but can also be used as a nurse.
S. aucuparia N (Rowan or Mountain Ash)	Very decorative pinnate-leafed tree with white flowers and large crops of red berries. Light, open growth.	To 30ft/9m. Short-lived on shallow chalk, but good on dry, light, acid soils.	Good small tree in groups in exposed position.
Tilia cordata N (Small-leafed Lime)	Rounded head, green leaves with paler underside, spreading bunches of scented white flowers in later summer.	To 80ft/25m	Ancient woodland tree.
T. platyphyllos (Broad-leafed Lime)	Rounded outline, flowers produced earlier than above.	Vigorous to 100ft/30m. Light, fertile soils.	Very handsome as a specimen in open ground.

3(iii). Fruit and Nut Trees

Apples, pears, plums, gages, damsons, cherries, peaches, nectarines, apricots and figs may be first choices, but several of the following make valuable additions.

Kentish Cob	Large nuts of sweet taste, but can be stripped by squirrels etc. before you can eat them.	15ft/4.5m	Best for hedgerow planting.
Filbert	Smaller nuts, but the above also applies.		
Medlar (*Mespilus germanica*)	Picturesque tree with crooked branches. Pinkish-white flowers followed by conspicuous brown fruits for jelly or dessert.	15ft/4.5m.	Charming small specimen near a house.

Morus nigra (Black Mulberry)	Again, picturesque and spreading tree. Round-headed. Dark red rich fruits after about 10 years old. Can make lawn very messy.	15ft/4.5m high and wide.	Often used as specimen tree but keep away from paths which the fruit will stain.
Portugal Quince	The best and most widely available variety. Pink 2in/5cm cupped flowers in spring, large golden pear-shaped fruits. Rounded outline.	Quite vigorous to 13ft/4m. Best in moist, lime-free soil.	A group is very decorative in inner garden.
Walnut (Juglans nigra)	Stately tree with very large leaves and large round fruit, usually in pairs. Named clones available.	40ft/12m. Fast-growing in rich soil in warm areas.	Avoid site where tree is subject to late frost. Ornamental specimen.

3(iv). Trees for Avenues

Virtually any tree can be chosen so long as it is as risk-free as possible in its situation. The choice must depend on soil, exposure, space, period of garden style (and house), length of run and general surroundings. Spreading trees, upright 'street' trees, classical trees, fruit trees and great forest trees are all possible. Here is a selection, many of which have formed the avenues of the past. Only a few of those below are suited to small gardens; and here, formal shrubs may be a better option.

CONIFERS

Cedrus libani (see page 196)

Juniperus chinensis	Greyish columnar tree of which there are many forms	27ft/8m. Good on chalk	For formal garden.
Juniperus communis 'Hibernica'	Dense, glaucous pyramid and may need tying to keep erect in age.	Slow to 20ft/6m. Good on chalk.	Formal garden.

Taxus baccata 'Fastigiata' (see page 200)

BROAD-LEAFED TREES

Acer platanoides (see page 202); for large avenues.
Acer pseudoplatanus (see page 201); for large avenues across the countryside, but invasively self-sowing.
Aesculus hippocastanum (see page 202); for large avenues across the countryside.

Carpinus betulus 'Pyramidalis' (syn. 'Fastigiata')	Fastigiate hornbeam, narrow when young, broadening into Ace of Spades shape in age. Formal outline.	50ft/15m. Good on sticky clay.	For large formal avenue.
Crataegus tanacetifolia	Pretty thorn with grey downy leaves, white flowers and yellow fruit.	16ft/5m.	Charming avenue in smaller garden.

Castanea sativa (see page 197); for large avenues across countryside

Fagus sylvatica (see page 202); as above.

F. s. 'Dawyck'	Fastigiate form of beech with short upright branches. Very narrow at first.	To 33ft/10m but can double. Best on well-drained soil.	Formal avenue; needs space eventually.
Malus hupehensis	Apple with stiff ascending branches, though lower ones are level. Prolific display of white flowers in early summer followed by yellow and red fruits.	Very vigorous to 33ft/10m.	Decorative in spring and autumn and suited to large interior garden.
Populus nigra 'Italica' (Lombardy Poplar)	Very narrow column with dense upright branches. Often used closely spaced for screen. Can be liable to die-back of crown from canker. Useful for quick effects but has drawbacks.	Very fast to 50ft/15m. Moist soil.	Not for exposed situations as it is not reliably wind-firm, nor for sloping land.

Prunus avium 'Plena' (see page 201)

Prunus subhirtella 'Pendula' (see page 199) Only for very large interior garden, where it will give sugary effect of lines of crinolines.

Quercus ilex (see page 199); only for milder areas and if you are prepared to wait for the effect. Can suffer in bad winters.
Sorbus aria (see page 203) and especially the form 'lutescens'; good for large, open, windswept places.
Sorbus aucuparia (see also other *Sorbus* – of *Aucuparia* group – on page 201.) In addition to these, there are forms with upright branches such as 'Embley' and 'Sheerwater Seedling'. These are suited to narrow spaces but have a highly municipal appearance.
Tilia cordata (see page 203); only for very large open countryside.

T. platyphyllos (see page 203); as above. Can be subject to aphid attack.

T. p. 'Rubra'	Red-twigged lime with semi-erect habit of branches. Dark red shoots in winter. Large greenish-white flower bracts. Globular outline.	To 40ft/12m, but can double in age.	Only for large areas.

Appendix II. Suppliers

Nurserymen or Seedsmen

Jack Drake
Inshriach Alpine Plant Nursery
Aviemore
Inverness-shire
Scotland
(An alpine nursery which also supplies some wild or woodland garden plants, and sometimes *Meconopsis* GS600 mentioned on page 61. They warn that it may not be a true blue in all areas but depends on soil and climate.)

Fortescue Garden Trust
The Garden House
Buckland Monachorum
Yelverton
Devon PL20 7LQ
(Source for *Acer palmatum* varieties, as mentioned on page 83. Also supply a wide choice of magnolias, choice shrubs and rare herbaceous etc.)

Plants from the Past
The Old House
1 North Street
Belhaven
Dunbar
(Source for period plants, some very rare. The owners, David Stuart and James Sutherland, are also co-authors of an excellent book on the subject, entitled *Plants from the Past,* Viking 1987.)

Potterton & Martin
The Cottage Nursery
Moortown Road
Nettleton,
Caistor,
Lincolnshire LN7 6HX
(Huge range of alpines, bulbs and also carnivorous plants including sarracenias in variety.)

Seaforde Gardens Nursery,
Seaforde,
County Down,
Northern Ireland
(Interesting list and possible source for *Cunninghamia lanceolata* and *Taxus baccata* 'Dovastanii')

Stapeley Water Gardens
Stapeley
Nantwich
Cheshire CW5 7LH
(Supplier of water-garden equipment, aquatics, marginals, grasses and also the waterlily 'American Star' mentioned on page 67.)

Trehane Camellias
Stapehill Road
Hampreston
Wimborne
Dorset BH21 7NE
(Suppliers of camellias mentioned on page 145 and 160.)

Trewithen Nursery,
Trewithen Gardens,
Probus,
Cornwall
(NOT a mail-order nursery, but if you are in the area in spring, a visit to buy camellias is well worthwhile.)

Graham Trevor
Sandwich Nurseries
Dover Road
Sandwich
Kent CT13 0DG
(Sometimes a source for *Cistus* 'Paladin' mentioned on page 13.)

John Chambers
15 Westleigh Road
Barton Seagrave
Kettering
Northamptonshire NN15 5AJ
(Wild flower seedsman)

Waterfowl, Ducks, Geese and Domestic Fowl

A very wide selection is obtainable in the late summer from
Tom Bartlett,
Folly Farm,
near Bourton-on-the-Water,
Gloucestershire

Information obtainable from:
The British Waterfowl Association
6 Caldicott Close,
Over,
Winsford,
Cheshire CW7 1LW

Dovecote Suppliers

Dovencote
Dove Cottage
Parsons Street
Adderbury
Oxfordshire OX1 3LX
(This supplier also sells doves.)

Rayners Garden Buildings
Llanaway Works,
Guildford Road
Godalming
Surrey GU7 3HR

Haddonstone Ltd
The Forge House
East Haddon
Northampton NN6 8DB

Suppliers of the Hydram (mentioned on page 185)

John Blake Ltd.
P.O. Box 43
Royal Works,
Accrington,
Lancashire BB5 5LP

Bridge Builders (mentioned on page 62)

David Baker,
Tiger Developments,
Deanland Road,
Golden Cross,
near Hailsham,
East Sussex